D0831217

Silent Shadows

SILENT SHADOWS

A NOVEL

Eva Maria Knabenbauer

WINDHOUND PRESS

Copyright © Eva Maria Knabenbauer 2003
First published in 2003 by Windhound Press
24 St Clements Rd
Ruskington, Sleaford, Lincolnshire NG34 9AF

Distributed by Gazelle Book Services Limited
Falcon House, Queen Square, Lancaster, England LA1 1RN

British Library Cataloguing in Publication Data
A catalogue record for this book is available from the British
Library

ISBN 0-9542292-0-7

Typeset by Amolibros, Watchet, Somerset
This book production has been managed by Amolibros
Printed and bound by T J International Ltd, Padstow, Cornwall

To Vernon

Author's Note

Aschersleben, quaint and medieval, nestles at the edge of the Harz Mountains. The Aschersleben in which I have set my story is not that town, rather it is an amalgam of the real and imagined. But while I have used licence in chronicling historical events and describing localities, I have endeavoured to be true to the feel and spirit of the place.

Acknowledgements

I would like to thank Juliet Bromley and Nicola O'Shea for reading and commenting on the manuscript, Martin Breese and Paul Sutherland for their criticisms of the early chapters, Jane Wallace for introducing me to word-processing. I am obliged to my local writers' group under the leadership of Dennis Winterburn for listening to extracts of the manuscript. Special thanks are due to Jane Tatam for her guidance, as well as editing, copy-editing and typesetting. Finally, I am grateful to Eric Mahler for his inestimable moral support and council during the writing of this book and for allowing me to display his paintings. The endpapers are a reproduction of *Beginnings* by Eric Mahler, while details from *Promenadenring* and *Gondelteich* (the latter used on the jacket) are reproduced at the beginning of each chapter.

Part One

Prologue

The train neared Aschersleben Station. Anni leaned out of the window and breathed in hard through her nostrils. Could she really identify the once so familiar air? She thought she could, even though she would not have been able to describe its properties.

Behind her in the carriage her friend, Victor, was assembling their belongings. As the train stopped at a red signal, he joined her at the window.

"It's been a long time," she said in a choked voice, without turning around.

He made no reply, but in a gesture of support put one hand on her shoulder. He knew that she had not visited her East German home for thirty-one years.

Again she went over the day's events in her mind. Only this morning they had been at their respective London flats, then they had met at the airport; the flight to Berlin had followed and now they were almost there…

On the day of her escape to the West, Anni had journeyed in the opposite direction, making her way to Berlin.

In the early morning she had walked several miles from her home town to the station in a neighbouring village where she was unknown and taken the train from there; in this way she thought the chances of anybody recognising her would be reduced. The particular circumstances she was in at the time made it imperative that she slip away unnoticed.

She had planned to cover the distance to Berlin in several stages, each one bringing her closer to the border; to have bought a through ticket and travelled without changing lines might have attracted attention—so much safer to go indirectly and use local commuter trains whenever possible.

Like most people intent on defection she had gone to the eastern sector of the divided city before attempting the border crossing; the year was 1960 and the Berlin Wall was not yet a reality.

She was twenty at the time, fearful whether she would be caught before reaching West Berlin, distraught at leaving her home, her parents and Rudolf. Unlike today, she was unaccompanied.

Full of hatred for the ones who had driven her out, but, having made it to the West, she had vowed that at the very first opportunity she would return to Aschersleben and seek out those who had made her suffer.

Nevertheless, when—after the fall of the Wall—she was able to make that journey without fear of arrest, she had wavered. Instead of getting down to organising the visit there and then, she had spent months deliberating about it and it had taken her until August 1991 before she went back.

So why had she not jumped at the chance of visiting her home town? Well, one reason was that over the years her desire for revenge had diminished as concerns of everyday living grew more important; once she had moved to England—just to study at first—adjustments to the new environment and the need to master the foreign language took priority. It was not so much that she no longer felt wronged, but having reflected on the issues they appeared to be more complex than she had imagined. She remembered revelling in the idea of physically attacking her former adversaries. Now she wondered what their motives had been for persecuting her and speculated on how to apportion the blame.

The unease she felt about the way she had conducted her private life in the former East was another reason why she had dithered. She worried about setting foot in Aschersleben, that it would overwhelm her. After all, everywhere she went there would be reminders of her younger days. What if she came across Rudolf? Her affair with him had hurt her parents, as had the secrecy with which she had planned her defection. Besides, had she taken the easy way out by leaving? Surely, it would have been more courageous to have stayed in the GDR and make a stand for her beliefs.

Without the niggling thoughts concerning past shortcomings, her natural curiosity at wanting to see the old home again would have impelled her to hurry back and look for the people she had known—especially her best friend from school, Karin.

❦

Anni and Victor were the last of the arrivals to pass the ticket collector and go out through the glazed swing doors of Aschersleben Station. Earlier she had been impatient to get a glimpse of the place, but now, suddenly, she was no longer in any hurry to get to the outside.

She put her bags down onto the forecourt and looked around. Victor followed her example. In front of them lay the town's large green, squarish in shape and intersected with wide paved pathways; vehicular traffic being restricted to its outside borders. Dusk was setting but several gardeners were still tending flowerbeds. She had never seen the grounds looking so smart. Even the areas near the station where a visiting circus had performed once a year, and where the Easter Fun Fair was held, appeared to have well-groomed lawns. All she could say was, "Well!"

"Yes," said Victor, picking up her appreciation, "definitely cricket-pitch material."

"Platz der Jugend, they called it. I wonder if it's got the old name back. Anyway, it was often filled with the town's young; blue-shirted Young Pioneers, and the FDJ, The Free German Youth. Red flags everywhere! Before that it was the brown shirts."

Victor grimaced. "I'd rather see crinolines; ladies listening to music, from that pavilion over there. Hussars riding by."

"It was a garrison town once," she emphasised.

In a more elevated frame of mind she indicated the direction in which her old home was.

The café was still a going concern—though a friend of her mother had described it as "neglected". As for the rest of the house, Anni had no idea what condition that was in. She was eager, yet at the same time apprehensive about seeing it.

"We can drop our luggage at the hotel and take a look," Victor suggested.

"It'll be dark soon," she stalled. "Why don't we go for

coffee tomorrow? Afterwards I'll show you around the town. You said you wanted to see the medieval watchtowers."

She picked up her bags and quickly led the way to their hotel. They passed the house Maria had lived in. "I wonder if she's still there?" Anni said. "Anyway, I'll find out when you've gone on your sightseeing trip."

Anni had mentioned Maria and Karin to Victor but had not told him about more personal matters like her doubts and worries concerning her visit. He was not aware of her need to come to terms with herself and she was not ready to trust anyone, not even Victor, with her innermost thoughts and feelings. *I suppose he thinks my trip is just a sentimental journey…*

Chapter One

W hat light there was filtered in through a small broken window high up in the rough stone wall facing them. Jagged pieces of glass protruded through the rusty iron bars which were set into the opening. Rainwater had seeped in and trickled down the stone work, leaving dirty rivulets of ochre and brown. Below the window, to the left, there was a black, leather-padded door. As soon as they were locked in the keep, her mother gave her a meaningful glance and held her index finger against her lips, so they sat in silence, waiting.

As time drew on, their anxiety grew. What if they were left here, imprisoned? What if the police conveniently forgot about them for the rest of the day? For tomorrow? For longer? Nobody would be able to hear their shouts for help, hidden away as they were. People had disappeared before, leaving no trace.

Anni shivered as memories which had been gathering dust for more than thirty years were unshelved.... She was sixteen again, tasting the dank, acid air of the cell. It was as if the intervening years had been swallowed.

It would've been easier not to have come back. And be a wimp? No! I needed to, to make my peace. Now it's possible, with the Wall gone. Should have been here ages ago....What've I got to lose? Fragments of Marx's Manifest, '...nothing...but their chains', strayed into her thoughts.

She drew her cup of coffee nearer. Without paying attention to what she was doing, she added a second lot of sugar, stirred the black syrupy liquid and stared into the steaming cup.

Several strands of soft blond hair had come loose and were hanging in wisps down the side of her face; the clip she had secured earlier to keep the hair from dropping into her eyes had slipped. She brushed the strands to one side and felt the elephant hair bracelet on her wrist sliding up her arm. A friend had given it to her as a present from a recent trip to India. It was supposed to be a lucky charm and she had decided to take it with her.

Silly little superstition, she thought, *but it can't do any harm and who knows, it might bring me luck.*

"I heard about the interrogation much later. My father told me, when he thought I was old enough to keep my mouth shut. I wonder if I would've been brave..." Maria was speaking quietly, almost to herself.

Brave? Anni thought. *No, that's not it. Obstinate maybe, even reckless, but certainly not brave. Funny how people see you.*

The woman facing her had been a lanky schoolgirl with pigtails when Anni left Aschersleben, and she had rarely given Maria much thought. The timid girl Anni had known bore no resemblance to the woman sitting there. Now, she exuded a confidence which took no heed of the oil paint smeared over her clothing; she had even managed to get it into her hair. Art, it seemed, had taken over her life. Her manner was direct but unassuming, giving the impression that she was content with herself.

What a coincidence, Anni thought, *that I should've stumbled across her gallery, of all places. And here we are, sitting opposite each other on the first morning of my return, yards from where I experienced such* Angst.

She rose to her feet, drawn by the display window, and squeezed out from between the chrome and leather contraption she had been sitting on and the massive dusty trolley Maria had clanked in from the storeroom. Cleared of its heaps of bubble wrapping, empty cardboard boxes and reels of string, it had been turned into a serviceable coffee table.

Standing between two small easels, displaying paintings for the public to view, Anni considered the former police building which loomed large, just a few houses away on the other side of the street. She had walked past it only half an hour ago, quickening her step, as had been her habit—a habit born of fear.

She watched as some workmen removed the iron grills from one of the windows. Modern double-glazed units were being unloaded onto the forecourt.

"Go ahead, civilise the place," she sneered.

The explosion of loathing had startled her, and as if to shield herself from the violence of her feeling, she gripped the edge of the wooden sill in front of her. She had anticipated that the visit would bring back painful memories, but she had never imagined feeling such anger again.

There had been warnings from her friends: "Are you sure you know what you're letting yourself in for?"

Well. She had not been sure; she had spent hours remonstrating with herself, but that was not something she had talked about to anyone. She had not even been able to open up to Victor who would be coming with her on the visit. She still had qualms about it when she finally decided she would go—though she knew she might waver and change her mind even then. She wanted to go? She had to! So, she had purposefully hurried the decision and let everyone know of her plans. This way, she would be obliged to deal with her ghosts and at the same time keep face with her friends.

A family had stopped in the street outside the gallery. While the parents were looking at Maria's painting, their two young boys pulled faces at Anni. She was not in the mood to respond to their antics and moved away from the window.

As she turned to rejoin Maria and Victor at the makeshift table she was assailed by the image of her one-time gaoler, Schulz. He was forcing her to stare down into a seemingly bottomless pit. She shuddered at the thought of the vision that had somehow been conjured up, then quickly pushed it aside.

"*Scheissdreck,*" she mumbled under her breath. *I've not been back five minutes and it's getting the better of me. I've got to keep telling myself: it all happened a long time ago.*

Victor had been very quiet, but now he cleared his throat. He shifted his sturdy frame and leaned forward in his chair. His shirt collar had tightened around his neck and his cheeks were rapidly turning a vivid pink. Under different circumstances this might have moved Anni to compare his colouring to marzipan piglets, just like the ones her father had so lovingly modelled in his bakehouse. Though—as she would have readily agreed—there was nothing remotely sugary about her friend's rugged skin. What struck her more was the concern in his face, but there was also puzzlement. She knew that he was going to ask a question and thought she knew what it was going to be; Maria's reference to the interrogation had seen to that. Waiting for him to ask it, Anni picked nervously at a piece of broken thumbnail, tearing it and making the thumb sore. She wished that she had told him about the incident with Schulz before.

If only I wasn't such a drip; a friend deserves openness. Must make him wonder if I trust him enough. Trust, she repeated to herself, then paused. *In my place he would've mentioned it, I think.*

"What happened at the police station, why were you there?" he said.

"It's a long story," Anni blustered.

"I don't mind," he said, giving Maria an enquiring glance. She shook her head.

"I'd like to know. I thought we knew each other quite well," he added, sounding a little resentful. He scratched self-consciously behind his ear.

"Of course we do," Anni said, studying her torn thumbnail. She looked up at him, "We're friends!"

Victor gave a searching look. She blushed in embarrassment, remembering how only a little earlier she had introduced him as her colleague. No wonder he feels hurt.

For reasons which Anni was to admit to herself later, she had played down her relationship with Victor to Maria. True, they were employed at the same further education college, but their friendship extended beyond work. Some evenings they would meet to see a film or a play at the local theatre and there were day trips on the odd weekend.

In his capacity as the senior technician, he had introduced himself soon after Anni joined the teaching staff. Victor—

renowned for his friendly support to all colleagues and nicknamed GOV, short for GOOD OLD VICTOR—had helped Anni with the setting up of some rather complex audio equipment.

They often spent their lunch breaks chatting together and it became obvious that Victor was exceptionally well informed about the former eastern bloc countries; he had been to Poland, Hungary and East Germany. In fact, one of his passions was travelling. Not being married and with no close family of his own he spent his holidays, including half-term breaks, abroad. Much to Anni's surprise, he liked to speak German with her.

"How come you speak German so well?" she had asked him.

"Ah," he smiled, "I've Granny Nowak to thank for that. She sparked my interest."

Of mixed Polish and German descent, with distant Hungarian roots, his maternal grandmother had come to live near her daughter. Victor was five years old then and spent whole weekends with his gran. At bedtime she would read to him, but struggling with the English she would invariably shut the book and continue the fairy-tales from memory, speaking in German, her native language. She was a first-rate storyteller and, knowing the storyline, Victor gave himself over to the sound effects she made of the various characters. Later, he began to understand a smattering of the language.

Anni took a sip from her coffee; it had gone cold and its sickly sweetness made her choke. Maria looked at her.

"Coffee's fine…wrong way down," Anni croaked.

❧

One afternoon, in the late summer of 1956, Anni's mother received a visit from the police. She was told to present herself for an interview at the station the following afternoon. No reason was given and she wondered what it might be about; it worried her.

The next morning Anni insisted on going with her. When they arrived at the reception desk, just before two o'clock, her mother was told that she would be seen shortly, that the questioning was a mere formality and would not take long. Anni was told to go home. "He won't want you there," the woman said.

"I said, 'Since it's not going to take long I'll wait.' She gave me a dirty look and shrugged. After about twenty minutes, a policeman came and told Mother to follow him. And—"

"Schulz!" Maria said.

"I know," said Anni. "I wasn't sure if you still remembered his name; I was ready to murder the bastard once!

"Anyway, Mother stood up and so did I!

"Schulz bellowed, 'We don't need you!'

"I said, 'I'm coming.'

"He said, 'Go home, girlie, this isn't a kindergarten.'

"He was breathing heavily into my ear and he pushed me towards the door. He stank; it made me feel sick. The arrogance, he treated me like an insect! No way was I going to leave my mother with him! I don't know how I did it, but I shouted: 'I'm coming, try and stop me and I'll make a scene!' I stuck my tongue out."

"What!" Maria giggled.

"Yes, Schulz was surprised," Anni said dryly, "he couldn't believe it. Mother gulped like a fish out of water. There was a horrible silence. My heart was in my mouth.

"He just looked at me, then he shouted, 'Right, through

here!' He grabbed my arm and shoved me through the door; he was livid. His face was all white and purple, and he was spluttering."

Anni became silent.

Despite her earlier resolve to stay cool she found the recollections unsettling, and for the first time since her arrival she wished she was back in London.

She realised she had fooled herself when she thought she had worked out how it would be on her return. After all, she had taken stock of the nasties she had experienced during her years under the regime. But that had been before setting out on the trip, from a safe distance.

She coughed self-consciously, wondering if her agitation had been noticed. Glancing at Victor, she saw that his jaw muscles were taut and he was biting his bottom lip.

I've even made him edgy, he's normally so calm. I really ought to get hold of myself.

❧

Schulz marched Anni and her mother out of the reception area, along a bleak corridor, then out into an untidy courtyard. They crossed it and entered a dilapidated building. Most of its windows were bricked up, making it dark and forbidding.

He led them up a flight of stairs and through what appeared to have once been an office. A single low-powered light bulb hung from a frayed cord from the centre of the ceiling. Tattered folders and their contents were strewn across the room. The remains of a desk, its legs broken and twisted on their fittings, was pushed over and up against one wall, splintered window frames were leaning one against another. Anni avoided stepping on the broken glass and crockery littering the floor, but her mother deliberately crunched it under foot. Schulz turned and looked at them. "*Schnell, schnell,*" he bullied, as he urged them on.

There were more corridors. Eventually he stopped before a battered metal door and unlocked it with one of the keys from a large bunch he had been tossing violently from one hand to the other. He pushed the door hard open. "Get in!" he sneered. Then he shut and locked the door on them.

Incarcerated in their inhospitable surroundings, with just a table and two chairs for furnishing, it was not long before Anni knew with the most horrible certainty that she would have to go to the toilet, or else! She cursed herself for not having gone before leaving home. Her mother had reminded her of it, but in the rush to get ready after her inopportune read of the final chapters of Thomas Mann's *Tonio Kröger*, it had slipped her mind. She did not have to say anything; it was plain to see as soon as she started to walk awkwardly around the cell.

"It can't be much longer," her mother said. But her voice carried no conviction. Even in her distress, Anni noticed that her mother was scanning the dismal room. She pointed to the rickety-looking table in the far corner. One of its legs had been placed inside a large dirty glass jar, obviously to steady the table. Anni understood and briefly lifted the leg up. They looked at each other and grinned.

A key was turned in the black leather-padded door. The handle creaked and the door swung inwards. Schulz appeared.

"My daughter needs to go to the Ladies," Anni's mother said as he came in.

Schulz gave a low whistle and, with unconcealed glee, sniggered, "That's funny." Then his eyes became icy and, pointing a finger at Anni, he exploded: "Who the hell asked you along anyway? Well, you can fucking wait!"

For a moment, her mother drew Anni close and squeezed her hand. And, as she stepped forward and positioned herself squarely in front of Schulz she seemed to grow in stature. He tried to avoid her eyes but she willed him to look at her. Speaking slowly, with great deliberation, she jeered: "You miserable little man! You pathetic excuse for humanity!" Her face radiated her loathing, and like a rabbit trapped in the glare of a car's headlights, Schulz was transfixed. He tried to look away but his eyes were held by hers. His feet began to shuffle uneasily as he fiddled with the seams of his trousers in an effort to regain a measure of control. But she could not bear to look at him any longer and turned away. The bulging shoulders of the man drooped.

"Let's get on with it," she said in disgust and strode into the interview room. Schulz followed unsteadily and slammed the door behind him.

Anni sat and waited, aware of the strip of sunlight moving across the wall with the passing of time. The interview room, with its heavily padded door, was almost sound-proof and however much she strained her ears—although occasionally she heard faint murmurings, and once a louder sound— she could not make out what was said. A number of times during that interminable wait she knocked on the door but received no answer. For long periods everything in the other room was quiet and she wondered if her mother was still in there or whether she had been taken somewhere else.

At one point during the lonely vigil, Anni's call of nature became desperate, and she had to heed it. She took the jar which they had discovered earlier and relieved herself in it, replacing the table leg afterwards. The liquid rose to the lip of the jar.

Four hours later her mother was returned to the keep. Again, mother and daughter waited in silence.

The town hall clock chimed seven as the rattling of keys heralded Schulz' return. He marched in, seething with suppressed anger.

"*Raus!*" he hissed. He did not speak again as he hustled them out of the room and back to the reception desk.

❧

"On the way home, Mother told me what the interrogation had been about. It was the damned magazine!"

"Magazine," Victor repeated. "What magazine?"

"Sorry, I should have explained," Anni said. "My aunt sent us parcels from the West. That was the problem."

Unlike the usual food parcels—they received one at least every other month—this one had had its contents wrapped in newspaper; and for padding—on top of the coffee beans, lentils, the packet of egg powder and chocolate—there had been a copy of *Der Spiegel*. Her aunt normally used plain paper for the parcels, but this time she had slipped up and forgotten about the East German paranoia of Western newsprint.

They had been surprised that the parcel had come through intact and had surmised that it had been let through deliberately. Everyone was aware that being in possession of such a magazine was an imprisonable offence.

"Well, Mother passed the magazine on to Maria's father. While she kept watch, he hid it in his briefcase."

"Worse than peddling drugs," muttered Victor. He frowned and looked at Anni: "How did the police come into it if nobody saw?"

"I can only…"

"Go on," Victor said.

"Well, to begin with, Mother said she never gave anything to anyone. Schulz called her 'a bloody liar'. He threatened to put me into care; showed her some photos of a correction centre. The girls were thin; some had bruises. He said he could make her talk. He enjoyed that. He told her to think about it. Then he laughed and said he'd got 'all the time in the world'."

With a self-satisfied smirk, Schulz sat in his comfortable armchair, towering above Anni's mother—the chair was raised on a wooden platform. He was grinning and looking down at her, but he said nothing more. He stayed that way for some considerable time. She, in turn, sat tight-lipped, just staring straight into his face.

He appeared to be uncomfortable under her gaze but tried to disguise it by pretending to be bored. Reaching for his newspaper, he turned its pages mechanically. Finally, deciding he had finished with it, he threw it hotly onto the floor and leaned across the table. Struggling to keep his voice calm and articulating every word, he said, "Have you thought long enough?"

It was unthinkable for Anni's mother to implicate Herr Klein, but she was worried what they might do to her daughter. Having considered the situation carefully, she decided she had to say something. She could not deny that she had received a parcel but gambled that Schulz was not in possession of the offending magazine so she told him that she had given something to Herr Klein but it had only been the *Church News* she had borrowed and then returned. "He was her friend, but also a church leader; an obvious target for the police," Anni explained to Victor.

"That's right," Maria said. "They were sore because Papa distributed the news sheets. He was only paid enough to cover his expenses."

Anni laughed sarcastically. "Schulz was playing with Mother, he knew about the magazine all along, he said so before he let her go!" She glanced across to Maria. "I think the parcel was opened but it was repacked and sent on to her, magazine and all! I think he was trying to trap her, hoping she'd lead him to some underground group. He should've kept the parcel when he had it, pulled Mother in and confronted her with it, but he gave her too much time to get rid of the evidence! She thought of that, so she told him she burnt the packing."

Anni tried to contain herself as she related how her mother had banged her fist on the table and shouted, "If that's a crime, what the hell is this country coming to!"

Victor was grinning and nodding his head. "Brilliant!" he said.

Anni pictured the scene, she and her mother hurrying home. Light-headed from being set free, they had fallen into each other's arms a stone's throw from the police station. They hugged and kissed right there, in the middle of the street, in full view of everyone. Passers-by had given them some very strange looks.

She remembered how her mother had laughed when she learned about the incident of the jar. And, after all the years, Anni took great delight in imagining Schulz knocking against the rickety table, perhaps days after their visit. She thought of him sniffing the air as he tried to discover the source of the vile smell.

She recalled smiling devilishly, savouring the moment…

"Just think, if their statements hadn't tallied," Maria said.

"They took your father in too, didn't they?" said Victor.

"Yes, but he told Schulz the same story. He said the only magazine he ever had from Anni's mother was the *Church News*. He lent it to her because he hoped she would subscribe to it. They searched the house, but they were too late, the magazine was already gone."

"It ended okay," Anni said, "but it wasn't quite that simple. We were sure they were watching us; we never thought they believed Mother's story."

"They didn't," said Maria. "They went through Papa's papers every time he printed something; they must have read every word he wrote, and checked the dots and commas. Then the Wall went up and they lost interest."

"I'm not surprised," said Anni, "everyone was as good as in prison then, so why bother?"

❦

"You going straight to the Vienna?" Maria asked as she handed Anni a slip of paper. "My home address."

"That's the plan."

"You must be itching to see it."

"Well, yes," Anni said, "but I'm a bit worried about…"

This is stupid, she thought. *I'm doing it again. I've been longing to see the place. Before 'eighty-nine I could only dream of it. I know it won't be the same.*

She took a deep breath and tidied her hair.

"You'll be all right," said Maria. "Off with you." She ushered Anni and Victor towards the door. "I really don't know how I recognised you from the window; must have been my sixth sense."

She turned to Victor. "Glad I met you," she said, shaking

21

his hand. "Anni says you're off to explore. Hope you enjoy yourself."

"See you soon, Maria. Maybe he will too, if he's back in time," Anni said.

"If I don't get lost," said Victor, doing a little skip.

❦

"Take this. It's a…just a local view; I did it recently." Still breathless from running after them, Maria thrust a cardboard package into Anni's hand. "I heard you tell Victor you liked it."

The next moment she turned and they watched as she headed back to the gallery. One of her rolled-up shirtsleeves had unravelled and was flapping about in rhythm with her movement. There was something childlike in the deliberateness of her gait and Anni felt like running after her to give her a hug. But she did not move. Then it was too late, she had lost the chance of catching up.

I really ought to be more spontaneous. Next time…

As Maria disappeared from view, Anni wondered, *how do others see me, Victor included? Am I stiff, aloof, boring…?*

"I hope she never dolls herself up," Victor said. "I like her, she's natural."

Chapter Two

The moment she entered the café, Anni had the uncanny feeling of stepping into the past. As she slowly walked the length of the room it seemed just as she remembered it.

She sat down in the far left-hand corner, near the spot where a tall Christmas tree had stood every year since she was eight years old. After early closing on Christmas Eve, the family celebrated. Presents were exchanged and opened—but only after she and her brother had sung their practised range of Christmas carols. It was one of those rare occasions when Wulf was not a pest. He refrained from his regular teasing: no smart yank of her pigtails, no sneaky pinches, no trying to trip her up. Moreover, out of sight of his school pals, he had even steeled himself to link hands with her, a soppy girl!

❦

Nostalgia was creeping in and she loosened the collar of her multi-coloured cotton shirt.

She looked around more closely, blew her nose vigorously and fixed her gaze upon the ornate ceiling before lowering her eyes and looking at the elaborate panelling which covered the walls from the floor to about two-thirds of the way up. She noticed several deep gouges in the reddish-brown wood nearest to her. She was sure they had not been there the last time she was in the café. On that distant morning she had made a mental note of the place—to carry away with her as a keepsake. She had not told her parents about the plan to defect, having persuaded herself it was better that way, easier. Easier for them, she had argued. Now, she found it painful to remember that she had chosen the early hours to hold in her mind those things that she would later wish to think of—she knew she would be alone at that time.

Now, in one of the window niches, partly concealed behind embellished glass, two white-bearded gentlemen were playing chess, keeping themselves alert with pots of pungent coffee. Within earshot of them a family of five feasted on king-size wedges of *sacher torte*.

The panelling looked dull. It could do with a good polish, Anni thought, and so could the parquet floor. Mother had always taken great pains to keep the floor in perfect condition; she would be horrified if she were to see it in this uncared-for state.

She suppressed a smile at her own disapproval; it was not usual for her to be so finicky in domestic matters.

While absentmindedly stroking the seat of the corner unit she was sitting on, she observed that the original white sign with its Gothic lettering, 'Toiletten', was still mounted across the top panel of the door leading to the corridor and cloakrooms. Curiously, it was only when her hands had come to rest on the seat that she became aware of the fabric of its covering. It lacked the thick velvety touch she remembered, although the design was very similar.

"Are you ready to order?" said Victor, who had joined Anni at the table. He had insisted on her having some time alone in the café. "I'll catch up later," he had said, and though she had protested, she was grateful for his consideration.

"I'll have a glass of beer, a couple of *Halberstädter Knackwürstchen*, piping hot with loads of mustard, and a thick slice of rye-bread, for starters," she said.

"Make that sausages and beer for two, please."

Herr Weitermann, the manager, gave an almost imperceptible bow in Victor's direction before striding quickly towards the kitchen.

"I'll show you around later. I'll take you upstairs where we used to live," Anni said. "I okayed it with the manager earlier."

She knew the photographs would no longer be on the landing; the ones her father had taken of the Tyrol when on walking holidays years before he was married. They had had pride of place. He was always dusting them and straightening them up.

"It's a shame Father didn't live to see the Wall come down," she sighed. "He didn't think it would ever happen; he called it 'my pipe dream'. *Vätchen*—" She swallowed hard. It was ages since she had uttered his pet name. Hearing herself saying it now conjured up the image of her father, cuddling her on his lap.

"*Turteltauben,*" her mother would say, with a mixture of pleasure and mild disapproval. At times the lovey-dovey bit got on her nerves: "Why don't the two of you get married?"

Anni's eyes became misty. She hurriedly bent down and

fumbled with her bag, busying herself with it while dabbing at her eyes with the back of her hand.

"Anyway," she continued, with false jollity, "what took you so long? I bet you couldn't tear yourself away from the model shop?"

"There was a really nice little engine," he said with the hacking laugh of a lifetime smoker.

She smiled. "You couldn't resist it."

"Quite right." His eyes were shining with pleasure. "You should've seen how it negotiated the curves, and it just glided over the points. A lovely little 4-6-4 German freighter, black. Beautifully reproduced in N-gauge. I've reserved it, didn't have enough money on me."

"I'll lend you some."

He gave a low whistle. "Creditworthy, am I?"

The Weitermanns' radio caught Anni's attention. Something about a "coup d'etat" and "Moscow" made her prick up her ears. "Ssh," she hissed, raising her hand slightly.

Coming from the Vienna's shop, the sound at times fading, they could hear the voice of a newsreader:

Since early this morning Yeltsin's supporters have gathered together outside the…Barricades are being put up to prevent the military forces, now apparently in control, from arresting Yeltsin… Gorbachev still appears to be under house arrest…there are rumours to the effect that he has been killed…

Anni sat upright, straining to hear more, but the announcer's voice was drowned by the noisy arrival of a group of customers.

"Gorbachev…dead? Did you hear?"

"Yes, I think so," said Victor.

She was staring through him. "It's ironic. I'm…" Her voice croaked.

For a moment, Victor looked at her, his eyes questioning.

"Yes, I'm back," she said, clearing her throat, and it's down to him."

Many thoughts went through Anni's mind.

The last time she was here her parents were running the café; on the face of it, in much the same way as they had done in the years before she was born. Back in the mid-1930s they had leased the premises and transformed the lower part into a small-town version of a Viennese coffee house. Local people, as well as visitors, gathered there, mainly in the afternoons and evenings, often to meet friends. The general atmosphere and surroundings—a mixture of elegance and traditional homeliness— encouraged conversations over steaming cups of coffee and plates of cakes, with or without heaps of whipped cream. Against the background of tastefully sweet music, the customers could relax and talk, read newspapers or just look out through the large windows and watch the people go by.

She thought of her defection, thirty-one years ago— the construction of the Wall was just over a year away. From the moment she had decided to leave she prepared for the possibility that she could never return, and accepted it.

It occurred to her that there were still half a million Russian soldiers and their families stationed in the eastern part of Germany. What would happen to them and to the population? What would be the consequences should the coup be successful?

As though Victor had read her thoughts, he said: "Watch out for the tanks tomorrow."

"Don't," she said, and she shuddered. "Don't even think it."

"Not to worry," he said calmly, "nothing's going to happen."

She felt Victor's reassuring touch on her arm and, just for a moment, her tension eased. "I'm really glad you're here," she said. "You've no idea."

Her lips moved again but made no sound. She realised she was on the verge of panic as she imagined the tanks rumbling along the streets. What if the regime did return? Her past would catch up with her and...

Victor seemed to sense her turmoil; he took her hand and squeezed gently.

"You make me feel safe," she told him, relieved that she had someone to share her fears with. But she had surprised herself, how easily she had let her mask slip. "Sorry," she said, "it's this place. It's full of ghosts." As she looked around the café towards the nearby window, a beam of sunlight caught her grey-green eyes, making them sparkle.

Victor reached out and brushed a strand of hair from her face. "Relax," he said, "it really is all right." Then, a touch of devilment crept into his voice, "You Krauts are all the same with your Teutonic gloom." He chuckled: " 'You are awful'."

Victor's little performance made Anni smile.

She remembered the first time she had met him. It was when he had helped her with a technical problem. That was just over a year ago when she was new to the college. Unfamiliar with the equipment, she had managed to work herself into a temper trying to set up a language tape for her evening class. She had been in danger of throwing it at the wall when, above the sounds of her frustrated mutterings, she had heard his good-natured: "Let me!" Clad in his technician's coat he had explained how to use the tape recorders.

That's typical of me, she thought. *I get aggressive so easily when I can't work things. I've plenty of patience with my students, but they're not inanimate.*

Not long ago, left to her own devices, she had broken a pair of pliers during an hour-long struggle to extract a nail from her living-room wall. Her language had been profane: "I'll bloody well do it if it takes me all day."

A rustling sound brought her back to the present. She turned towards Victor. He was fumbling in his shirt pocket for something. His freshly washed greying hair had curled up at the back of his head; it had refused to be flattened and rose up like frozen steam from a locomotive. She also noticed the triangular piece of toilet paper stuck to his chin where he had cut himself shaving that morning. *That's just like him, unselfconscious. On most other men the hair alone would look ridiculous. But on him that sort of thing is rather endearing.*

"Would you like one? No sign of any food." Having successfully retrieved a packet of Polo mints from the pocket, Victor popped one into his mouth, then passed the packet to her.

She helped herself and slid the packet back across the table, then watched as his dextrous fingers upended the roll of mints before tapping it against the smooth wood as though he were handling a cigar.

"Don't worry," he said, looking at her with a disarming

smile, "I won't start smoking again, not even my pipe. And that's a promise."

Feeling comfortable with each other, they sat in silence, crunching.

He really is a friend, Anni thought. *Why the hell did I introduce him as a colleague?* "Just a slip of the tongue," she had explained to him, apologising. But she had not even convinced herself.

Herr Weitermann arrived at their table. "Sorry it's taken so long," he said. "A technical hitch," he laughed, putting their plates of steaming sausages in front of them.

Chapter Three

I enjoyed the food. You did, didn't you?" Victor said. He picked up the bill and Anni's contribution to it, before helping himself to one of the cardboard beer mats from the table. "Very tasty, those sausages."

Anni did not answer; she was staring vacantly across the room.

He tapped her on the arm. "Wakey, wakey! Time for the guided tour you promised me."

Anni opened the door to the cloakrooms and, followed by Victor, stepped into the now rather dilapidated corridor. The *Damen* and *Herren* toilets were still in their original places, and in front of them was the winding staircase leading to the two upper floors. In her mind's eye she pictured the narrower stairway from the second-floor landing leading to the large attic. It had been used mainly for drying the laundry and as a general storage area. Like the corridor, the once heavily polished staircase was also in need of attention—two of the curved uprights were missing from the beautifully crafted handrail. To their left, a freshly painted white door opened onto the inner courtyard.

"I'll show you the front door," she said proudly. "It's rather grand."

Victor gazed at it as they rounded the bend of the corridor. "Hmm, very impressive," he said. He had always liked very old wood, particularly when it was skilfully worked. Because he wanted to see it from a changing perspective as they approached it, they walked slowly, their footsteps reverberating on the large stone flags. He was looking at it when sounds of a commotion came from the street. The grand door was flung wide, almost knocking Victor over. Two youths thundered in, dressed in hiking clothes. In spite of the warm weather they were wearing calf-length boots. Heavy backpacks strained against their shoulders.

"Catch me!" jeered the smaller and more agile of the two.

"Wait for me, damn it!" yelled his companion. He was breathing noisily. Perspiration stood out on his flushed face. Moments later they were lost from sight around the curve at the other end of the corridor, but their rapidly stamping feet orchestrated their progress up the staircase. Thump, thump, thump…the wooden steps resounded under the assault. Something about the frantic urgency of their ascent made Anni look up as she and Victor retraced their steps along the corridor. Images were beginning to form, one in particular. She sharpened it. It was as though she were looking through binoculars and bringing distant views into focus. She recalled the chase she had witnessed many years ago. As they came to the staircase, only steps away from the door to the inner yard, she stood still, stiffening and resting her hand on the banister for support.

"What is it?"

"Nothing really," Anni said. She looked around, trying

to bring back the scene she had witnessed long ago. She let go of the banister her hand had been resting on. "Those youths, they reminded me of something from the Russian occupation."

❦

Anni's father had not yet returned from the war and her mother was running the café unaided; she had only recently been allowed to re-open it.

One evening, trouble erupted between Max, one of the German locals, and Igor, a Russian soldier.

Later, whenever the incident was discussed, it was not clear what had instigated the insult, but at the point when Anni's mother was carrying a tray of drinks into the café, Max called Igor "a foul-smelling barbarian".

The Russian just grunted and spat vehemently on the floor. Slowly and deliberately he got up from his chair, placing it carefully, almost gently, back at the table. Then, spinning easily on his heels, his face blood-red, he lunged at Max.

The surprise on Max's face turned to horror as he realised that he had unleashed something terrible, but being quick on his feet he dodged between two tables. In his efforts to escape the inevitable attack, he ran into the shop part of the Vienna, trying to reach the street that way. Unfortunately, just as he got near the door, a frail, elderly man who was entering blocked his exit.

With Igor right behind him, Max appeared to be cornered, but he must have noticed the open service hatch to the kitchen. There was no other choice. He took it. Diving through the opening head first, he landed on the kitchen floor behind it. By the time he had picked himself up, Igor was closing in on him. Desperate now, Max ran along the passage to the bakehouse and from there into the inner yard.

Had he known, he could have turned left, slipping through the connecting building and out into the market square. Instead, in his confusion, he turned right. But being unfamiliar with the premises he could not see his way to the street. The only route that now offered him the possibility of some place to hide was the stairway.

❧

At first, when the fracas started, Anni had been very frightened, but her little-girl curiosity got the better of her. Crouching as low as she could and keeping close to the railings, she sneaked after the two men as they raced up the first flight of stairs. By the time she reached the landing, she heard Max hammering on Fräulein Vogel's door one floor above—he had obviously seen the strip of light shining from under it. Very distressed, and with his voice high-pitched, he was pleading to be let in.

The ageing Fräulein Vogel aspired to gentility, but she had one weakness: she was a nosy "old bird". She opened the door, just a fraction, and pushed her long thin nose out from behind it.

Hearing Igor's heavy breathing coming nearer, Max must have decided the time for niceties had passed and in his growing despair he pushed his way inside the old lady's living room.

Staying low, from her position near the top of the stairs, Anni peeped between the railings and saw, right in front of her, as though it were happening on a stage, a mighty and awesome struggle. The light from the room appeared to flicker as Max kept trying to shut the door, which Igor was straining to force open. It swung to and fro as each man fought to gain the upper hand.

"Baldrian!" Anni mumbled under her breath. She sniffed. *"Baldrian!* Yes!" Her nose twitched again.

"Beg your pardon?" said Victor.

"Baldrian!" she repeated. "Sorry, valerian. That's the smell that was coming from Fräulein Vogel's living room. I got a strong whiff each time Max tried to shut the door."

"Weren't you scared?"

"Not at the time. I was too busy watching."

" 'Curiosity killed the cat'. How old were you?"

She thought for a moment. "I must've been six or seven; anyway, before Father returned. Yes, that's right," she said, and sat down next to him on the stairs.

"Who won?"

"Igor."

"So what happened after the door was shut?" asked Victor.

"It wasn't shut," said Anni. "Igor won!"

Anni had crept closer to the now wide open door. The two men were chasing each other around the dining table in Fräulein Vogel's living room. The normally ethereal-looking old lady had lost all colour from her cheeks. She was attired in a long flannel night-dress displaying dainty frills around the neck yoke. Her white hair, which was normally rolled up into a bun, had fallen free and was draping in strands over her chest and shoulders. Flailing her arms and trying to reason with the intruders, she pursued them around the table. Only, she took small, stumbling steps and in her confusion kept changing direction, obstructing Max in his attempts to escape and hindering Igor in the chase. It took the skill of both men to avoid colliding with her.

As Igor's frustration mounted, his temper grew hotter and his shouts more threatening. Suddenly, he stopped running and jerked out a short knife from his belt. Fräulein Vogel emitted a horrified shriek and Max, his whole body trembling, his face turning a deathly white, threw himself under the table. He rolled over and picked himself up on the other side with the most amazing speed. As a result of his quick reaction he had gained a little time; just enough to make it to the door and out onto the landing.

Anni managed to scramble out of the way. She scurried to the far end of the landing and huddled in the corner.

Igor stormed past in blind and furious pursuit.

She had been hiding for only a few moments when Fräulein Vogel, shaking with terror, succeeded in shutting and bolting the entrance to her flat.

Then there came a most tremendous crash from somewhere below. According to what Anni heard her mother later tell Fräulein Vogel, Max, after tripping on the stairs, had tumbled down and landed at the feet of the people who had gathered in the corridor soon after the trouble started. Among them were his drinking partners, Igor's comrades, Alexander Satow as well as Anni's mother— she had been befriended by Satow who was an officer in the Russian Military Police. It was the time he usually called.

Igor, still in pursuit, was brandishing the knife, intent on getting to Max, now lying helplessly on the ground.

Satow decided it was time to intervene. He placed himself between the two men. "Drop the knife," he ordered. When Igor did not respond to the command, Satow pounced, shoving him hard back against the stairway. The knife spun out of Igor's hand and stuck harmlessly into the banister.

The various people assembled in the corridor had been

eager to give their versions of the event but Satow had
heard and seen enough, so when, recovering from his fall,
Max picked himself up and began to accuse Igor of starting
it all, it was a big mistake. Ignoring the protestations of
innocence, Satow, who by now was tired of the affair,
smashed his fist into Max's face. "That's for insulting my
comrade and trying to lie your way out of it."

An appreciative murmur went up in the corridor; one
of the soldiers pulled the knife out of the banister and two
others placed themselves, one on each side of their winded
comrade. They lifted him up into a sitting position on the
bottom step of the stairs, while Max's drinking partners
helped him as inconspicuously as possible away from the
scene.

Anni's mother, Satow and the rest of the people went
back into the café and only the soldiers were left in the
corridor.

❦

Anni, still hiding upstairs, was afraid to come down and
pass the Russians.

She remembered the whispered stories she should not
have been listening in on; tales she only half understood;
yet their horror was undiminished. She, too, could be stabbed
to death and thrown into the Gondelteich. It had happened
to two teenage sisters, kidnapped by a group of soldiers.
The girls' naked bodies had been found floating in the lake;
Igor's knife, glinting in the light of Fräulein Vogel's living
room was still fresh in Anni's mind.

*Sitting on the stairs with Victor and talking about
the incident, Anni recollected how she had felt that
evening.*

Alone on the landing, with her mother out of reach, with no one else to turn to and forced to rely on herself, she was feeling very small. In her loneliness she had started shaking, her little feet trembling on the floorboards.

Her teeth were chattering so hard that she feared the Russians might hear. She climbed up onto the windowsill and wrapped the heavy curtain around her head, hoping they would all go away.

As she cowered there she wished she had not been born. It was the first time she had had such thoughts and she kept them firmly to herself.

Was it then that she had begun to sense the precariousness of existence—not that she had thought of it in abstract terms? She was too young and, in that instance, not in any state for any kind of reasoning. Her fear had not been irrational for a small child, but all the worse for its reality.

❧

It seemed ages later that Anni realised everything downstairs was quiet. Coming out from behind her curtain, she slowly climbed down from the windowsill and crept to the top of the stairs. Listening intently, she could hear no violent sounds from below.

Thinking that it was now safe to come down, she ventured halfway down the stairs. Not seeing anybody about but still fearful, she took a chance and sprinted the rest of the way, running into the back room where Alexander Satow and her mother were talking.

She sounded anxious, relieved and angry all at once when she asked Anni where she had been. Anni did not reply, instead she dived onto the floor at her mother's feet.

"It seems hilarious now. I grabbed hold of her legs and hid under her skirt."

An amused smile crossed Anni's face. "After that I was always doing it. She was very embarrassed, especially when I hid under her nightie. It really annoyed her."

"I'm not surprised," said Victor, "she—" His head turned as the door from the café was pushed open. One of the white-bearded chess players stepped into the corridor. Seeing Victor and Anni perched on the hard staircase, he acknowledged them with a little smile before disappearing into the Gents.

Anni had become aware of her uncomfortable position and she eased her left leg from beneath her, massaging it vigorously. "You were saying?"

"Oh, yes! Actually I've forgotten but...never mind."

"Well," she said, wiggling her ankle, "I've never told anyone about mother's nightie; mind you, she always said I was secretive. Maybe I was; maybe I still am. Oh, I don't know..." She breathed in slowly. "I've just told you, haven't I?"

Chapter Four

The Vienna, which overlooked Wallenstein Street, was in one of two U-shaped buildings, connected to form a rectangular courtyard in the centre. Facing in the opposite direction, the second building looked out onto the market square. At one stage this inner yard had been divided into two halves. The Vienna's part of it was still used for the storage of crates, empty bottles and refuse.

As Anni and Victor stood in the café's yard, she felt dwarfed by the darkly towering walls all around them. Only when she tilted her head back could she see a square of pale blue sky. A dividing fence had been installed between the two halves of the courtyard. It was still there. Anni looked at its heavy vertical panels and wondered if it could be the same one. Yes, there was the rusty metal gate halfway along it. And because in the past it had never been locked, she walked up to it and tried the latch; it opened. There had been many occasions when she had used it to take short cuts to the market.

They stopped before an arched door to the left of the entrance to the bakehouse. It still had its original stout tumbler lock. "The old beer and wine cellars," Anni motioned to them, and she gave a small shudder.

"The whole place looks medieval," said Victor.

"Yes," she replied, "it is. There should be a plaque on the market side, 1540, I think."

Standing in front of the door, she recalled the apprehension and unease she had felt as a girl whenever she had been called upon to go down there to fetch something.

Even then she had sensed horrors of the past. What foul dramas had been acted out during its four hundred years of turbulent history? What unfortunate souls had been dragged down there and made to suffer unspeakably? Maybe the stone walls held echoes of their screams, spectres of grotesquely mutilated bodies?

She had grounds to be scared. It was fortunate that she had not learned of the skulls and other bones until much later. They had been found behind a bricked-up shaft which had once connected the beer cellar to the crypt of a now derelict monastery in the nearby Monks' Walk. When the ruined shell was dismantled, for safety reasons, the underground shaft had been discovered and traced through.

She thought of the worn stone steps, beyond the locked door, made smooth by the tread of many feet. The steps, flanked by rusty metal railings, descended steeply and wound gently to the left at the bottom. No daylight ever penetrated the darkness of those catacombs. The ceilings always seemed to her lower than they actually were and the roughly hewn walls added to the overall gloom.

She recalled the chill—even on the hottest summer's day it had felt cold—and she could smell the dank and musty air, but always mixed with the welcome aroma of spilled beer.

Through long and winding tunnels, she had passed the widening used as a general storage area and where the winter potatoes and coal supplies were kept. At the far end of it there was another door, also locked, leading further down and into the wine cellar.

Wooden racks reached from floor to ceiling, and here the silence lay heaviest. Before electric lights were installed the only barrier against the darkness were oil lamps, bracketed to the walls.

She had never volunteered to go into the cellars, but when her various excuses and protests had failed she found herself going down the steps. On these occasions a strange tingling sensation would spread from the base of her neck and down her spine. Her legs had felt wooden as she walked, very rigidly, along the narrow passageways. Despite her dread she could never bring herself to run to safety. She always felt compelled to walk slowly, back through the tunnels and up the steps, keeping her eyes fixed straight ahead for fear of seeing something horrible following her. Her nerves were *taut but she knew that the moment she started running she would go to pieces. Only when she came near the top of the stairs did she rush out, tearing across the yard before turning around to look; breathless, her heart pounding.*

Apart from her relief at being safely out in the open air, there was something else—she became aware of it only gradually—it was a peculiar sense of elation and a puzzling feeling of something akin to disappointment that her ordeal was over, for now.

❧

After Victor had walked around the café's yard several times, paying close attention to the uneven walls and warped window frames, Anni took him to see their former air-raid shelter. It was situated on the market side of the courtyard. "The place felt like a tomb, but we rushed to it as soon as the sirens started. When they sounded at night, Wulf and I were often half asleep, so Mother wrapped blankets around us and led us to safety. Well, comparative safety anyway."

Victor and Anni made their way carefully down some dangerous-looking steps and filed through a dimly lit network of intersecting passages. She remembered that electric lighting had been installed just after the war, so there was no need for torches.

At one intersection a torn silk shirt, obviously used by somebody as an oil rag, was hanging from a rusty nail. Stepping to one side to allow Victor to pass, she brushed against the smooth fabric. A splintered piece of button became entangled in her hair, and as she freed it she noticed, beneath the accumulated grime, the shirt's still discernible delicate pink tint.

The colour stirred in her memories of Rudolf. He had worn silk shirts of just that shade. His elegant clothes, good looks and worldly manner had impressed her so much.

I was very young then, susceptible to such things, she reasoned. *I was naïve, but that was only part of the story. Those weren't normal times and had things been different, events might have taken a different turn. What the hell! I've gone over the rights and wrongs of it often enough. This isn't the time or place for another round of self-recrimination, or speculation.*

❦

"The benches are still here!" Anni exclaimed as she and Victor entered the shelter's main chamber. But gone were its erstwhile trappings: a grey steel table, shelves and chairs which had been piled high with blankets and cushions. There had also been a medical kit and some candles. Apart from the benches and a large crate in one corner, the chamber was now empty.

"There were seven from our building sheltering here, including Fräulein Vogel and Frau Stuber with her two children. The rest were from the market side." Anni sneezed, then grew silent. She sniffed the air.

The aroma of overripe apples came to her. She looked around the chamber; the sickly sweet smell was coming from the corner to her left. Fräulein Wagner had kept crates of them in here. Obviously, like her, somebody was still using the place as an apple store.

The smell had other associations too; Frau Kamm, who was reputed to have never washed. Her pungent smell had mingled with that of the apples. Anni had always tried to hold her nose for as long as possible to shut it out.

Then there were the whispered conversations of the adults; one in particular held its horrors for her.

Frau Stuber had told of the bombing of the aeroplane factory on the outskirts of the town: some of the bombs had fractured the outlet pipes from the metal-cooling baths. The water, which had been scalding, had flooded the nearby air-raid shelter, killing all of the workers in it.

Fräulein Vogel's voice had been shrill with morbid excitement: "They must've screamed like lobsters in a cooking pot."

Even Anni's mother, in hushed tones, had voiced her fears about being buried alive should their shelter be hit.

After hearing those gruesome tales, whenever Anni was in the shelter listening to the bombers droning overhead, she would sit frozen to the bench in terror, imagining the walls being blown in on them.

❦

Anni had left her bench seat and was walking slowly around the chamber.

"You must've had a bad time," she heard Victor say.

She turned to look at him. "No more than others," she said.

"No, I suppose not," he said softly. He was still sitting on the bench, leaning casually back against the wall, his legs crossed.

There's something different about him today. She looked at him more carefully and it dawned on her. *That's it; I didn't notice before—not like him at all; why didn't I see it earlier? Too preoccupied, I suppose.* She looked again, at the sharp crease in his smart, new-looking trousers, his hand-tooled shoes. *Well polished too. Is he trying to tell me something? Wonder what worldly Brenda would say! "Dressed to kill", no doubt. "Anni's new fella" would be all round the canteen before you could blink twice. Doesn't really go with the bit of toilet paper on his chin though, and the sticky-up hair.*

Anni smiled inwardly as she walked across and sat down on the bench next to him. Picking up the thread of their conversation, she asked, "Did the Blitz affect you?"

"Too young." His voice held a trace of humour. Then more seriously, he said, "I wasn't even evacuated. But my boarding-school days were bad enough, I suppose. I was sent away in 1950. I was only six then. Very grown up I was." He laughed artificially.

"Where?" she said.

"Yorkshire."

"Oh, miles away from home then?"

"Yes, up north. I wasn't told I was going."

"You hadn't been told!"

"No," said Victor. "In those days it was common for children not to be told anything. I only remember bits of it anyway. The train journey: miles of open country, snow-covered fields; lots of sheep." He grinned. "At the end of that, a ride in a taxi with my father." Victor drew in a deep breath, exhaling slowly. "So, we got to the school—if that's what you call it. An old woman met us at the main door— I thought she was old, anyway!" He laughed heartily, "I thought she might be a witch!"

"Too many fairy tales."

"I expect so," he nodded, calming down again.

He remembered being led along a dark corridor and he wondered where he was—his father was no longer with him. The old woman ushered him into a large, sparsely-lit room furnished with many beds. She undressed him and unceremoniously put him into one of them. Then, without a word, she turned off the light and was gone. He shivered between the cold sheets as he lay in the strange room, aware that he was not alone only because he heard the occasional cough and the rustling of bedclothes. Eventually sleep overtook him.

"How awful," Anni muttered under her breath.

"Yes, not very nice, but people were like that then; very severe, particularly at that school." He paused, remembering… "The night lady was the worst!"

"The old witch?"

"No, Mrs Hedgley; she was deadly with a slipper. Used to thrash anyone who wet the bed. That's what woke me up next morning; the little lad next to me was getting a walloping." He looked at Anni and grinned, then shuddered. "Damned glad I didn't wet the bed." He rummaged in his shirt pocket. "Cruel, those people."

"All of them?"

"No, not all." He popped a mint into his mouth and offered Anni the packet; she took one.

"Mrs Hedgley would've made a good Nazi g—" Anni was about to say "guard". *How could I compare her to one of them*, she thought, *or even the Stasi, however nasty old Hedgley was?*

"You were going to say 'Nazi guard', weren't you?" His eyes narrowed. "Well, maybe. Cruelty always finds an outlet."

It became quiet in the shelter, each of them occupied with their private thoughts.

After a while, Anni said, "How long were you there?"

"School? Oh, about five years." He sat up straight on the bench. "Bad memories, they follow you like shadows." He sighed and his shoulders sagged a little.

She could not remember an occasion when he had talked so much about himself. "You never said you were at boarding school," she said. "Actually, I don't know very much about you at all."

Victor did not answer but quickly stood up and, yawning loudly, he stretched his arms. "Come on," he said, "let's get some sunshine."

As they came out into the daylight she noticed some cobwebs hanging down the back of his shirt; some of the threads were clinging to his black trousers.

"You should've worn jeans," she said, gently brushing away the wispy fibres. She refrained from taking a dig at his elegant trousers.

Again, the image of Rudolf came to her. She remembered his smile; it had made her feel special. *No wonder I couldn't resist him!* She chuckled as she thought of the meticulous Rudolf emerging from the dust-covered cellar. *He and cobwebs! Would I have brushed him down?*

"What're you giggling at?" said Victor.

"Nothing." She pushed the image of Rudolf aside and patted Victor on his tummy. "You're putting on weight, fatty!" she said. Then she hastily took her hand away.

"Oh, thanks a lot, flatterer, 'But I like you'!" He grinned broadly. "I know I'm getting fat, I'm going bald too." He bent down and kissed her on the lips.

In the past Victor had given her an occasional hug and the odd peck on the cheek, but this, Anni thought, was a little different. She wondered what to make of it. *I enjoy our visits to the galleries and antique markets. He's easy to talk to; we talk about a thousand things, and I respect his opinion. But is it enough?*

It had seemed a good idea to travel together to her old home town; she knew she would be glad of his company. He planned to go off on his own for some of the time— ever since she had met him he had spoken of visiting

Dresden and Weimar. She would spend that time looking up people she had known, and hoped would still be there. After his return they would be going back to England. No strings attached—that made good sense, or so she had thought. Anyway, it was ages since she had had a close relationship.

They went up the last few steps and into the courtyard. Anni tried hard to think of something ordinary to say to break the silence that had ensued between them after the kiss, but nothing came to mind that seemed natural. So she was relieved when she noticed the windowsill of Herr Wagner's workshop. "I used to sit here," she said, walking up to the window ledge. "I loved watching Herr Wagner work."

Still trying to divert her thoughts, she busied herself at the window, wiping off the grime with a tissue. Through a gap in the dirty white paint daubed over the glass, she peered into the room. All that remained from the once cluttered workshop was the bench, a three-legged chair, lying on its side, and some broken crockery, which had been dumped in one corner.

"This room was magical," she said, still feeling flustered.

Victor tried to look through an adjacent windowpane. "Can't see a thing."

"Try this one," she said, stepping back to make room for him. "His workbench was littered with all sorts of things. You should've seen it."

She described the finely shaped tools, Bunsen burners and boxes with glinting stones of diamonds, pearls, gold and silver. Magnifying glasses and dusty leather-bound books had been strewn all over the bench, and looking the absolute ruler over his treasures was Herr Wagner. He was a short man, plump, wobbly-cheeked, his head covered with fine white hair. It had been white from birth; his eyebrows and eyelashes were white too, so people called him "the albino".

His clothes were old-fashioned and ill-fitting, handed down to him by his father, giving him an odd appearance.

He was very good at his work; Anni understood that even then. He did not seem to mind her watching him, but she was never sure whether he noticed her at all. When occasionally he glanced up from his work he never spoke—not that it would have been easy to talk through the window, it was always closed. A fixed squint kept his magnifier in place as he worked simple strands of gold and silver, transforming them into delicate patterns of nature-based jewellery.

He had no friends; the only person he was close to was his sister. Like him she was considered strange, unworldly and impractical in the extreme. It was said that her husband left her on their wedding day.

"I liked the Wagners, they were easy going. I used to take their afternoon coffee to them; he even let me handle his work."

Anni's thoughts turned to the ring and necklace he had designed for her. "After we get home I'll show you some of the things he made."

Chapter Five

Victor was only half-listening to Anni, but not for any lack of interest in Herr Wagner's former workshop. His thoughts kept returning to the episode of a few minutes ago. How had he allowed himself to kiss her?

Friendship, he had convinced himself, was all that he required, he had been sure of it! It was something he had decided long before he met Anni—he did not want to get hurt again and had vowed not to get emotionally involved with anyone.

He shook his head. *It doesn't make sense, unless…could I still be harbouring a subconscious desire for something more? After all, romantic involvement was once important to me. Maybe Anni's sparked off something…*

Nonsense, nothing's changed, I still think of her as a friend, and that's all.

Rationalising in that way made him feel easier in his mind and, leaning against the partly cleaned windowpane and squinting into Herr Wagner's former realm, Victor now paid full attention to what Anni was saying about the toy-like tools she remembered. Herr Wagner had always neatly arranged them on his workbench; precious stones had not been given such preferential treatment.

But then, as he stepped aside and continued listening to her, he became increasingly aware of a forced jollity in her manner and he became distracted again.

She seems nervous and her face is flushed, I didn't notice it earlier, I should have, but I've been worrying about my own feelings. She's definitely trying to hide something though. Maybe it was when I kissed her...she didn't seem upset at the time, but that could explain it.

All at once he was annoyed with himself for having been so forward, but it had been an impulse!

He went over the incident again trying to see it from her point of view. But no matter which way he looked at it, he was forced to the conclusion that at least she had seemed at ease when she patted his paunch.

So then, it isn't that she is afraid of physical contact—the odd peck on the cheek hasn't bothered her in the past. In fact, at times, she's been quite familiar, as I have! Perhaps there are other similarities with myself, maybe she's also been hurt...

He decided that her nervousness had started after the kiss and he, clumsy fool, had broken a taboo. Maybe she was afraid of emotional involvement.

He had felt particularly relaxed and kissing her had been the most natural thing to do; impulsive, but normal. He had not planned it, it had just happened. But even as he tried to justify his action, he knew he was not convincing himself. He had to admit that his motive was more complex.

Who am I trying to kid? If I believe it was so straightforward, why am I still worrying about it?

He turned towards Anni and saw that she was fidgeting with the piece of tissue paper she had used on the grimy window. Eventually, she crumpled it into a ball and stuffed it into her shirt pocket before going on to talk about Herr Wagner's sister.

I wish I knew how she feels about us. We can't go on as we are. Well, I don't think I can, not really. I should talk to her about it. He smiled to himself ruefully, *but I know I won't.* He lowered his eyes and looked down at his feet. On the ground, near his toe-cap, he noticed a small pebble; he kicked it into the cellar shaft. The pebble clunked noisily on the steps as it somersaulted down. *The truth is, I'm too afraid to discuss it, I might lose her.*

❦

As Anni led the way back to the Vienna's courtyard, Victor's thoughts were still occupied with what he saw as a new situation.

I've been here less than a day, he reflected, *and everything's changed, for me at least. I don't know how it happened because we've never talked about ourselves, not intimately. That's probably my fault; how silly of me to think I knew her—I never really knew Helen either—somehow I've avoided sharing my experiences with anyone; even friends do that.*

Anni had reached the dividing fence and stopped in front of the metal gate. She pushed it open.

As the gate creaked on its rusty hinges, Victor was unaccountably reminded of his father, whistling: "It's the loveliest night of the year".

❦

In his younger days Victor had always been falling in and out of love. He attracted, and in equal measure, was drawn to fun-loving girls. The light-hearted affiliations he formed with them suited him, as he had no desire to settle down.

Unfortunately for him, or so he thought at the time,

53

the unalterable fact of ageing would not allow him to continue in his carefree way for very long. That is to say, as he and the pool of his partners grew older—he preferred them to be roughly the same age as himself—they increasingly looked for stability and commitment in their relationships. So, when he was not prepared to engage in anything more serious than an affair, he found that the women tended to look elsewhere and he felt rejected—for he was not without feeling.

It was witnessing the disintegration of his parents' marriage and seeing his mother's suffering that ultimately had the effect of making him look critically at himself and revise his perspective on life.

He was in his late thirties or early forties before he came to develop a more mature attitude, and he regretted much of his former self-indulgent behaviour. He could see the vacuity in striving for excitation and pleasure and was now ready to admit that it was no longer enough.

Then, a few years on, he met Helen. His experience with her turned out to be disastrous and was to scar him deeply. It also made him wary of women, to the extent that on making friends with Anni he let himself look upon her rather as an honorary male.

❦

Helen had ditched Victor, emptying his bank account and taking his beloved collection of Japanese lacquer boxes with her, shortly before their planned marriage.

He had met her while he was on a home visit from Nepal, where he was teaching English as a foreign language. His contract had had six months to run.

They had kept in touch by letter, and halfway through his remaining time in Nepal she had come out to visit him.

He realised then that he loved her, and she said she felt the same.

On her return to England, she stayed in his small London flat, which he had bought and kept on during his foreign work contracts. "Why spend half of your earnings on a bedsit when my place is empty," he had suggested, knowing her budget was tight, being based on earnings as a supply teacher. "Anyway," he reminded her, "it'll soon be our home. You might as well get used to it."

He had not had the slightest inkling that she was an adventuress, taking advantage of his good nature—enjoying her all-expenses-paid holiday in Nepal and then living it up in his flat.

Days before his return she had reassured him of her love, so he was devastated when he found it had all been a sham. She said so in a curt note left on the mantelpiece:

Sorry. It was good while it lasted, but no thanks.
I'm after bigger fish.

To get over his hurt he had busied himself completing a teaching handbook. He had taken on his present, less demanding, job as a technician to give himself more time for the book. He was still working on it when Anni joined the staff.

Recently he had started to edit his travel diaries. She had encouraged him in this after he had told her about his work in Nepal, though he did not mention Helen.

Actually, Anni had done more than encourage him; she had spent hours reading his manuscript and had suggested a number of improvements. Driving home after one particularly exhausting work session with her, he had chuckled to himself: *in Anni's place, Helen would probably have charged me for her time.*

Chapter Six

Anni climbed the stairs to the first floor landing ahead of Victor. She was very conscious of him now. She imagined that he was gazing at the back of her neck, which, only minutes before, she had bared by tying her hair into a pony-tail.

Noting the disconcerting tingle on her skin, she remembered a recent telephone conversation with her mother. *She often senses things before they happen,* Anni thought. *I wonder if she knows something I don't.*

"Hmm, I suppose it's safe to return," her mother had said. "They won't arrest you now." Before that conversation she had disapproved of Anni's plan to visit their old home. "Why go back?" her mother argued. "What's the point of it? Why bring back painful memories? The past's dead. I don't ever want to see the place again."

Not wanting to touch upon the subject of her parents' defection, and just to reassure her mother, Anni had said that there was no need to worry. "Victor's coming with me."

A long silence had followed and she wondered if they had been disconnected. But her mother, sounding concerned, had finally cut in: "Is that wise?"

"I'm old enough!" Anni had laughed.

"Just wait and see," her mother had replied, "this visit, it'll change you life." She had sounded very mysterious.

❦

Anni had forced herself out of her earlier mood, having diagnosed it as a temporary aberration. Her return to sanity, as she saw it, had been hastened when, on following an irresistible impulse, she had turned around on the stairway. Victor was not, as she had imagined, paying any attention to her at all. He was much too busy looking at the ornate handrail, fingering its curves.

Persuading herself that her strange mood had really passed, and knowing that Victor would follow at his leisure, she made her way to the old living quarters.

"The living room!" Anni said, as Victor came into the now bare interior. "Used to be well-furnished; good old-fashioned wood."

Victor's eyes lit up and he immediately wandered around, touching the panelled walls, running his fingers gently over them. "Still in good condition," he remarked. "Lovely." He turned towards the mantelpiece. "That's classical, cast–iron, black leaded!" He continued around the room, inspecting the stained glass doors leading onto the balcony. Coming back to the entrance door, he rapped it hard with his knuckles. "Solid oak."

"I was standing just where you are now when the American burst in, right there. I nearly got flattened! We heard them running up the stairs."

The day that Anni's home town was occupied by American troops had started unusually quietly. There had been no air raids but that in itself did not altogether account for the hush. She had sensed a general air of apprehension and restlessness; her mother as well as many others appeared preoccupied and unwilling to answer her questions.

Anni had been a shy little girl, thin and long-legged, clutching at her mother with small clammy hands. She was even paler than usual, her bright eyes peering, overlarge, from behind a curtain of dishevelled hair.

Later that morning they heard the sound of shelling in the distance. A little after midday the sounds became louder and more threatening. Then came the din of heavy vehicles approaching. When the bullets started to ricochet from the walls of neighbouring houses, Anni's mother shouted at the children to throw themselves onto the floor. From above them they heard the splintering of glass, followed by a louder crash as it fell onto the pavement. Shells screamed against the brickwork. The firing seemed indiscriminate, and, even after it had moved on towards the other end of the street, they kept their heads down.

In time, the sounds grew fainter and Anni's mother crawled on all fours to the nearest window and looked out. Wulf and Anni came out from behind the settee and stood huddled together in one corner of the room. Their mother took some white tablecloths and flew them from all the first-floor windows—she was praying that there would be no resistance by some last-stand heroes.

There had followed an eerie calm but they waited, knowing that it was not over.

In the early hours of the afternoon they heard tramping

feet, then shouted orders coming from just below their front windows. Fists pounded the heavy entrance door to the house and it was flung open. This was the same door, which, because of its fortress-like appearance, had only the day before saved everyone in the house from the vengeance of a group of freed prisoners. They had battered wildly against it with axes, knives and spades, when all they needed to have done to gain access was to press down on the door handle and it would have opened.

There were more shouts, followed by the thud of feet on the stairs to the first-floor landing and higher up.

Anni's mother anticipated the soldiers' next move. She rushed towards the living-room door and unlocked it. Moments after she did so, a big American threw his weight against the door. The catch gave way and as the door flew open he was propelled forward across the living room, narrowly missing them all.

"A right old comic strip," said Victor. "I wonder if the GI thought so."

"Probably," Anni replied, "but we didn't." She remembered how the soldier's perplexed expression had changed into a grin as he caught sight of her and her brother.

More Americans piled in. Two soldiers stood guard over them in the living room while the others stomped past and searched the rest of the flat. Judging from the sounds coming from above, it was obvious that Frau Stuber's and Fräulein Vogel's apartments were also being turned over.

Anni watched through the open door of her parents' bedroom and saw the mattress being probed; the bedstead was also thoroughly checked. Drawers and cupboards were pulled open and their contents emptied onto the floor. The clothes were heaved out. Every item was handled, pockets were turned inside out and everything was thrown onto a pile. One of the soldiers was eyeing her father's prized camera. He looked at it appreciatively before returning it to its case and looping the carrying strap over his shoulder.

After the search a superior officer arrived with two juniors. He commandeered the whole building and placed it at the disposal of the military. The two junior officers were allocated most of the flat. Anni's mother was told to keep all doors unlocked as the army would be setting up regular day and night patrols, checking on all the houses around the market.

The young officers politely introduced themselves, but the children were treated with smiles and jokes. Obviously, Anni and Wulf could not understand the humour, but by the expression on the officers' faces, they realised that something comical was being said. At one point, Anni turned to her mother and said, almost in a whisper, "They speak funny."

The officers proceeded to double-check the premises, especially the café, shop and bakehouse downstairs. They immediately seconded the last of these as their washroom.

Before they retired a guard arrived for the night duty.

Next morning, the Americans had all left early, Anni and Wulf crept downstairs and looked cautiously around the bakehouse. On one of the cake racks they saw some soap and chocolate. Wulf wanted to eat the chocolate but Anni was afraid and told him not to. "We must ask Mother." But ever-cautious, she told them to leave it alone.

The following morning the soap and chocolate were still there, along with a short note: "Das is for du."

"Generous to a fault, the Yanks," said Victor. "No chewing gum? Well, mustn't be petty. Did you talk to them?"

"Not exactly," Anni said. "They were usually gone before we got up. Except one morning. Wulf dared me to go downstairs."

Anni edged down the stairs and, hearing the sound of men's voices, she entered the yard and stopped outside the open door of the bakehouse. The two officers were standing bent over their makeshift washbasins, splashing water over their bare shoulders and chests. They stopped when they noticed her. One of them said something to the other and beckoned her, with a huge grin, to come inside.

Taken by surprise at finding them still there, but encouraged by their friendliness, she stayed where she was, twiddling the hem of her dress nervously. The soldier with the big grin who had gestured to her, playfully splashed water towards her. His companion held out a bar of chocolate and said something in broken German. But Anni, remembering her mother's warnings, scuttled away, still clutching the hem of her dress.

"Not the best way to make friends," said Victor. "Mind you, I suppose there wasn't much time."

"No," said Anni. "The Russians took over. Otherwise, everything would've been different. I would've been different."

She had often wondered how things would have been had the Americans kept possession of the area. She was convinced it would have become part of the West and she, along with everyone who was dear to her, would not have ended up under the regime.

She had tried to cope with the propaganda, the flag-waving, and especially, the continuous surveillance.

In consolation she had told herself that she at least aspired to the higher ideals in life which, without the suppression, she possibly would not have valued in the same way.

All the same, she had felt weighed down by the system

and as she grew older the turmoil in her mind mounted. The idea of getting out became stronger and she knew, sooner or later, she would have to make the attempt to escape.

❦

Victor had opened another packet of mints. He had consumed great quantities while listening to Anni's story. "It's these or my pipe; it's damned hard to give up." He sighed. "Tell me to shut up and stop feeling sorry for myself."

"I'll have one," she said, "better a Polo junkie than a tobacco addict."

"I'm not so sure about that," he said. "The accepted wisdom keeps changing." Assuming a stiff schoolmasterly stance he raised his index finger, and imitating the querulous voice of one of their work colleagues he whined, "Don't say you haven't been warned." He sighed again and, feigning reluctance, held out the packet.

"I'll risk it," she responded. Grinning wickedly, she popped a mint into her mouth and, exaggerating his habit, crunched as noisily as she could.

He dipped one eyebrow and winked at her. "Touché!" he said.

Instantly she felt the ease return, the ease she had felt before he kissed her, and she was convinced she could cope with whatever the situation should bring.

I'm as comfortable with him as I've ever been, she told herself, and she believed it.

He leaned towards her as if to kiss her again. But he must have thought better of it—after all, his earlier overture had not brought a definite response, at lease not one to encourage him. He turned away and studied the stained glass again. Unconvincingly this time.

After a while, he said, "Back to the café then, shall we?"

Chapter Seven

W hen did you arrive?" said Herr Weitermann taking the keys from Anni. She was standing in the doorway with Victor and looking back into the Vienna.

"Late last night," she said.

"Are you staying long?"

"About two weeks."

"Good, come again, on early closing night. We can have a chat and a glass of wine. Did you have a good look upstairs?"

"Yes, thanks," said Anni.

Frau Weitermann thrust her head through the service hatch. "Have a quick peek at the back room and the old bakehouse."

"Love to!" said Anni. "But I don't want to invade your privacy and…"

"Ach! Don't worry about that," interrupted Frau Weitermann.

❦

Stübchen they had called it. It was the back room behind the shop and they had lived their day-to-day lives there. It held many memories for Anni.

She pictured her father sitting in his leather swivel chair, taking a rest from the baking. Her mother would join him when business was slow, using the time to do household chores, ironing, sewing, silver polishing; on rare occasions relaxing with a book.

Anni saw herself, doing her homework.

The faces of relatives and friends passed fleetingly through her mind; figures from the past settled around the big solid table, talking…

"Follow me," said Frau Weitermann. "If Herr Darrenbach comes in," she called over her shoulder, "give him the package next to the cash register."

"Darrenbach!" Anni went rigid. "Impossible!"

She became aware that Frau Weitermann and Victor were looking at her.

"Yes!" said Frau Weitermann. "He phoned in an order just now. D'you know him? I've never met him. Karl has." She seemed intrigued by Anni's excitement.

Anni collected her wits. "Where's he living? Is it local?"

"Yes! Bahnhofstrasse, number thirteen. Lovely house, painted pink."

"How old is he?"

"Karl says he'd be fifty-something."

"Can't be Rudolf," Anni muttered. He'd be over seventy now. But the surname… ." She shrugged her shoulders.

All the same, 13 Bahnhofstrasse was a house she intended to call on.

Anni was taken aback as she and Victor entered the Stübchen of the Vienna. *This isn't it*, she thought; *it's not the room I remember.*

Frau Weitermann stood, her hands clasped over her ample tummy, proudly surveying her domain.

There's no atmosphere, Anni thought.

"Everything in here's new," beamed Frau Weitermann. "We did it as soon as we could. After the Wall, you know. For a start, I got rid of that awful hessian wallpaper." She gave a shudder. "Then we painted the walls a nice bright pink. When we took over, there was no furniture, until the State supplied us with the basics. But recently we bought our own."

Frau Weitermann was so sure of her improvements that she did not ask for any opinion. But Victor who had noticed Anni draw in her breath, and had seen how her eyes flashed towards the ceiling, knew she was appalled.

"Excuse me, I've forgotten something!" said Frau Weitermann, tapping her forehead. "You carry on, I'll be back shortly."

"What happened to your furniture?" whispered Victor. "Your parents couldn't have taken it with them."

"No, they didn't. Most of it was rifled by the officials. My cousin told Mother about it later. Maybe I'll come across some of it one day."

She pointed to the middle of the room. "Our big oak table stood there. You could really lean on it. Not like this flimsy thing."

Memories were racing through Anni's mind, like wisps of cloud blown across the sky.

Mother, sitting at the table facing the open door to the shop, weighing out five grams of precious coffee into tiny home-made reusable paper bags, her target being a hundred portions for every half kilo.

Mother, sitting behind the shiny letter balance, concentrating; her intelligent blue-grey eyes occupied with the task. Slim and shapely with her tiny waist, blond hair and smooth-skinned face with its high cheek-bones. Beautiful, and so much younger-looking than her years.

The difficulty with the coffee had been that in the first few years after the war it was extremely hard to get hold of. It was smuggled in from the Western Zone or bought on the black market, and both practices were illegal. So, real coffee could only be sold to trusted customers. But the sale of it was an open secret. The aroma of it brewing could not be disguised and masking the smell of the roasting process was impossible. Once the real coffee had run out it was back to selling ersatz.

The image of her mother faded and was replaced by one of the whole family sitting around the table gluing down ration stamps for butter and sugar which customers had exchanged for cakes and pastries. She saw the small bowls of flour and water, used to glue the stamps in blocks of ten by ten onto sheets of newspaper. Later, they would be handed in to the council receiver.

This image faded too, and she was surprised by the mundane picture which replaced it. Gooseberries were on the table; piles of them; and she and the rest of the family were cutting off the stalks to prepare the fruit for jam making.

Anni brushed the hair from her cheek and looked at Victor. "Just think," she said, "all those subversive activities going on here. My parents could have gone to prison just for telling political jokes. Everything was risky; nobody could be trusted."

"Dangerous times," said Victor.

"Yes. Mother would have been worried sick if she'd known what I heard; in case I let something slip to the teachers."

"Did she think they were Stasi?"

"She couldn't take that chance; the Nazis planted snoopers…I was always looking over my shoulder. Karin was one of the few people I could talk freely to."

"D'you think you'll find her?"

"I hope so. I really want to know what happened to her. There's so much to… ." Her voice trailed off as she started walking around the room, looking indifferently at some of the Weitermanns' expensively framed prints; she was remembering an incident during a German lesson when Karin had been the only one among her fellow pupils to stand up for her.

"Just to give you an idea," Anni said, turning to Victor, "we were reading Anna Seghers' *Das Siebte Kreuz* in class. One of the characters in the book, a young boy, had his bike stolen. The Gestapo got involved. They suspected that an escaped prisoner from a concentration camp had taken it and they wanted a detailed description of it. The boy had scraped every penny together to buy his most treasured possession, but his memory suddenly became rather vague as he realised that the price of its return would be the recapture of the prisoner. He didn't want that.

"We all agreed that the boy had done the right thing and our teacher considered this was the end of the matter and moved on to another topic. I kept thinking about the story. I put my hand up. 'Would you praise me if I were to help a Stasi prisoner to escape?' I said.

"A hush fell over the class. Parmenides—that's what we called our teacher, a classic scholar who loved to baffle us by quoting from the *Way of Truth* in the original Greek— was taken aback. He screwed up his eyes. He mumbled ineffectually.

"Red Sybille jumped to her feet. 'What a stupid question! Any prisoner of the Stasi is an enemy of the people. Everybody knows that.' Her neighbour nodded wildly. They whispered to each other, wrote something in their exercise books. Other voices came out in support of Sybille.

" 'It's not stupid at all,' Karin shouted, to make herself heard. Why don't we discuss it?' she challenged the teacher.

"He had composed himself. He stood up. 'Silence!' he commanded. 'Anni will stay behind. The rest of the class is dismissed.'

" 'Why put yourself in danger, and me as well?' Parmenides asked very quietly once we were alone in the classroom. I'd expected an angry telling-off but for the next few minutes he just sat there studying me closely. But underneath his composure I sensed he was worried. I could tell from the way his eyelids twitched. I kept thinking: you're not a Party disciple so I might be lucky.

"After what seemed ages, he said, 'You're a bright girl, you ought to have known better. You must realise, I shall have to report this. If I don't, they will,' he gestured to Sybille's corner. 'I'll do what I can, but be circumspect in the future.' He smiled at me and stood up, tapped me on the head as if I were a pet dog. 'Promise?' he said.

"I promised."

"Were you all right?" Victor asked.

"Yes, eventually—after a grilling by the headmaster, and after his severe warning. Parmenides though was moved to a village school where, finally, he retired.

"I did become more careful. Don't really know what possessed me to ask that question in the first place. On the other hand... ." She gave a crackling laugh. "It must have been the weather; I felt exceptionally high spirited at the time." (On her way to school she had enjoyed slithering through drifts of powdery snow. Lazy soft flakes of the white stuff were still falling and she had chased after them, trying to catch them on her tongue.)

When did cautiousness become part of my character, she thought? *I suppose being guarded became second nature, I learned too well. Anyway, I probably had the potential for being secretive. Well, whatever, it must have happened quite gradually, and later I didn't know when being vigilant became automatic. Introducing Victor as a colleague was all part of the same thing. I might as well admit it; I didn't want Maria to ask personal questions about us. I wonder if he realised it. He keeps telling me I'm nice, but—!* She sighed.

"Anyway, I kept my promise to Parmenides but that didn't mean I changed my attitude, you know. I was an expert at putting on an act."

As she elaborated she felt some of the agitation she had known so well, and her words came out rapidly. When she had reached her late teens it became a game to recite the official line to her parents after coming home from school.

She did it with such conviction that it worried them. They wondered if, finally, she had been brainwashed. But those were the only times the slogans crossed her lips.

"Do I sound self-righteous?" she asked, but she did not allow Victor time to answer. "In those days I was so certain." Seeing his raised eyebrows, she continued, "No, I haven't changed my views. But I wonder if they would have been the same if my parents had been Party members."

He shook his head. "You're not the flag-waving type."

With a little embarrassment she said, "No, but I used to be a day-dreamer."

Victor grinned. "Weren't we all?"

As a girl Anni had imagined herself in heroic situations. In one recurring flight of fancy, she had joined a resistance group and been given an important mission.

Sometimes, often during dinner, her eyes would glaze over and she would be oblivious to her surroundings. It was then that her mother nudged her to bring her back to reality. At those times, her father merely smiled, saying, "*Anni ist wieder am Dösen.*" Something which invariably prompted Wulf to chant: "*Döskopf! Döskopf!*" After which he stuck his tongue out at her.

"And you can stop laughing: 'Dozy head!' indeed."

"Sorry," Victor chuckled, and raised his hands to protect himself.

His mirth was just one of the ways he had of making her feel comfortable with herself. It seemed natural to trust him with the minutiae of her earlier life. Not long ago, inner warnings of possible regrets would have been enough to make her wary of revealing too much of herself. Now there was a craving, almost, to share her experiences with him.

Anni's reflections were interrupted by the sound of footsteps approaching. "Must be Frau Weitermann," she said.

Victor was studying a small bronze figurine of a dancer. It was exquisite and as such stood out from the rest of the displayed knick-knacks. "It's got to have been a present," he said under his breath.

As Anni glanced at him she noticed that the little piece of toilet paper he had used to cover the cut on his chin was gone. It was now lodged on the inside of his shirt collar. She considered the tiny piece of shrivelled paper, a minor detail in itself, she knew, but she felt a wave of affection come over her.

"Sorry I deserted you," said Frau Weitermann rushing into the room. She took hold of Anni's hand and steered her towards the shop doorway. "Herr Darrenbach's just come in. See for yourself."

Anni looked into the shop. Leaning against the cake counter was a tall, broad-shouldered man, casually dressed in blue jeans and black cotton shirt. His thin dark hair was greying at the temples. Strands of it were held together at the nape of his neck by a thin rubber band.

"D'you know him?" said Victor.

"I'm...not sure," Anni said slowly.

She studied the man carefully. Was there a resemblance to Rudolf? She recalled the fine features of the man she had known, his aquiline nose and long narrow head, the almost Mediterranean colouring. This face, at the counter, was of a rugged kind with an upturned nose.

"Wait a minute!" she whispered. "It could be Rudolf's son—Rudolf's someone I used to know—Darrenbach isn't a common name and he did have a son, as I remember. Fabian, I think it was. I even saw him once, long ago, at Rudolf's flat. Well, not quite see; that's an exaggeration. Had a glimpse of him's more accurate."

He scared me witless, she thought, *no other word for it.*

She gently touched Victor's arm. "I'll tell you about it sometime."

"Sounds interesting," said Victor.

Herr Darrenbach was getting ready to leave the shop. Anni's eyes followed him as he made his way awkwardly to the door.

Of course! All at once she was sure. Yes, it had to be Fabian. She had forgotten about the artificial leg. Rudolf had told her about the childhood accident.

She closed her eyes and listened intently for the metallic click of the knee as it locked firm when he transferred his weight onto it. Yes! Just like the sound she had heard before, from her hiding place… .

❦

"I've got some photographs of the café and shop," said Frau Weitermann, "from just after we took over." She rummaged around in the drawer of her small desk. Not finding what she was looking for, she pulled the drawer right out and placed it on top of the desk. "They must be here somewhere," she said, opening the first of several fat brown envelopes and spilling its contents onto the desk.

Appreciating the trouble Frau Weitermann was taking, Anni and Victor looked on in silence while the envelopes were systematically sifted.

It was the small matter of picturing her child's bed as it stood pushed against the wall of the Stübchen—at about the spot where Frau Weitermann was searching for the illusive snaps— that made Anni think of her early fall from grace, and of Walter Ziegenbart.

She had been almost nine years old when she fractured her leg during physical training at school. The leg was in plaster from the toes right up to her thigh. Because the café and shop were open and running, her bed had been moved downstairs into the back room so that she would not have to lie upstairs alone. But as her parents were busy, and she was often left with nobody to play with, she had become bored.

She discovered something to pass the time; she found if she squeezed her thighs together it gave her a warm pleasurable feeling—naturally she kept on doing it.

One afternoon as she was once again engaged in this agreeable activity—she was lying on the bed, her face flushed and making the usual noisy breathing sounds—her mother came in. Anni thought nothing of it and continued with what she was doing; until her mother's thunderous voice made her stop abruptly. She had never sounded so angry. "Stop it! Stop it at once! Whatever d'you think you're doing? Don't ever let me see you doing that again!"

Looming above her, Anni saw her mother's eyes full of horror and distaste. But Anni, in her innocence, could not understand what she had done that was so bad.

Her mother had stormed out of the room and Anni lay there, confused. Only slowly did it dawn on her that her entertainment must have been something really terrible for her mother to be that disgusted. Anni cringed at the thought of her father being told.

For many years afterwards, anything to do with that part of her body, or anyone else's, became taboo. So it was not surprising that she did not tell her parents about the incident with the elderly Walter Ziegenbart.

He had moved into one of the flats opposite, and before long he had become a regular customer at the café. He seemed to spend half his time dropping in for a "quick drink". He was a heavy drinker. According to Anni's father he was never sober, not even in the mornings, though at the same time he was never what could be described as incapable. From the start he was generally disapproved of. His motives were suspected when he struck up a rather unlikely relationship with a retired schoolmistress who lived nearby and on whom he allegedly sponged.

Until the day he said to Anni, "I've got something to show you," she had not taken much notice of him. Her parents had always discouraged his attempts at familiarity, and on the rare occasions when he installed himself in the back room, he had not spoken to her.

She had just come home from school, alone, when he called out to her from the archway to the courtyard, directly opposite the café. She hesitated. But wondering what he wanted, and being nosy, she walked towards him. From the entrance of the archway he gestured to her to follow him. With Anni close behind, he picked his way across the large uneven cobblestones of the courtyard, passing an old broken-down carriage before coming to a disused stable.

The door creaked as he pushed it open. Stepping inside he invited her to come in. She stopped at the entrance; something did not seem quite right, and when he called out to her from inside the stable there was an urgency in his voice she mistrusted.

She was looking from the sunny courtyard into the interior of the stable and it took her a few seconds to adjust her eyes to the dimness before she could make out his figure clearly. He was facing her and, for the first time, she noticed how ugly and bloated his face was. His unhealthy reddish colouring accentuated the coarse and heavy nose.

While she was looking at his features she realised that he was fumbling with his trousers, and when he lowered his eyes she looked down too. He was standing, legs slightly apart, with his trouser fly open.

She backed away from him and saw the sneering grin on his face. He laughed at her shocked expression. As though under some horrid compulsion she looked again and saw him take *his reddish looking 'Hammel', as her mother called this part when she mentioned it to her brother, into his hand.*

The incomprehensible size of it made her gasp with horror. "Come and touch it," he said, and he took a step towards her.

Hearing him speak broke the spell; while only seconds earlier she had stood rigid, unable to move, she now turned and dashed across the yard and back home.

Life, Anni thought, is a whole series of accidents. You happen to be in the wrong place at the wrong time and there you go, repercussions, inhibitions...

After the Ziegenbart fiasco, Anni grew even more neurotic. She would not undress in the common changing room for swimming lessons but put on her swimsuit at home and change back into her clothes in the toilets. The other girls did not mind showing themselves. They romped about in various states of undress. She was out of it all.

Rudolf encouraged her to look at herself in a new light. He did not see anything dirty in being naked. How fortunate that life's accidents work both ways.

❦

"Penny for your thoughts," said Frau Weitermann trying to attract Anni's attention. "It's typical, I can't find those photographs, I was sure they were here." She sighed. "I'll have to show you next time."

She walked over to the glazed side door and beckoned to them. They followed her into the kitchen. It too had been modernised. The atmosphere of its once unfussy functionality had gone. The bulky black coal-fired stove, which had stood against the wall on one side of the kitchen, had been taken out and so had the small gas cooker. None of the heavy cast-iron pots and pans which had hung from large hooks all around the stove were there either. The kitchen, Anni had to admit, was practical, but still she could not help feeling a little sad. She noticed that the white ceramic sink unit under the window to the inner yard had been exchanged for one of gleaming stainless steel. And because new modern wall units had been fitted, she was hard pressed to remember where the shelf had been on which her budgerigar's cage had stood.

"The bakehouse hasn't been touched," said Frau Weitermann apologetically as she led them along the passage towards it. "Everything there's the same, only we've never used the oven, we didn't need to. We did suggest that it be kept in working order, but it wasn't up to us."

"So, who's doing your baking?" Anni said.

"The State Bakery used to, but since the Wall came down, the Kaisers down the road supply us. It suits me fine, especially since we're retiring soon."

"But the new furniture…"

"We'll take it with us of course," said Frau Weitermann.

On entering the spacious bakehouse, Anni walked all around it. She stopped briefly at the door to the yard and looked across to the empty laundry and storerooms. She went over to the oven and laid her hand on one of its iron doors. In the winter she had always enjoyed the oven's warmth. Her room was directly above it and was kept cosy by a time-honoured version of underfloor heating. In comparison, the room above the laundry and stores was an icebox. A large part of the bakehouse was taken up by the oven with its metal runners. Piping hot baking trays full of delicious cakes were left to cool on them until needed in the shop. She opened the door to the main baking compartment and remembered her father as she had seen him shortly before she left.

Competing with the noise of clattering trays, he was whistling an old tune from the 1920s, as he often did. She tried to remember the tune but could not. He was dressed in his customary black and white check trousers, white tunic, white apron and wearing a high, white, cylindrical hat.

It occurred to her that he had been about as old then as she was now. With a sudden twinge she recalled thinking that he was getting old. His black hair was losing the battle against the invading grey and he had started to put on weight around his middle.

As it happened he did not mind being teased about his increasing girth; she had heard him say, good-naturedly, as he patted his tummy, "It's what's cost me most of my money."

❦

"D'you mind if I take this?" said Anni, picking out a teaspoon from a bucket of assorted cutlery.

"Take what you like. I'm scrapping it anyway. We can't take everything," Frau Weitermann said. "I had a sort-out the other day."

She stopped speaking when her husband stuck his head through the door. "Sorry folks," he said, "but the wife is needed in the shop." She excused herself for the second time.

Holding up the spoon to Victor, Anni said, "It used to be my brother's, I'll send it to him. He'll remember it."

Wulf had firmly believed nobody knew about his little spoon. He was never without it. He kept it in the pocket of his leather trousers. But he did not always push it far enough down and the A-shaped end of the handle would stick out.

He was between eleven and twelve when he was at the peak of his "spooning career".

For a boy of his age he was very short and extremely thin. Spindly legs and knobbly knees protruded from the short lederhosen he regularly wore. Despite his thinness he had a voracious appetite, and because he had a particular penchant for anything sweet he was continually on the lookout for the odd "spare" piece of cake, pudding and fruit tart filling.

On entering the bakehouse Wulf would look around for would-be observers and, at the same time, seek out his objectives. Seeing a dish with one of his favourites, stewed gooseberries or cherries, he would casually walk up to it and, when within striking range, he would whip out his little teaspoon and plunge it into the fruit.

The lightening speed with which he moved had reminded Anni of the striking motion of a cobra. She had spied on him on one of his escapades, and afterwards watched him cleaning the cherished spoon, smoothing it in his hands, gently rubbing it with a piece of soft cloth until it gleamed. He had even given it a name. "'Engel A'," she heard him whisper. The shape of the handle was the reason for the 'A', but she could never understand why the 'Engel'. There was nothing angel-like about it.

Wulf did not know that Anni had ever seen him on his raids. The return of his spoon would make him think.

"Your brother…" Victor paused to crunch a mint; "he's still got a sweet tooth?" He laughed.

"As far as I know, but I don't see much of him."

"Where's he living nowadays?"

"Down south, near Frankfurt. When I go to Germany it's to visit Mother and that's where I tend to stay. He comes up to her place and we see each other then."

"Your mother lives in Westphalia, doesn't she?"

"Yes, that's right, quite a distance from Wulf." Anni walked over to an antediluvian piece of apparatus bolted to the floor; her father had used it for whipping cream and mixing dough. "Anyway," she continued, leaning her shoulder against it, "for many years Wulf and I haven't been close. But I have the feeling things might change. Recently, he seems to have mellowed, probably Helga's influence. Since he married her he's stopped being a workhorse; they only married just over a year ago."

Anni elaborated on Wulf's newly discovered interest in gardening and wildlife. In years gone by he would not have dreamed of single-handedly digging out the ground and installing a thirty-foot pond, and of worrying about the frog population. All he was concerned about was his computer business.

Then they heard Frau Weitermann approaching through the passageway.

"Maybe we've taken enough of her time?" Victor suggested.

Anni agreed. But before they all went back to the Stübchen, she just had to go over to her father's old worktable. The uneven surface looked dull and grey; it had lost the fresh amber sheen it had in the days when it was cared for. She pulled first on one handle and then on the other of some containers under the work surface. They still slid easily on their metal runners.

Chapter Eight

Anni and Victor came into the market square from the alleyway which led from Wallenstein Street.

It was market day, but even though some of the stallholders had started packing up, the square still buzzed with activity. If the barrow-boys were to be believed, apples had never tasted sweeter, pears never juicier; "*Birnen zum Austrinken*," a stub-nosed, freckle-faced lad shouted, outdoing his neighbours with his salesmanship. He grinned cheekily when he noticed Anni looking at him. In a small alcove across the isle from the boy, she saw colourful skirts hanging from rails, waving in the slight afternoon breeze. Close by, roasting sausages spat grease into the hot coals.

She gazed at the stalls and remembered the sparse displays of old. "See what you can get," she heard her mother say. "Accordingly I'll decide what's for dinner. If it's carrots it'll be stew." *Got some bananas once—I saved mine; it was all squashy when I got round to eating it.*

She looked at the faces of the people milling around, but there was nobody she could recognise as anyone she had once known. Then she realised, the people she was looking at were young; she was thirty years out of date.

They walked on further into the market as Victor (who had been quiet and appeared to be preoccupied) fumbled with another packet of mints. He stopped and offered her one. "I think I'll stay another day," he said hesitantly. "I don't feel like going tomorrow. D'you mind?"

"Mind? No, that's fine!" Anni said, giving his hand a squeeze. "I'm glad."

He looked at her questioningly.

"Really!" she said.

Immediately she wished she had bitten her tongue. *That's fine!* she mimicked to herself. *I'm glad! Really! Is that the best I can do? I should've told him it's wonderful.*

She was enjoying being with him more than she would admit. She felt a flush of headiness at the thought of spending an extra day with him, but it did not last; doubts kept creeping back. She wondered if she was allowing herself to be pulled in a direction she was not ready for. The trip was supposed to be a sort of pilgrimage, and she had not meant to get into an emotional muddle over Victor. *Maybe that's what Mother had warned me of.*

※

I'm not an ogre, surely, Anni thought. Nevertheless, she could not deny that he seemed much relieved after owning up to his wish to stay another day.

She was fingering the dark-green silk scarf Victor had bought for her from one of the stalls. ("The colour will complement your eyes," he had said when, with a flourish, he had presented it to her.) Walking next to him she could see he was back to his lively, inquisitive self, humming as he looked up at several slate-covered roofs sporting rows of dormers. Then, apparently remembering something, he rushed towards the nearest doorway. It was the entrance to the Vienna's connecting building, and on a plaque above the doorway's curvature was displayed 1540, the date she had mentioned in the café's yard.

As Anni joined him in old Wagners' doorway, Victor was intrigued by a street of houses leading out of the square, which seemed suitable only for midgets. From behind the toy-like buildings, and in contrast to them, rose a high tower. "That's one of the watch-towers," she explained; "fifteenth-century, they're all around the town."

Before leaving the square they passed the town hall and, on its south side, they looked at what Victor had taken to be a spear hanging from the wall. It was in fact an ancient measuring instrument used by the townsfolk of the time to check that the traders had not cheated them in the length of cloth they had bought. As he was inspecting it, the town hall clock started to chime; its gilded clock face crowned by a black and gold globe showing the moon phases. Anni pointed out the two he-goats above it. It was three o'clock, and each time the clock chimed the goats butted their heads violently together.

They walked towards St Michael's Church. Extensive renovation and rebuilding was in progress all around them.

"And I thought everything was the same," said Anni, skirting around a pile of new bricks. "It isn't."

"Traffic jams must be new," said Victor.

"Yes, too many cars. You can't play in the streets any more."

"We used to do that in Bury St Edmunds."

"I thought you were a Londoner!"

"Well, I am, almost; we moved to Wimbledon when I was ten. Not much left of Bury in me now so I don't have your sentiments."

"I remember horse-drawn carriages, and sleigh bells," she said dreamily as they stood at the kerb and looked at the slow-moving traffic. And she wondered, *is Rudolf in one of the cars? He could be standing over there in the crowd...*

❧

Demolished houses became more frequent as they came nearer to the church. Once they had been good, solid houses and had stood for decades, even centuries.

Passing some boarded-up cottages only steps away from the church, Anni stopped abruptly. "Steinstrasse's gone, there's nothing left, the cinema's gone too! It's a wasteland!"

Sticking out from a clump of weeds, a board announced that a branch of the Dresdner Bank was to be built there. Anni was looking at the board when a young couple came over to ask for directions to the travel agency. "The one near the town hall," the woman said.

Anni had noticed the busy new agency earlier and seen the window display offering travel to exotic destinations.

"*Nachholbedürfnis,*" she said under her breath after the couple had gone.

"That's a mouthful," Victor mumbled. "*Bedürfnis* is a need or want, *nachholen* is to make up for something, I see what you mean."

❧

Inside St Michael's Church it was very quiet. Anni and Victor were alone except for an old woman kneeling and praying silently near the altar.

Every so often, Victor stopped to look at the stained glass windows, wooden carvings and stone figures; he took a long time over the elaborately worked pulpit.

They talked in whispers and when they became aware of it they smiled at each other.

Victor had come along to see the inside of the church under protest. He disliked churches, all churches; to him they were symbols of indoctrination and repression, but he admitted to admiring the workmanship and beauty of the artefacts.

Anni was not a believer either, but she liked the peaceful atmosphere and the serenity she was able to absorb from the revered buildings. She never forgot that while she was growing up, and even as an adult, there had been times when she wished she could believe. But there were too many nagging doubts. She had cursed her inability to accept without question. Others did, yet she would turn every religious claim over in her mind.

She had asked herself why it should be that honesty and integrity were seldom rewarded, whereas opportunism was. The argument that the just rewards for the choices we make are to be reaped in the hereafter initially consoled her. But it lost all plausibility when the priest giving religious instruction had no answer to the contradictions she thought she had detected.

She had wrestled with the problem for some time; at first on her own, but eventually she had asked the priest. Exactly how she had phrased her question she could no longer remember, but in essence she wanted to know how it could be reconciled that each individual is said to have choice and is free to act, when it is also supposed that absolutely nothing happens without the will of God. She reminded the priest that he had told the class: not a single hair on his own head, or anyone else's, would bend unless God willed it.

She had put up her hand and asked the question during one of the lessons, and she could not understand why the priest was angry with her, had scolded her, told her sharply to sit down and stop being troublesome. Then he proceeded to preach to all of them about the need to have blind faith.

The need to have faith…Anni repeated to herself. As if it were possible to order oneself to have faith! The idea was contemptuous.

She had continued to attend the lessons which took place out of school hours and within the church grounds. Attending them was strongly discouraged by the teachers at school, so it was something which had given her a chance to thumb her nose at the system—and of course, she continued with the lessons because her parents insisted on it. However, she never again asked the priest for clarification.

Chapter Nine

Victor's extra day in Aschersleben promised to be scorching hot. So, following Anni's suggestion, they were pleased to spend it out in the open. Soon after breakfast they started to explore the tree-lined walkways of the Promenadenring encircling the inner part of the town. They were situated just beyond the ancient town wall on the site of the former moat—over the centuries the 1200-year-old town had vastly increased in size and, eventually, had outgrown the confines of the wall.

As they ambled along the quaint and leafy walkways, which stretched for more than three miles, they stopped to look at particularly interesting parts of the wall.

At times the river flowed swiftly alongside them. Victor was pleased when, on deviating from the pathway, he discovered the ruins of a water mill which lay almost totally hidden under the lush vegetation and which Anni had completely forgotten about.

The only thing that marred the out-of-time feel of the walkways were the trenches, dug up by local workmen for the renewal of crumbling water pipes. Many a time Victor was in danger of falling over heaps of new piping and work equipment when his inquisitiveness overcame caution. Occasionally, the trenches carried on into intercepting streets—with all the traffic disruption that entailed.

Outside Anni's former grammar school—located within the circular walkways, as were many of the town's schools—building materials were piled so high that they obstructed the view into the school grounds.

While they were crossing Schiller Street, Anni saw the house where Rudolf had lived, and her steps slowed as she recalled the last time she had been there. She glanced at Victor who was taking some photographs; he had not noticed her hesitation.

No, I won't tell him yet, she thought, *and then not all of it... .*

❦

When the heat of the afternoon became overpowering they rested on a bench in the welcome shade of a group of broad oak and chestnut trees. Leaning against Victor's shoulder with her eyes closed, Anni said quietly, "I've often wondered what would've happened if my father hadn't returned from the war."

"We probably wouldn't be sitting here," said Victor.

"Alexander wanted to take us back to Russia with him."

"We definitely wouldn't be sitting here," Victor said very quietly.

"No," said Anni, "but he did come back. Mother always thought he would. I asked her once how close we'd come to living in Russia."

"And?" said Victor.

"She didn't really say, but we never saw Alexander again, not after Father came back."

89

The heat had become even more oppressive as they relaxed in the dappled shade and Anni's head began to droop. As her chin touched the collar of her blouse, she sat up with a start.

"Why not have forty winks," Victor suggested. "Go on," he encouraged when she seemed hesitant. He reached behind for his jacket and spread it across his lap. "Get your head down."

In the transitory moments before sleep, Anni glimpsed Alexander's ephemeral figure. He was short and stout with broad shoulders, often using his massive strength to toss her and Wulf playfully, in turn, into the air; catching them just before they touched the ground.

In her drowsiness, she saw him playing with their model toy shop—opening the little drawers and weighting up sugar and flour on the tiny scales.

He turned his open, pleasant face towards her and she saw the abundant freckles, especially around his eyes.

She could smell his distinctive scent which came from the cloves he always carried with him and frequently chewed.

He was singing a Russian folk song in his native tongue. He winked, and his image dissolved.

❦

At dinner that evening Victor returned to the unfinished topic of the afternoon, when Anni had been talking about her father who had suddenly come back from Russia in the June of 1947. He had been a prisoner of war there and, unable to announce his release to the family, had just turned up at the house.

Anni was playing ball with Wulf and some other children, a few streets away from home, when Christa, an older girl living nearby, shouted to them from across the road, "Wulf! Anni! Your father's home!"

Wulf hesitated, then stuck his tongue out and shouted back, "I haven't got a father!"

Anni took a while to take in the message, but then she realised the significance of it and started to run home.

Wulf followed, keeping a few steps behind, still protesting, "I haven't got a father! I don't believe it," he muttered over and over.

As they neared home their pace slackened.

Very gingerly, they made their way towards their back room. Anni stopped just inside the doorway, not knowing what to do next. Out of the corner of her eye she noticed Wulf turn on his heels and scamper away, repeating obstinately, though on the verge of tears, "I have no father! I have no father!"

She took an uncertain step forward. She could hear her mother's whispered exhortation: "Go on, greet your father, go on!"

Anni looked at the stranger standing in front of her with his arms held wide.

Is that him? He did not look at all like the man in the photograph; nothing like the father she had imagined.

He was painfully thin. His head, covered with long unruly black hair, seemed too large and heavy for his pitifully scrawny neck. His cheeks were hollow and a stubbly beard gave his face a haunted look. His clothes were hanging on him, making him look like a scarecrow.

"But his eyes," she said, "were reassuring. They were warm, and they lit up as he gave me a big happy smile. He held me in his arms and…"

A tear was slowly running down Anni's cheek. Victor had seen the drop of liquid well up in her eye, watched it grow bigger, overflow. Carefully, with the back of his hand he wiped it away. "It can't have been easy…for any of you," he said haltingly.

"No." She stared at their empty plates and began to fidget with her serviette as the waiter cleared the table.

> She had got used to her father's presence around the house, his appearance stopped being strange and she took to following him about—at first from a distance, then she became bolder and did not miss a chance of jumping onto his lap whenever he sat down.

> She remembered imitating her favourite green budgerigar. It had loved sitting on her shoulders to peck away at her earrings. She had nibbled her father's earlobes in a similar way and with just as much enthusiasm, making them into elongated fleshy things…

Still engrossed in her thoughts, she took a sip from her brandy glass, then set it down, twiddling with the stem. Composing herself, she pushed the glass aside.

"Father slowly recovered," she said, "except for the nightmares; they went on for years. He couldn't talk about what happened, not even to Mother. I was fourteen before he said anything to me."

From the start he had hated the idea of fighting, war. He just wanted to be left alone to build his business, to live happily with his family and see his children grow. But, he was conscripted into the army. To make the best of a bad job, he volunteered to work in the kitchens.

He was posted to Denmark, from there to Poland, and finally to Russia where he was taken prisoner near Moscow. "I never fired a single shot, so at least I can be sure I haven't killed anyone," he would say.

He felt extraordinarily lucky, and at the same time guilty, to have survived the prisoner-of-war camp. So many of his fellow inmates perished; hunger and disease were their enemy. Anni never forgot his matter-of-fact account of an outbreak of dysentery in the camp. Sick men, weakened by their illness, fell into the latrines and were drowned in the stinking slime.

There were memories which were a burden to him all his life: he had witnessed brutalities by some of his comrades whom he had thought of as decent human beings. Others had denounced fellow soldiers on trumped-up charges, just to gain some small favour.

"Anyway," she said, straightening up in her chair, "during his years under the GDR regime he came to detest the Stasi informers. One of them reported him for tearing up a picture of Stalin. He should have hung it in the café, but he wouldn't. He said he'd have no propaganda. 'I'll have nothing to do with it. I didn't in Hitler's days, and I'll be damned if I'm going to start now.' He got three months in prison for that!"

"Good Lord!" said Victor.

"Well, that didn't stop him. After he came out he refused

to let conscripts in; he had a thing about uniforms. He wouldn't even make an exception for his nephew, told him to go home and change his clothes."

"What about your brother when he…?"

"Oh, Wulf escaped before they could get him; that was way back in 'fifty-nine."

"That must have caused problems?"

"Well, no. For some reason his disappearance wasn't noticed. Mind you, he was working away from Aschersleben, staying with friends. The officials never came to enquire. Somebody wasn't doing his job."

"No," Victor grinned.

"We knew Wulf was going. He didn't say much about it but we knew; he never was a big talker. He was fed up with all the restrictions. He wasn't allowed to travel, that hit him hard. I'm sure you'll understand his frustration at that," Anni said, looking up. "He never regretted going. He saw the world, worked hard for it mind, and advanced himself by studying. But as I said yesterday, he became a workaholic, with no time for anything else—until recently that is."

The waiter arrived with a pot of aromatic coffee and set it down on the table.

Anni poured the steaming liquid and handed Victor his cup. "Sorry," she said, "I've been going on again. You must tell me if you're getting bored." Her eyes were questioning him as she spoke.

"I'm honoured that you're confiding in me," he said simply, openly meeting her gaze.

"That works both ways," she smiled. Realising the challenge in her voice, she felt herself blushing, and she quickly bent over her cup.

❦

For a while Anni and Victor had been quiet, intermittently sipping their coffee.

She knew he was mulling over her words. *I should have let him be*, she thought. *If he wants to tell me about himself he will do, in his own time…*

He cleared his throat. "You said once before that you didn't know much about me. The trouble is I'm tight-lipped." He coughed again. "I haven't always been that way. But something happened that made me distrustful of people, well, of women in particular. Oh dear," he said, noticing her puzzled expression, "I don't mean you. Sorry, I'm not doing very well, am I?" Under his breath, he added, "Could do with my pipe to clear my head."

"Look," she said, "tell me another time. I shouldn't have brought…"

"No, it's all right, the person I'm referring to is Helen. I met her in 'eighty-seven, during my home visit from Nepal. You know I was out there. Well, I fell in love with her. She said she felt the same. She didn't mean it though." He looked at Anni from under knitted eyebrows.

He's not finding this easy, she thought. *Just telling me the minimum, to get it out of the way.*

"I was terribly upset and it took me a long time to get over it. In short, she ditched me."

He raised his hand to attract the waiter. "Can I have the bill, please?" he said, when the waiter came.

❧

I wonder what happened with Helen, Anni thought as she and Victor walked along the hotel corridor to their respective rooms. She had wanted to ask him in the restaurant but he had effectively closed the subject and they talked of other things.

Stop speculating, she told herself. *I'm sure he will tell me, eventually, now that he's broached the subject.* But Anni could not easily divert her thoughts; not for the first time since dinner her mind returned to the topic of Victor and Helen's relationship. *What on earth had this woman done to him? He says that it took him a long time to get over her, but has he? He can barely talk about it. I must not read too much into that. Nobody likes to admit defeat. Anyway, when did the break-up happen…after he came back from Nepal?*

"I suppose it's time to say goodnight," Anni heard Victor say, interrupting her ponderings. They stopped outside her door.

"Yes," she said, facing him. "Sleep well! Don't forget you've an early start tomorrow, so have I. And no more arguments," she quickly added, "I will come with you to the station."

He took her hand. "I…" he started but did not continue. Still holding her hand he looked into her eyes.

He bent forward and, this time, she was not surprised when he kissed her on the lips.

He drew her close and she responded, not for long. *This isn't right*, she thought. *I'm losing control. I don't know yet what I want, but I don't want to be swept away by the moment. I let it happen in the past, but Victor's too precious…*

Gently but firmly she disengaged herself. "Right, time for bed!"

The expression on his face was a mixture of disappointment but also understanding. But what puzzled her was his look of relief. Thinking about it later, before she went to sleep, she wondered whether he had decided that intimacy might have been a little premature for him.

Chapter Ten

At lunchtime the next day, Anni sat alone in a small restaurant waiting for the sandwich she had ordered. Her table near the window overlooked Linden Street and the newly opened, bustling Hong Kong, though she was too preoccupied to take much notice of the trendy take-away.

After their breakfast, she had seen Victor off at the station. They had been in a rush to catch his train, but he managed to extract a promise from her to let him know if any problems arose. "I'll ring you," he shouted from the window of the departing train.

As she drank her coffee, her eyes wandered over a group of people standing just outside the entrance door. There were several men in uniform and a couple of young women in floral-patterned summer dresses.

The moment it registered that they were Russians, she felt a sudden apprehension; and immediately she wished for Victor's presence.

That's silly, she remonstrated with herself, *why should I be so nervous about seeing Russian soldiers, in this of all places? It was only to be expected. Panicking over the Gorbachev thing*

*when I first arrived might be quite excusable, but not this
childishness. Whatever's the matter with me, why the need for
Victor all of a sudden? I've been living on my own since I was
twenty, so who am I kidding? I know the answer. I might as
well admit it: my friendship with Victor is changing; it's progressing.
He's becoming part of my life.*

The ham sandwich arrived, and as she munched it she
considered the events of the previous night—particularly,
Victor kissing her for the second time.

For a moment she had wavered as to whether or not
to invite him in…

"See you tomorrow," he had said.

She remembered the thoughts that followed. For many
years she had been free of emotional entanglements. She
had been quietly content and assumed it would continue
that way.

Lowering her gaze, she noticed her empty plate and began
wiping her thumb and forefinger on the paper serviette.

*Well, I've learned to be sensible, and not before time! I'm too
old for wild abandon.*

※

Anni concentrated on the foreign sounds that were filtering
in through the open door.

She had recently bought a set of language cassettes, but
it was years since she had actually practised her Russian.
Apart from the occasional revision exercises in the early
days after leaving school, she had badly neglected it.

She had enjoyed her lessons at school and prided herself
on her working knowledge of the language. But now, even
though she listened most carefully, she could only understand
the odd few words. She could make no sense at all of the
conversation that was taking place outside.

When the Russians walked away, her eyes followed them. Even after they had disappeared from view, she was still looking in the direction they had gone, remembering…

What exactly am I remembering? The images I suppose. Without the words describing them? Anni thought about that for a while, wondering about "wordless images". *Are there such things? What does articulation add to them when one is old enough to talk about early experiences; does it alter them? Probably. But the raw images are all one has to work with, they are the "silent film" on which memories are based. I really must remember that when I think of my past…*

The Americans had left and there had been a short interlude under the British. Of them, she only had a vague memory, though one scene had stayed with her: a couple of uniformed men walking in step, erect, purposefully, and tucked tightly between elbow and waist they each held what she now knew to be a swagger stick.

Then the Russians came.

The common soldier looked very different from his American ally: poorly clothed, untidy and dirty. Many were pimply-faced youths. Their trucks looked uncared for, encrusted with dirt and mud as they were. Behind the trucks came open-topped lorries, and following these were vehicles which had dirty brown tarpaulins partly stretched over the rear. They were filled to the brim with men who were sitting on simple wooden benches along the sides, and also on the floor. As they drove over the cobbled street, the soldiers were thrown about en masse.

Looking down onto the tops of the vehicles she had been reminded of fields of wheat, tossed by a succession of sharp gusts of wind.

Some of the lorries had their floors strewn with brown sacks. Straw was spilling out through the sack ends and ragged holes; some soldiers were asleep on the improvised bedding.

The Russians came in very slowly, slow enough for the horse-drawn carts to keep pace with the trucks.

Towards the end of the processions were two more vehicles with tarpaulins. They carried the wounded; some with their arms in slings; others had head wounds or carried crutches. Several columns of foot soldiers completed the motley band. Compared to the way the Americans arrived, the Russians moved in as though they were defeated troops rather than victors. There was only a little heavy weaponry; most of the big stuff came in later.

Everyone from Anni's part of the building had come together to see the Russians move into the town: her mother, Frau Stuber, Fräulein Vogel and all the children.

Apprehension hung in the air and Anni sensed that this occupation was expected to be calamitous, more frightening than anything that had happened so far. After the arrival of the Americans the general feeling had been that the town was fortunate to have fallen into Western hands. But from the

Russians, the adults agreed, no mercy could be hoped for—fear had been fuelled by dreadful stories of pillage and rape told by refugees from Silesia and Prussia.

Once the vehicles and soldiers had passed, Frau Stuber with her children and Fräulein Vogel went back to their own flats.

Anni's mother took her scissors and hacked away at her blonde hair. Glossy strands of it were soon sliding to the floor. "They look like soft little birds," Anni said quietly. Then her mother sorted through her husband's clothes and put on the tattiest suit she could find. She covered her head with an old dark-blue plumber's cap a workman had once left behind, and which for some reason she had kept. Having made herself look as plain as possible, she turned her attention to their food provisions.

She systematically removed almost all of the tins, packets and jars from the kitchen and carried them down into the cellar, making several journeys of it. She also transferred the flour, which she had saved, into a couple of strong paper sacks. She moved these down, too. At the time, they still had plenty of coal, and by putting the food provisions under the top layers she judged she had found a safe hiding place. When there was no more room in the coal pen, she used blocks of firewood, which were stored next to the coal, as an additional hiding place.

Next, she went into the wine cellar and surveyed the remains of the stock. She took the last bottle of cognac and some of the wine bottles and hid them in a hole in the wall, behind a number of stacked empty beer barrels. The rest of the wine was left on the racks. She had tried to offload more of it into Fräulein Wagner's cellars, but the request was refused.

When all possible precautions had been taken, they settled down to wait, but nothing more was seen or heard of the Russians for the rest of that day.

❦

On her first evening alone in Aschersleben, Anni sat in her hotel room, bent over her journal. She had intended to record the days' events and thoughts in it before, but until now the pages had remained blank.

THE VISIT, she wrote, AUGUST 1991. She printed it, in capital letters, on the label of the front cover. She turned the next two crisp white pages over, wrote "Day Three" at the top of the third one and began with her systematic chronicling.

She described Victor's hurried departure that morning, her lunch in Linden Street and the group of Russians outside the door of the restaurant.

She stopped writing, pen poised…images of pimply-faced soldiers and muddy army trucks, scenes of primitive horse-drawn carts advancing as if in slow motion started to surge through her mind again.

Relaxing her grip on the pen and leaning back in the chair, she deliberated on how to proceed. She reached for her glass of whisky and took a sip. "I know," she mumbled.

Turning to the next page she set down a different sub-heading altogether: THE RUSSIANS, THEIR ARRIVAL PROPER.

Expanding on the memories she had reclaimed in the restaurant, she wrote about the day she came face to face with them.

So that the events would stay sharp in her mind, and also in order of occurrence, she made the following entries:

Our Russian occupiers had vanished—or so it seemed. Eventually we went to bed, fully clothed.

We were woken early the next morning—loud noises in the street. Looked out from our living-room window—saw neighbours herded out of their homes. They were made to stand in a line on the pavement facing the houses.

More soldiers arrived—watched them get out of their truck. They bypassed next door—stopped at ours—stampeded in. Everybody in the block was ordered out. We were manhandled down the stairs. Fräulein Vogel tripped and tumbled down the last few steps—saw her hobble out into the street with an injured leg. Earlier, I had heard her frantic prayers coming from the floor above.

Outside, the soldiers made us to understand that we had to obey orders—a rifle was fired into the air to show us what would happen if we didn't. I sobbed quietly—wouldn't stop till Mother ordered me to. We stood pressed together for what seemed an eternity. Our guard kept pushing us closer against the wall of the house. He shouted at us and I grew more frightened.

The looting seemed unimportant. I looked on as the soldiers ransacked our belongings. Boots were favoured objects, as were blankets, quilts and food, but most of all, alcohol. Bottles of wine were carried away like trophies. Everything, except for the wine and the things the soldiers stuffed into their pockets or hung round their necks, was dumped at the side of the road—fragile items were flung with the rest.

From down the street came a piercing scream— we thought it was Renate. Later we were told, her new doll had been taken from her by one of the soldiers. Her mother tried to retrieve it but she was pushed back and beaten. Renate's sister, Heidi, came to her mother's aid and all hell broke loose. We heard the soldiers yelling at each other; the sounds growing louder, more excitable, uglier. A superior officer sped by—breaks screeched. Afterwards the soldiers quietened down. Before long all of them were gone. From outside our house they had picked up armfuls of the booty. Left behind on the pavement was a trail of sugar, a solitary boot, odd pieces of clothing and three wheels of a toy train.

❦

As Anni outlined the bare bones of those distant events, the past returned to her in even more vivid and disquieting detail. Sitting in a tired wicker chair and writing feverishly, she paid no heed to its annoying creak or her discomfort.

She recalled how they had gone back into the house and walked through the devastated rooms, stepping over clothes and photographs, an upturned coal bucket and broken plates and glasses. Her mother did not even cry, and without uttering a word she picked up her valued oil painting from the living-room floor and leaned it against the balcony door; it had been torn out of its frame and carelessly thrown across the room.

Downstairs in the café, shop, back room, kitchen and the bakehouse, a similar sight greeted them. The entrance to the cellars had been forced but, miraculously, in the storage area, neither the pile of coal nor the heap of firewood had been disturbed. Of course, not a single bottle of wine was left on the racks and even those which had been hidden behind the beer barrels were gone. The barrels had all been smashed to pieces.

Abruptly, Anni's writing came to a halt with the tip of her fountain pen still touching the paper. The full stop at the end of the last sentence was fast turning into a blob; she noticed it and quickly let the pen slip from her grasp. Her stream of memories of that day had run dry and no matter how hard she tried she had no recall of how it had ended.

She thought of the days and weeks that had followed, and she came to the conclusion that much of what she knew of that particular time in her life was second-hand, having been told to her by her mother.

The flour, hidden away in the cellar, was not discovered during later searches either, and it helped them to get over the worst of the food shortages. Every morning and evening they ate flour and water porridge, a sort of gruel. Sometimes an egg and a little milk were added to it. Occasionally her mother bartered some flour for rabbit meat.

Like the other townies they called on farmers in the nearby villages to exchange valuables for vegetables and smoked sausage.

Some time into the occupation a rudimentary order was established, and with it came a rationing system. Things got a little better then. Also, the black market was flourishing and, once again, money was in demand—the trouble was her mother began to run out of it.

To make a living for the family, she needed to open the café again. It had been closed since her husband's call-up in 1940 but, with the help of a former accountant, she managed to get the necessary permit. To begin with, all she had to sell were dry bread rolls and ersatz coffee. Then she was granted a licence to sell a limited amount of schnapps. This turned out to be a mixed blessing. It was dangerous to collect the fortnightly allocation from the local wine trader as many publicans were robbed by soldiers lying in wait for them.

Her mother came up with the idea of using their old pram to transport the alcohol, instead of using the handcart—an old pram pushed by a mother accompanied by her two small children seemed an adequate camouflage—and when she actually employed the tactic it worked out very well. She only lost her supplies once, and that was not because of a robbery but a street accident.

The schnapps caused other problems. It was strictly forbidden to sell it to the Russians, but on a number of occasions drunken soldiers, having finished their own supplies, demanded more from her. For her own safety she sold them the schnapps, with the result that some of them got so drunk that they fell asleep on the floor of the café and lay there until they were collected by the military police.

The telephone shrilled.

It was Victor. He had made his way safely to Dresden...

"Let's not talk about me," he said, changing the topic of conversation. "How was your day?"

For the rest of the call he concentrated on Anni's concerns, asking her about every little thing that had happened since his departure, down to the choice of dinner menu.

"You couldn't be more keen to know if you were my mother," she said and laughed. She was surprised about his inquisitiveness—it verged on nosiness, she thought—but also pleased by his interest.

Chapter Eleven

For several days Anni had tried to make contact with Fabian Darrenbach and her old school friend, Karin.

On ringing the bell at 13 Bahnhof Street, Anni had received no answer. "Fabian and Elisabeth have gone away," the lady from next door said, leaning over the fence. "They'll be back on Monday."

Anni went to the house where Karin had lived but found only strangers there. She lost count of the number of doors she knocked on in the neighbourhood but she was out of luck. She did not learn one thing that might lead her to Karin. And when she visited the places they both had known, she did not fare any better. The answer to her question was always the same: "She doesn't live here." Nobody remembered Karin, or her family. But Anni was not going to give up easily. *She saved my life, for God's sake! That must mean something.* When she went back to the Weitermanns, and when she visited Maria again, she engaged them all in her search. And, of course, whenever she came across someone she had known in the past she asked about Karin.

Christa—the girl who, many years ago, had told Anni and Wulf of their father's homecoming—still lived in the same house; on the spur of the moment, Anni had tried her door. "I haven't seen Karin for at least ten years," the matronly woman sitting in an electric wheelchair said. "I know the two of you did everything together, inseparable you were, you even dressed alike." She laughed. "Remember the zebra skirts!"

At Christa's suggestion, Anni talked to a few former customers of the café; they were old men and women now. They told her that Frau Stuber had died six months earlier and that her children had moved away years ago. Anni learned that the Wagners, brother and sister, were dead also and that Frau Kamm was now living on the outskirts of town. One of the old ladies gave her the new address of Frau Lang, one of Anni's former teachers. With Frau Lang's help, she was able to recall the names and faces of many of her fellow pupils. However, disappointingly, she too could not help in the search for Karin, though she suggested Anni might place an advertisement for missing people in a local monthly publication. This sort of thing was often done, it seemed, after the Berlin Wall had fallen.

❦

Stopping off at an Italian ice-cream parlour on her way back to the hotel, Anni reflected on some of the people and places she had visited during the day.

The teacher's flat situated on the edge of the town had not been easy to find. It was a couple of minutes walk from the open-air swimming pool and, though she had avoided going near the place since she was fifteen, for her near drowning experience had put her off the pool, she had enquired at the ticket kiosk about the address.

It would have made more sense if I had developed some sort of water phobia, Anni thought...*Maybe it's because my scare somehow got tied up with the place, but not with swimming...*

On the morning of the incident, Anni and Karin had been revising together for school tests. But the weather being beautifully warm and sunny, the girls led each other astray and slipped out from Anni's room to go swimming instead.

They had never seen the pool so quiet. "They're all swotting at home," Karin said, as she dived into the water. She was a strong swimmer and confidently covered the pool several times.

After a while, she said, "I'll get out and get some ice-cream." She left Anni enjoying herself in the water.

"It was stupid of me to go so far from the handrails but something possessed me to try swimming the whole length," Anni admitted later. She had not attempted it before, and finding herself alone in the middle of the pool, she panicked. Thrashing about wildly, and gulping water, she went under. She struggled to keep afloat but could not. Eventually, a strange calmness engulfed her. She felt comforted by the water, and as she took in more she was sure she could hear melodies from Mozart's Eine Kleine Nachtmusik. A thousand tiny stars seemed to be glittering all about her.

"If you had not returned in time I would have drowned," Anni said. "The attendant was nowhere."

Because they were not supposed to have been at the swimming pool they decided not to say anything to their parents. "Let's keep it to ourselves," Karin suggested.

❦

At the hotel, Anni borrowed the local telephone directory from the reception desk and proceeded to leaf through its pages. The directory contained surprisingly few listings of telephone numbers for a town of that size—though many more telephones were being installed.

She spotted Karin's family name twice. With great excitement she rang the numbers but the people she spoke to were not related to Karin.

Nevertheless, a careful study of the directory provided Anni with some information of interest. Hans-Dieter Baumann, Friedrich Dreifuss and Peter Hopfenstange were listed. She tried Hans-Dieter first. He had been in the sixth-form class with her and, since they had lived close to each other, they often walked to school together. Unfortunately, Hans-Dieter was away on holiday and was not expected back for another two weeks; too late for her to meet him. When she discovered that she was speaking to Hans-Dieter's son, she introduced herself and left her home address and telephone number. "Maybe your father can help me to find Karin."

She then tried the number for Friedrich Dreifuss, but only managed to speak to his younger brother. He seemed to think it very strange that she should want to contact a fellow pupil after so many years. And, voicing his suspicion, he said several times, "How do I know that you're who you say you are?"

After this experience she almost did not ring Peter

Hopfenstange. In any case, she had known him less well than the other two. If it had not been for his name, she might even have forgotten him. Hopfenstange, hop-pole, certainly was not the right name for him. He was the shortest pupil of his year—maybe even the shortest in the whole school.

Hopfenstange answered the telephone when Anni rang a little later. When she asked him whether he remembered her he assured her that he did. He almost seemed hurt that she should have thought he might not. He kept repeating how pleased he was that she had contacted him and would not take "no" for an answer when he invited her to his home, so she agreed to visit him after dinner the next day. "It'll give me a chance to check around," he said.

Hopfenstange was still short; his height, or rather lack of it, did not come as a surprise. But what startled Anni were his cold, shifty eyes and his constantly moving gaze. His long, thin nose seemed even longer now; it was in sharp contrast to his tadpole-like mouth. Dark colouring and heavy eyebrows gave his face a menacing expression which his gushing friendliness was unable to disguise. Anni could not help feeling uncomfortable in his presence.

Standing in front of her, maybe to compensate for his shortness, he rhythmically elevated his slender frame by shifting the weight alternately from the tips of his toes to the backs of his heels. On her arrival, he had invited her to take a seat on the living-room sofa. He had sat in what she assumed to be his personal armchair. But he seemed unable to stay in it for any length of time. He was constantly getting up and sitting back down. Amazingly light on his feet, he moved around the living-room floor like a bouncing tennis ball, forcing Anni to follow his movements with her eyes and making her feel quite giddy. She could not help but make comparisons to the spectators at Wimbledon where all heads move in unison in pursuance of the ball.

Frau Hopfenstange's appearance was the opposite of her husband's. She was big and round and at least a head taller. She seemed ill at ease from the start and spoke very quietly and slowly. She soon excused herself to make some coffee and seemed noticeably relieved when she left the room. Anni had not even had a chance to inquire where she came from. But moments after Frau Hopfenstange had departed her husband volunteered the information: Brunhilde came from Brandenburg.

Once in full flow, Hopfenstange kept on talking. He recounted classroom events Anni had long since forgotten. He remembered quite a few of their fellow pupils and knew the married names of at least half of the girls. But he, too, could shed no light on Karin's whereabouts.

Trying very hard not to show her disappointment Anni only half-listened to his continuous flow of anecdotes. But when he referred to her disastrous demonstrations during their chemistry lessons, she felt annoyed.

When it came to performing practical experiments she had invariably been the first to be called to the front of the class where she was required to repeat Herr Baer's most recent experiment.

She had never liked chemistry; it was her weakest subject and she considered herself useless at handling test tubes, litmus paper, chemicals and at working the Bunsen burner.

She was sure it gave Herr Baer sadistic pleasure to shout at her and see her with shaking hands,

near to tears—of course, the rest of the class erupted
into merriment each time her name was called out.

Hopfenstange's voice sounded gleeful and Anni's irritation increased as he continued to gloat over her past inadequacy.

What a jumped-up little twerp, she thought. Normally she would have contained her animosity but looking at him standing there, full of pomp and self-righteousness, she felt impelled to remind him that he had only been average, and was that in all subjects, whereas her only failing had been in chemistry. "To be average," she said, "is to be mediocre, and if I couldn't be top, then I'd rather be bottom! If I remember correctly, Peter, you never excelled at anything, did you?"

Hopfenstange's jaw dropped, just as Brunhilde reappeared with the coffee. She glanced at Anni, then her husband, and timidly placed the cups on the table.

Anni looked across at the large woman opposite her and wondered how she, Brunhilde, had come to be married to Peter Hopfenstange. She felt a liking for Brunhilde and was just a little guilty at being partly responsible for her discomfort. *She must have heard the exchange between me and her husband*, Anni thought. And, trying to put her at her ease, she asked how life had changed since the fall of the Wall.

Brunhilde winced, and made a choking sound as she dropped the teaspoons. "I…I don't know…" she managed to mumble, and she looked to her husband for help.

Anni noticed that Hopfenstange squirmed at what seemed a perfectly ordinary question, and she wondered if it was because of her question or whether he was still smarting from their earlier exchange. She looked more closely at him. He was once more sitting in his brightly coloured armchair, but shifting uneasily in his seat. When he spoke he did so in a measured way, carefully weighing his words. His manner was no longer confident.

"There's really not much to tell," he said, answering for his wife. "After school I joined the technical drawing office of the State Tool Plant in Nord Strasse, and I worked there until…anyway, I worked there until recently, and now I…" Shaking his head, he propelled himself from his chair.

"Why don't you say you were made redundant?" Brunhilde blurted out, in what seemed an attempt to be helpful. But when the attention became focussed on her, her face showed alarm again. She turned abruptly and busied herself with the coffee.

"All right," Hopfenstange said, "I will! I was made redundant! And that after I worked my way to the top!" He laughed coarsely. "I used to be second-in-command, you know. Didn't miss a day, except for when I was in the Volksarmee." He slumped back into his chair and picked at the braiding on the armrest.

How pathetic he looks sitting there, deflated, Anni thought, and she wondered: *have I been a bit hard on him? After all, he's lost his job, and I do quite like Brunhilde; despite her size she gives the impression of being vulnerable.*

Her attitude having softened and feeling somewhat less antagonistic towards Peter Hopfenstange, Anni asked him how difficult it would be to find work.

He looked at her gloomily and shook his head.

"Maybe your old company will recover and you'll get your job back," she suggested.

He did not reply.

"I'm aware of the problem of unemployment," she said, "but—"

"I don't think I'll work again," he cut in defiantly. But he spoke quietly, almost under his breath.

"At least you're near retirement, it's much worse for the young," Brunhilde pointed out.

Hopfenstange sprang from his seat and glared at his wife. "You think so do you? What do you know?" His face turned a deep purple; he was breathing hard. He spun around to face Anni. "Those promises they made at unification sound very hollow," he hissed. "All lies!" His voice was shrill as he rammed home his grievances: "We're the poor cousins of the damned Wessis, that's what! Our factories are closing. All of a sudden, nobody wants our products. They tell us our industry's outmoded. Shoddy goods," they say. The ones who still have a job are paid less than in the West. To top it all," he screeched, "they come here in their Mercedes and expect us to thank them on bended knee. I didn't ask for any bloody favours. I was all right before the uni—" He threw his hands in the air.

Anni had been shaking her head in disbelief at his outburst, her anger mounted. Before he could say any more she challenged him: "Shouldn't you give the economy time to pick up?" She did not wait for his answer. "Nobody should expect miracles overnight—anyone who does must be naïve, stupid! Look around! Forty years of neglect! You can't put that right in a few months." Her knuckles were white as she gripped the side of the sofa. "Have you noticed the pollution?" She jabbed a finger accusingly. "Your stinking factories polluted everything. That's being reversed, and not at your expense!"

Anni took a deep breath. *Why shouldn't I say what I think; guest or no?* Looking straight into Hopfenstange's eyes, she said, "D'you want the Stasi back?"

Keeping her eyes fixed on him, she sank back into the sofa.

The silence that followed was too much for Brunhilde; she left the room with a strangled squeal.

Anni waited for Hopfenstange's reply.

He went over to the window and stood there, looking out; occasionally elevating himself in his former manner.

She was well aware that there were many who wished the regime back. Certainly, the ones who had lost their advantages did; and the opening of the Stasi files had shown how widespread the involvement of the population was.

She tried not to think about that when she mixed with the locals. She could not go about suspecting everyone she met; it would not be fair, and it would spoil her visit. But in Hopfenstange's case, she could not quell her suspicions. There had been such hatred of the new order: "I was all right before the uni—" She knew he had meant unification. She could still hear the passion in his voice. *But would he really have been so careless and shown himself up if he had something to hide?* Others—recent investigations had shown— were expert at covering their involvement. *But was he just a sympathiser, or had there been more to it?* How was she to know? One thing was sure, he felt hard done by. And as for ideological commitment, he had not spoken of any.

In her mind, she repeated what he had said, several times. He was still facing the window. *How much longer is he going to just stand there*, she thought?

When he did turn around, after some minutes, he spoke quietly; his tone full of apology. "No, of course I don't want them back. You're quite right to remind me. A short memory's a failure of human nature. I know I ought to be counting my blessings…"

Anni noticed how the words flowed more easily from his lips the longer he spoke, and when he finally came to a stop, his face held the beginnings of a smile. He raised his eyes to look at her again.

She was not taken in by his sudden accommodation. *It's*

too much of a turn-about. She was sure he had meant what he had said earlier.

It occurred to her that he might have thought she would be more sympathetic if he complained about his difficulties. *But why should he have thought that?* Maybe he considered her a foreigner, somebody he could appeal to as though she were someone emotionally uninvolved?

Hopfenstange's spinelessness, his efforts to ingratiate himself, had left a bad taste in her mouth. And when, a little later, he tried a more outrageous ploy and professed that he had opposed the old regime, she was convinced that his rebuke of the new situation ran deeper than just his worries about unemployment and rates of pay.

Anni suddenly realised that Hopfenstange was speaking again: "...particularly as we were always friends in our schooldays. Let's have a little drink to better times. Brunhilde," he called out, "bring in that rather nice cognac we've been saving, and the good glasses."

Brunhilde gingerly pushed the door ajar. "Would you two like some savoury snacks as well?"

"Yes, dear, why not?"

Anni was sickened by Hopfenstange's cynical display of a friendship to which she had never been party.

For his own reasons, he's trying to sweeten me, she thought.

He had tried ridicule and attack, humility and, now, a hospitality that was not, on his part, genuine.

Although she felt most uncomfortable in Hopfenstange's presence, she stayed just long enough so as not to hurt Brunhilde's feelings and at an opportune moment she announced that it was time for her to leave,

❧

Later that evening, Anni asked Heinz, the hotel barman, about Peter Hopfenstange.

After some hesitation, Heinz told her that there were certain rumours. Apparently, Hopfenstange's name never appeared on the official waiting list for the town's prospective car buyers but, all the same, he had a new Wartburg every other year. Also, he was not among the applicants who had wanted to buy the house which he somehow later acquired. "Mind you," Heinz whispered, after furtively glancing around the bar, "I think it's poetic justice. The people who owned the house are suing him. They escaped when the Wall went up but now they're back."

In her room, Anni opened her diary. She turned the pages until she came to the end of the entry for Day Eight. She wrote across the whole of the next page:

Day Nine

HOPFENSTANGE!   CREEP!!!

Chapter Twelve

Y ou take care, too,"Victor replied. "Sleep tight." He heard the disconnecting click but did not replace the receiver immediately. Instead, he looked at it in disdain as if it had been at fault.

He had meant to tell Anni about this afternoon's incident. It had bothered him sufficiently to want to tell her. What if something similar happened to her? Knowing how forthright she could be, what difficulties might she get herself into? But, rightly or wrongly, he had kept quiet.

Anyway, I didn't get a chance, he told himself, lamely; *I kept waiting for the right moment.*

His chest expanded with a heavy intake of air—its deflation being accompanied by a loud sigh. *Maybe it's just as well I didn't come out with oodles of advice. Watch it, Vic, old boyo! She doesn't take too kindly to being nannied.*

Back at his lonely table in the restaurant he downed a large whisky and ordered another. It was ten o'clock, everyone but himself had company.

Dining alone had never bothered him in the past. He had got used to it on his travels and his spells of living and working in the far-flung places of the globe. But today, he did mind.

What if he were to… . As the idea grew he started to feel happier. *Yes, why not? Go back early and surprise her; it'll stop me fretting. I won't mention the young man…*

By the time he got up from his table, he had decided. He would return tomorrow morning.

※

The incident which had sparked off his worries had happened in Weimar. After visiting the Ettersburg Castle where Goethe's *Iphigenie* had had its first stage performance— with Goethe playing Orest, next to Corona Schroter—Victor had returned to the town.

He had finished his lunch and was standing outside the Schiller House, near the picturesque fountain on the esplanade. His weighty guidebook told him that the house had been reconstructed in 1946 after suffering bomb damage in February 1945. Schiller had lived there from 1802 to 1805 when Weimar, through Goethe's influence, became the centre of German classicism.

As he was looking up at the first floor windows where Schiller had lived, worked and died, Victor's concentration was disturbed.

"Don't mind me, general dogsbody, me!" the sweeper's disgruntled voice complained from nearby; he was scooping up a cigarette butt before depositing it on top of a pile of dirt and waste he had already collected. His comment was directed at a curly-headed young man, standing a few yards away from Victor, on the other side of the fountain.

"Sorry," said Curly-head, looking guiltily at his discarded cigarette end.

How young, seventeen, eighteen at the most. Victor was

intrigued by the white silk suit and long Pre-Raphaelite hair. *He would've made the perfect model for Rossetti; actually, he looks a bit like him.*

"Yeah, you tell 'im!" somebody screeched from behind Victor. A skinhead, clad in dirty jeans, orange shirt and purple sneakers materialised from nowhere. He was advancing towards Curly-head, dribbling with his feet like a footballer, jeering, and punching at the air.

"Who's a pretty boy then!" he jibed, prancing menacingly around his prey.

The sound of a clattering can came from down the road and a second bald-headed youth approached. The bottoms of his rough black leather trousers were stuffed into army-style boots. Giving his empty beer can a final crushing with his boot, he kicked it against a lamppost. He joined his comrade; they nudged each other knowingly and briefly clapped hands as if engaged in a Bavarian Schuhplattler routine.

" 'Is motor," the newcomer grunted, giving the sweeper a sideways glance and indicating with his head in the direction of the car parked at the roadside.

"Yeah!" the first skinhead said, breaking into a chant: "We wanna ride, we wanna ride! Gimme the keys, gimme the keys!" He held out his hand to Curly-head. When the car keys were not forthcoming, he shuffled closer. "Now!" he threatened, "the keys!"

The joke was no longer a joke.

Looking to Victor for support, the sweeper started towards the group. "Look," he said, "we don't want trouble, leave the kid be."

"That's gratitude for yah," the one in the dirty jeans said, and ignoring the sweeper, he grabbed Curly-head's floral tie and started pulling him about.

As far as Victor was concerned, things had gone far enough. "Let him go!" he commanded as he moved nearer.

Dirty-jeans loosened his grip for a moment. He glared at Victor as though sizing him up. He seemed undecided, then, suddenly, he thrust his hand into Curly's jacket pocket.

Victor's arm shot out and he grabbed the skinhead by the front of his orange shirt—there was a ripping sound as he heaved the youth off the ground—with his free hand he screwed Dirty-jeans' right ear, kneeing him in the groin as he did so, then shoving him aside.

Black-leather came forward, measuring himself against the surprise adversary.

Victor was taller, sturdily built, and he was serious. He had always hated bullies; the thought that Anni could easily be attacked by louts such as these had made him furious.

Black-leather looked at Victor, wondering if he could take him. Scuffing one boot against the pavement, he glanced quickly at the sweeper who was now holding his broom in a threatening way. "Ach," grunted the skinhead. With a dismissive gesture of his hand he tried to give the impression that he could not be bothered. He went over to Dirty-jeans and pulled him to his feet. Swearing and spitting on the ground, they made their exit—Dirty-jeans hobbling away.

Watching the hooligans retreat, Victor recalled his early schooldays. He had been rather small—he did not develop his physical prowess until he was thirteen—and was regularly teased, set upon and beaten up. Later, when he was able to defend himself, he never let anyone get the better of him; bullies then left him well alone. Now, he could never stand by and see others victimised. He was well aware of his protective streak; particularly when it was to do with Anni...

"Sign of new times," said the sweeper. "Price of freedom I suppose." He was leaning on his broom and giving Victor the thumbs-up.

"You could've brained those louts with that broom," said Victor, and he went to pick up his guidebook from where he had dropped it near the fountain.

"Wish I had. Not German, are you! English? Thought so," the sweeper said, when Victor confirmed it. "Good, this job," the sweeper continued, "get time to think. Used to be a flautist, professional. Long time ago." For a moment his eyes took on a wistful expression, then hardened. He looked at Victor then turned his head away. "Fell out of favour, critical of the Party, see. But, I'm playing again, just for fun." He looked down at the broom head and nudged it with his shoe. Then, straightening his back, he said, "Used to crawl with police, this place. No trouble then. Do what they like now." He started to sweep again, haphazardly, then he stopped, shook his head and sighed. "Didn't think I'd be sorry. Regimentation, you know. Good for them, it was."

The sound of squeaking leather made both men turn around, Curly-head was approaching. "I want to thank you for helping me," he said, giving Victor an awkward deferential bow and a nod of acknowledgement to the sweeper. "They would have beaten me up, I know the type." He flared his nostrils. "If there is anything I can do, please…" he implored both men, handing over his card before leaving. *Otto Orsini & Son Autovermietung*, it read. "Car hiring service, I see," Victor said.

☙

For more than an hour Victor stayed on the esplanade, talking with Amadeus, the sweeper.

Encouraged by Victor's interest, Amadeus spoke of his life as a musician. An unguarded comment to a fellow player had changed everything for him. But he had not allowed his demotion to crush him, and recently he had started performing again.

When Victor finally went on his way, he felt the eyes of his new friend following him; turning to take one more look at the Schiller House he saw Amadeus, still leaning on his broom, waving his cap to him.

Walking on, Victor reflected that until his stay in China, on another work assignment, he could not have fully appreciated half of what Amadeus had told him about the conditions in the East. He knew that before he had observed repression at close quarters he would have been angered at how someone like Amadeus could meekly accept his fate. Five months in China had taught Victor to doubt whether he would have been any different.

Despite the privileges that had been heaped upon him as a foreigner, he had come to the conclusion he could not carry on with his job of training Chinese students to be teachers of English. Being paid more than six times the normal salary did not compensate for witnessing the subjugation of the people around him.

A large group of Japanese tourists passing by—their guide babbling excitedly and pointing to the esplanade—reminded Victor of the time he himself had been taken on a sightseeing trip, soon after his arrival in Beijing. *I could've got used to being stared at and followed by crowds everywhere I went*, he thought. *Maybe even the spitting?* He shuddered involuntarily as he remembered encountering it. Chinese men—invariably they were men—did not just spit; they made a ceremony of it. Noisily, they would bring the phlegm to the surface and then discharge it in an arc without apparently looking where it might land. Yet he had never seen anyone being struck by the viscous substance.

What had been unacceptable to Victor was the discouragement—but it was more than that—it was the suppression of any individuality. Things were done en masse. The day started with the half-past-six loudspeaker call to get everyone out of bed. That was followed at seven o'clock by exercises and running. The whole college was put though their paces—all except him. "One, two, three," screeched the public address system. But worse still was the lack of choice: at the end of their course, the newly qualified teachers had no say over where they worked—unless they had a "guanxi, back door". The college committee even had to approve if males and females started courting. If approval was not given, as was the case with one couple, they were sent to separate schools, hundreds of miles apart in the countryside.

"Under our regime, I wouldn't have dared speak to you…" Amadeus' voice echoed in Victor's ears. How similar the systems of the East Germans and the Chinese were, he thought. To begin with, he had wondered why his Chinese students rarely sought contact with him outside of the classroom. Then he realised, the gatekeeper in the teacher's block checked and kept a record of their identity cards when they did visit him, which was never singly.

❦

The next morning Victor took a train back to Aschersleben.

Anni had not expected him until the following evening, at the earliest. She bumped into him in the hotel corridor and could not hide her surprise: "Why didn't you say on the phone…?"

"I can go, if you'd rather…" he clowned and started to zigzag away.

She responded, "Cut. This isn't the Ministry of Silly Walks. No more silliness." She giggled. "Seriously though, how come you're back early?"

"I've seen all I wanted to," he said. "Besides, I'd rather be here with you. Missed you," he added, but so quietly that she did not hear him.

⚜

In his temporary hotel room—Victor's premature return meant that he could not yet lay claim to his old one—he unzipped his travelling-bag and started to unpack the few things he had taken with him on the trip.

He was humming to himself, delighted to be back—not least because of Anni's obvious pleasure at seeing him.

He was looking forward to their outing later in the afternoon. They were going to visit an open-air antique fair, set up beyond the old town wall near St Michael's Church. They had hardly finished their hellos before starting to make plans, picking up easily from where they had left off.

He recalled Anni's enthusiasm. She had been to the fair the previous day but had run out of time. She had been sure that he would enjoy going. "You'll love it, you'll see," she had said. "It's very much like the Suffolk one."

"The 'good old days'," Victor said aloud to himself.

He zipped the bag shut and stood still for a moment. *Now there's an irony. I don't want to go back to the way we were.* His jaw muscles tensed and he sat down on the bed, leaving the shirt he had been about to store away on top of the chest of drawers.

"The old days, eh?" he mocked as he lay back on the bed, mumbling to himself. "Not so good 'good old days'."

He stared up at the ceiling.

A succession of images passed through his mind: Anni in Maria's gallery talking about Schulz, contempt in her voice: a different, vulnerable Anni in the Vienna, hiding her tears. Scenes from the cellar...the start of *the* situation.

He combed his fingers through his hair then slapped his forehead. *Stop it,* he thought. His obsessive thinking about *her* was exasperating him. But actually he liked nothing better than to think about her; she was constantly on his mind. He had even telephoned Maria from Weimar just to talk about Anni and speak her name, eventually finishing the conversation by commissioning a painting of her old home.

He sat up, picturing himself kissing her outside her hotel door. His pulses raced a little at the memory of it. His intentions had not been entirely innocent...

I nearly frightened her off that time. Well, I frightened myself anyway. At least I was better today; didn't blurt out just how much I've missed her. And last night on the phone...I kept stumm about my worries. That could've blown it too.

I mustn't force the situation, he reaffirmed to himself as he got up from the bed. *Let her go at her own pace; if she wants us to go anywhere, that is. What am I saying? I don't even know what she really thinks about us; I may be getting fired up about nothing.*

Chapter Thirteen

On the last day of their visit, on impulse, Anni suggested showing Victor the places where, as a girl, she used to ski and ice skate during the winter months. "It's not far from Maria's, so we'll be in time for coffee."

They set out in the direction of the ruined castle on the hilly outskirts of the town. After walking for about half an hour on the flat they reached the uphill stretch. Twenty minutes later they were at the halfway mark, and here the gentle climb along the cobblestone paving came to an end. The steep, final part of the ascent lay before them. To reach the top they would have to follow a much narrower, meandering pathway lined with trees and thick bushes— along the paved stretch they had just climbed there had been widely spaced detached villas.

Anni spied a metal park bench, and let herself sink down onto it gratefully. She sighed. "How times've changed; I used to run up this hill. I didn't need a rest then."

Victor joined her; he too appreciated the pause. "Gives me a chance to look at the lovely houses we've just passed."

"I've sat on this bench before!" she said.

It was the same one Herr Lirkyrp had taken her to after one of his classes at the evening institute. She had been attending his English class for several months and he had asked to walk her home. On the way they had made a stop at the bench.

Anni had not thought about him for a very long time; once, she had found it difficult to keep him out of her mind.

On that lovely balmy evening she felt so light on her feet that it seemed to her she was walking without effort. She was just eighteen and had been dreaming of being alone with him. She had learned that his first name was Oliver and she used it privately to herself when she thought of him. It made her feel closer. Walking at his side she felt blissfully happy. She was only vaguely aware they were going the long way, the very long way to her home. As they walked, the light breeze occasionally blew the hem of her thin summer skirt against him, making her blush; she felt compelled to avert her eyes then. Their conversation had long since dried up, and apart from his few occasional remarks, they walked in silence.

All she could think of was that their being together should never end. She was enveloped in magic. In the fading evening light he had sat down on the bench, and she next to him.

She remembered that they were sitting, each with one hand resting on the bench; his left hand and her right hand lay side by side, very close, but not quite touching. Time seemed to stand still.

She turned to look at him, her wide liquid eyes pleading. With a sudden movement of his head and shoulders be extricated himself from her gaze. Looking down, she saw his hand twitch and very slowly he slid it closer to his side, away from her. As if trying to prevent his hand from distancing itself from her, she made hers move in his direction too, just a little way, jerkily, as though she were moving a heavy load. When her hand came to rest she turned it over, offering him her palm. He did not move. All at once she felt horribly alone.

As she relived those moments, she experienced the painfully vivid image again: a huge wooden cartwheel revolving, slowly at first, then faster, at ever-increasing speed. She heard it clatter, excruciatingly loud, travelling farther and farther away from her.

Eventually Oliver Lirkyrp broke the silence. Speaking in his melodious and darkly vibrant voice, he asked her to promise him only to get married if she was completely sure of having found the one person she could be really happy with. If she were to find herself in a situation where it was hard to make a choice between prospective husbands, she should marry none of them.

Looking at her earnestly he took her hands and pulled her up from the bench. He walked her home with one arm protectively placed around her shoulder. They stopped on the way only once, when he told her bluntly that East Germany was not the *right place for her. When she agreed, he said only that she must leave. He also mentioned—and this was a by-the-way—that he was married and had a baby daughter.*

Anni arrived home, her feelings and thoughts in turmoil. For days afterwards her behaviour was so distracted that it prompted her mother's perplexed inquiry: "Whatever's wrong with you, girl?"

That emotionally charged and memorable evening was the only time she spent alone with Oliver. Afterwards, he was careful not to be with her unaccompanied.

She pictured him as she had last seen him outside the institute, a striking man in his early thirties, of medium height, walking elegantly with his head held high. The way he...

She felt a nudge, and like a piece of elastic snapping, her reverie came to a halt.

"Look!" Victor was pointing to a woman waving her arms, heading towards them.

When she came closer, they realised it was Maria.

"I saw you passing," she said. "What're you doing up here? You haven't forgotten, have you?"

"No," Anni laughed. "We're early. We're going up to the castle and the ski run first."

"Ach so," Maria said, but she looked disappointed. "Maybe you could do that later; Papa has got something interesting to show you."

As they headed towards the villa with the Swiss–style

balcony, the house that Maria had inherited some months ago, they grew quiet. Walking single-file along narrow pathways, familiar only to Maria, did not make for easy conversation.

Anni thought of Oliver Lirkyrp again, and in the process of her thoughts, she saw the summer's evening she had spent with him in a different light.

How silly I was. I felt rejected but I shouldn't have done. I think he actually cared. He could've taken advantage of me but he didn't. Not because he wasn't attracted to me; he more than liked me, I was sure of that. Even I wasn't too innocent to sense it. If I'd appreciated what his situation was I wouldn't have felt so miserable. My imagined rebuff only added to the rest of the frustrations; if it hadn't been for finishing school, I might have left then—especially after he'd said the East wasn't right for me. I suppose it was also bravado… . Anyway, Rudolf appeared on the scene. I wonder, Oliver, then Rudolf?

Maria had started giggling and could not control herself. Standing in the middle of the pathway, she turned to Anni and spluttered, "Remember, you and bossy-boots Heidi?" She paused to catch her breath. "You took me tobogganing near the ski run, yes?" She tried to say something else but another bout of giggling got in the way. "I was only five; you didn't want to take me along." Still giggling, she walked slowly on.

"You had a little accident, didn't you?" Anni exclaimed from behind her. "You piddled yourself!"

In the bitter cold of that afternoon, Maria's trousers had frozen solid. Later, at home, when her mother took them off, they stood up on the floor like a sculpture. It was Anni who got the blame.

Wondering if they had bored Victor with their tale, Anni looked over her shoulder. He was not even within earshot of them, but following behind at a distance. *He's probably been looking at something or other,* she thought. *Just as well perhaps, nothing worse then listening to other people's anecdotes.*

Near the villa, the two women stopped in front of a cluster of pine trees. They looked at each other and Maria pointed. Then, as if of one mind, they burst out laughing like a couple of silly teenagers, it was the spot where they had played the game with the banknotes. They were still laughing, when Victor caught up with them.

"That was your idea," Maria said, sniggering at Anni.

❧

They had finished their afternoon coffee and cakes when Maria's father pulled his chair closer to Anni's. He opened a worn leather briefcase and took out a large brown envelope. From it, he produced two torn-out pages of a newspaper. "Have a read," he said. He waited until Anni's glasses were firmly perched on her nose before handing them to her. "The columns marked with red."

Near the top of the first page an arrow pointed to Herr Klein's name. Above it, Anni saw the heading: "Letter to the Editor." Featured that week was a reply to Herr Klein's submission of the week before.

The printed text was lengthy; it filled the page and continued on the next. Anni hesitated, eyeing the long columns. "D'you mean ... now?"

"Please," he said. "Don't worry about them over there. They're fine," he added, glancing again at his daughter and Victor who were engaged in conversation.

From the first paragraph Anni was hooked; the topic was like a lure and she was eager to take it.

Good, she thought; *Herr Klein has spoken out against the*

Stasis. Judging by the response he touched a raw nerve. I see, that's one way of putting it: "Saddened by the article".

Hmm, the argument's described as "cold-hearted railing"; the bit about Stasi "misdeeds" didn't go down well either. Too bad!

Raising her eyes and peering over the top of her glasses, she saw that Herr Klein was studying her. "I'm enjoying this," she said, nodding approval, "especially his quotes from your letter. Or is it a woman?" Anni's mouth creased into a smile.

"Actually it's a man, but read on," he said, unmoved by her appreciation.

Herr Klein's solemn voice puzzled her and she shot him a quizzical look. *Why is he so serious,* she wondered? *Hmm, definitely not amused. Does he think I'm being flippant?*

"Sorry," he said. "I'd better explain." With an expression of contempt he pointed to the pages she was holding. "This guy's cunning; you'll see, just read."

Somewhat chastened by these remarks, Anni concentrated on the rest of *Letter to the Editor.*

The man's manoeuvring, she thought. *He's clever, but I think I know what he's up to! He's admitting just enough to give the impression of honesty. He agrees he's implicated, but says it's not his fault. He must think we're stupid. He's trying to cover himself.*

Having finished the article, Anni put the pages down. She took her glasses off. *That was an exercise in logic. With Hopfenstange it was raw emotion.* She looked up at Herr Klein.

She picked up the pages again. "Slippery," she said, slapping the paper with the back of her hand. "Top marks for sophistry, but he's dangerous. No wonder you aren't amused."

Noticing that Maria was not in the room, she said to Herr Klein, "I'd better explain to Victor."

She took the article over to him and pulled up a chair.

"This man," she said, shaking the pages, "admits working for the Stasi, but not the responsibility; blames his superiors."

Victor took a few minutes to read the opening paragraphs, tracing the text with his finger.

"So, the Party bosses made the laws which the Stasi safeguarded, is that it? And this guy says he only followed order, claims he was small-fry?"

"Exactly!" Anni put her glasses back on and skimmed the paper. "Here," she said, pointing further down the page.

> "'Contrary to Herr Klein's belief, it was not the majority of the Stasis but our superiors who made it possible for Honecker's regime to stay in power. Our superiors knew the conditions in the country, knew about the discrepancy between propaganda and reality. They knew about the embellishment of the truth and the deception by the SED-bosses.'"

Victor looked up. "Who're the SED?" he asked.

"Ruling Party," said Anni.

"Right," he said, and continued.

> "'They protected the Party hierarchy who caused the problems which ruined the country— insulating the Functionaries from unrest and giving them a feeling of security. On the orders of our superiors alone, we investigated the writers of critical leaflets and arrested them. Some of us pulled protesting citizens, who were enemies of the State, from celebratory demonstrations so that the authorities could operate unhindered. And some hounded people who occupied themselves

with the questions of environmental pollution,
travel restrictions and supply problems...' "

Looking over Victor's shoulder and following his finger
along the text, Anni absorbed it for the second time. Her
cool was beginning to desert her.

"Pass-the-buck time," she muttered, giving vent to her
growing antagonism.

She started to crumple the sheets of paper, then she
stopped. *That was rude*, she thought, and flattened the creases
out. *Herr Klein obviously wants to keep the article for future
reference, and Victor hasn't finished with it.*

Anni had wondered if Victor would have difficulties with
the letter. But he was coping very well. She knew from
experience that students with a larger vocabulary than his
would have been struggling. But his efficient handling of
the language served to remind her of his resourcefulness.

"You're good with the vernacular," she told him. "You
could've gone far with Honecker's lot!"

"Oh, thanks a million!" He turned back to the letter.

He breathed audibly." Listen to this," he said, keeping
his eyes on the paper: 'The Stasi, it needs to be said, was
no mercenary army but an organ of the State, founded on
a legal basis.' "

"Legal basis! Where does it say that?" Anni scoffed.

"Here," Victor said, "the small print."

She moved closer and looked to where his finger was
pointing. "I missed that bit."

Her eyes moved quickly over the text. "Founded on a
legal basis! Whose law's that?" She flung the pages down.
"That's supposed to make it all right, is it!" The letter
slithered across the table and onto the floor.

"My sentiments too," said Victor.

The flicker of a smile crossed Herr Klein's face, but the look in his eyes told them: I know how you feel. He cleared his throat. "We aren't finished yet, there's a postscript." He picked up the pages and turned the second one over.

"The postscript," he said, grinning, and read aloud.

" 'I am not ashamed of my association with the Stasi. I did not apply to join; I was chosen by selection. The approach came from them after a long process of screening. Only then did I declare my commitment to the Service. They picked the best, i.e. in respect of qualifications, training, profile, and personal characteristics. Among other things, I was selected for my exemplary service to the local constabulary.' "

Herr Klein paused. His fingers drummed on his knee. He looked straight at Anni and she knew...

When he came to the writer's lament about privileges of the departmental heads, as compared to the hardships of the ordinary employees, such as himself, who ate their meals in canteens infested with cockroaches while the bosses enjoyed high salaries, cars, luxury houses and hunting grounds, Anni could bear it no longer.

"Schulz!"

Herr Klein held the page closer for her to see.

The signature at the end of the postscript read: Kaspar K Schulz.

"Schulz! I knew it!"

She had always sworn to take revenge. She had thought that given the chance she would throttle him.

She took the page from Herr Klein and stared at it. After

a while she waved it gently towards him. "It's not even worth slapping his face, is it?"

"Get a couple of heavies," she heard Victor mumble.

Anni saw herself standing in front of Schulz…

He's old now, possibly frail. No, it's too late. Funny how you think you know what you'll do, until it comes to it.

She turned to Herr Klein. Your way's best, writing about it, letting everyone know. Maybe next time people won't be so ready to comply."

"Don't worry," he said, "I shan't let the matter rest. I've not finished with him yet!"

❦

As Anni and Victor continued on their climb to the castle ruins they discussed Schulz' letter, until the efforts of the ascent forced an end to conversation.

Maria would have acted as their guide had she not been expecting her husband back from a training course. She had told them about the changes in and around the castle grounds. Some of the old pathways were now part of a zoo which had not been there in Anni's days. There were also newly built-up areas and Maria had warned Anni that she would be hard pressed to find her way about.

But, upon reaching the top of the hill, the enjoyment of the view across the beautifully rolling countryside to the distant mountains shrouded with darkly enigmatic forests, and the jewel-like reflections of the Gondelteich below made Anni forget the rigours of the climb. Looking at Victor's rapt expression, she knew he felt the same way. Sensing her gaze upon him, he took her hand.

It's hard to imagine just now, she thought, *but tomorrow night we'll be back in London; life, as the saying goes, will return to normal… . Or will it, return to normal, that is?* She came out of her reverie with a jolt, suddenly remembering her mother's mysterious prediction: "This visit," she had said, "it'll change your life." *Well, she would say something like that, wouldn't she? She's always hoping I'll fix myself up with someone suitable; she knows Victor's a colleague, not married, no children. No, it's just wishful thinking on her part, that's all,* Anni confirmed to herself, relieved to have come up with a feasible explanation. *Anyway, it's up to me, isn't it? Okay, okay,* she smiled inwardly, *"Thou protesteth too much, Caesar." Things will be what I want them to be, and at the moment I'm all for normality. It avoids all sorts of complications. I'm not saying everything will be perfect, and anyway, maybe I'm taking him for granted. One thing is sure; I shan't forget what we've had together...*

Standing close to Victor, she felt at peace, free to let her eyes travel, beyond where she could see; where she knew the watchtowers used to be and where a border no longer divided East from West.

Part Two

Chapter Fourteen

When the letter arrived, Anni looked at the sender's name and address, printed in bold letters on the back of the envelope. She turned the letter over several times. She was intrigued. She did not know anyone called K Meyer, living in Düsseldorf. But, interestingly, when she opened the envelope, the handwriting was vaguely familiar. By the time she had read the first few lines she was jubilant. With shaking hands she read the rest of it. In the letter Anni discovered how it had come to be written, over two months after her visit with Victor to eastern Germany.

One of Karin's friends had been to Anni's home town, had picked up an out-of-date copy of the local magazine by chance and had seen the advert requesting Karin to get in touch.

Anni could hardly believe her luck. She had almost given up hope of hearing from her friend, in spite of having been optimistic at the outset; she had not thought the advertisement would lead to any response after such a long time.

In her letter Karin gave a short summary of the events of the intervening years and Anni had responded by doing the same in her reply. Soon they were engaged in lively correspondence, each trying to fill in the long silence between them.

They decided to wait until after Christmas before meeting. Anni was to fly to Düsseldorf on the second weekend of the new year; arriving on the Friday evening and staying until Sunday.

❦

Karin proposed to meet Anni at the airport, and because they had been doubtful about recognising each other they had exchanged recent photographs. After all, their last meeting had taken place decades ago, when they had bumped into each other near Aschersleben Station.

That was about a year after they had both passed their high school diplomas. Karin, who had gone on to medical college in East Berlin, was on her way back there after spending a couple of days with her family. There had been little time to talk then and they had arranged to meet on Karin's next visit home. That meeting never took place; on the date they had arranged to meet, Anni had already escaped.

The last time they had seen each other, Karin had been quiet and her usually glowing dark-brown eyes had looked dull and vacant. She had seemed distracted and Anni had commented on it. She had asked whether the cutting-up of bodies had been too upsetting. "Oh, no," Karin had replied, "that's nothing. I've got used to that; even the smell doesn't make me feel faint any longer."

❦

Anni walked into the airport's reception hall, searching the people's faces. It was not difficult to pick out Karin from the crowd. Quite soon after casting her eye over the groups and individuals, Anni noticed a tall dark-haired woman dressed in the pillar-box red coat Karin had said she would be wearing. She was standing at the other end of the hall, with her head slightly turned to one side. Anni moved towards her and as she drew near, the woman's head turned. The years had added character to her face and there was a self-reliant, practical air about her which had the result of making Anni feel the younger of the two, although she was actually a year older.

The next moment they were in each other's arms, hugging and squeezing, laughing, with Karin almost lifting Anni off the ground. The embrace was repeatedly interrupted by Karin, who briefly but vigorously pushed Anni's head back so that she could look at her.

Anni, who had always been more reserved than her friend, found, to her surprise, that she was returning the exuberant greeting.

"God," she said eventually, "you haven't changed." She tried to disentangle herself. "Let me breathe."

※

Anni sank easily into the comfortable passenger seat of the convertible.

"You know," said Karin after she had started the car, "you're as soft as I remember. And all that long golden hair."

"You haven't seen the grey ones yet," Anni laughed.

"Grey!" Karin chuckled. "Mine already is." She pointed to her short thick curls. "This is out of a bottle."

It was not the first time Anni had been complimented on her appearance. She knew she looked younger than her years, and though in one sense she was pleased by such comments, Karin had revived some thoughts that had been nagging for a while. It had occurred to her, not long ago, that her face, little marked by time, might not be something worthy of compliment, rather, it could signify detachment from the experiences of life. She had wondered whether, in recent years, she had erected a screen around herself.

"It's really good to see you," Anni said, as the car crawled through the heavy evening traffic. "It's a lifetime since we sat together in school."

"Yes," said Karin, "and we don't know much about each other any more, do we? We've a lot of catching up to do, but we can talk when we get home. I've already prepared dinner, and I haven't forgotten what you wrote about claret."

❦

"That was delicious," said Anni, "and you didn't forget my liking for red cabbage!" She stretched her arms and walked across the living room towards the balcony. Through the glass doors of the third floor apartment she could see the lights of the city ablaze below her.

"It's very pleasant on a summer's evening; feet up, looking over the window boxes," said Karin. "D'you still miss German food? You wrote that it was difficult to get pumpernickel, and salami."

"That was years ago," said Anni, returning to the table. "Culinary deprivation. No sausage, no schnapps. Now you can…get it…all," she said haltingly. "But," she hesitated again, "I told you that thirty years ago. You must've got my letter…the one from England; when I first got there." She searched her friend's face. There was no reaction. In the few seconds since Anni had mentioned the letter, Karin had gone quiet. She seemed remote, her eyes gave no clue as to whether she had even heard. "I wrote again later," Anni continued, "to your halls of residence. When I didn't hear from you I wondered. I told myself you never got them; my letters. Maybe they were…"

Karin looked at her, then looked quickly away again.

Anni was puzzled, then something occurred to her. "I didn't write about politics," she said, "or anything, it was all harmless stuff."

Karin got up from her seat and paced restlessly around the room. She took a few steps towards the table, stood still for a moment, then went back to her chair.

Watching her had given Anni time to think. "Were you afraid to write? That's not a reproach. Please…" she put out her hand, "I mean…I know what things were like."

Karin remained silent. She avoided looking at Anni but her mouth twitched. She seemed on the point of saying something.

Why doesn't she come out with it? Unless, is there something…? *No!* Anni dismissed the thought. Immediately, she was ashamed of her suspicions so she continued talking, almost blabbering.

"You sent a couple of postcards while I was still in West Germany, but once I got to England…well, I thought, an East German writing to an English address!" She leaned forward in her chair. Karin still avoided looking at her. "Anyway, when I didn't hear from you, I stopped writing, but I sent a birthday card. Oh, and one for Christmas. When that came back saying you'd moved—that was written on the back—I gave up. But a few years later I tried again. I wrote to your parents. That came back as well, stamped 'verzogen'."

" 'Moved away?' Lies!" Karin burst out, startling Anni with her ferocity. Karin's right eyelid started to twitch as she continued, and her agitation made her repeat herself. "All lies, all of them! My parents didn't move. Last year, when my father died, Mother went to live with her sister. They didn't move!"

"Yes, I know," Anni murmured. She took one of Karin's hands and clasped it in both of hers. "Years ago, my mother showed me a letter from her friend who visited your parents' house. The same place they'd always had." Anni paused, and inconsequentially, she said, "Did you know that my parents left a year after me?"

"I heard about it," Karin said, "but..." She shook her head. "I shouldn't have lost touch, I shouldn't have." She stood up, sat down, and brushed her hand across her forehead. "I suppose I could make it easier," she said slowly, "and tell you that I did write, couldn't I? You wouldn't know. But I didn't..."

"Look, it's all right," said Anni. "Don't beat yourself over the head."

Karin did not seem to hear.

Eventually, she said, "They called me into a meeting. A couple of my lecturers were there, and someone in uniform. They asked me about my friendship with you; your letters, you see. The one in uniform said you'd undermined 'my socialist convictions'. Socialist, my foot!" She slapped both hands hard onto the table. "I should've said what I thought of their rotten state!" She slapped the table again. "But I didn't!"

The wine glasses wobbled. A dinner fork, which had moved across the table with the vibrations, fell onto the floor. As Anni bent down to pick it up, Karin said, more calmly now, "That was the trouble, we all kept quiet. Things might have been different otherwise."

"You would have been expelled," Anni said, wiping up some of the spilled wine with her tissue.

"I know," said Karin. "It's no excuse; I was as spineless as the rest." She was staring past Anni, looking towards the balcony. Her eyelids were twitching again. "I made myself an accomplice. I don't know what I was hoping for; I thought the problem would go away and I could avoid making decisions, I don't know." She looked directly into Anni's eyes. "When your Christmas card arrived, I got another girl to write the note and I sent it back to you. Soon after, I had a letter from the Youth Committee saying how pleased they were about what I'd done."

"I caused you problems," Anni said. "I should have thought about it, but I was anxious to keep in touch. I thought that writing to your East Berlin address would be all right. Oh, what the hell, they were only letters."

"Only letters? In England, maybe. No, I should have left," Karin said. "I should have had your courage. I did think of it but I waited too long. Then it was too late, and it became virtually impossible."

"Yes…my parents just made it before the Wall went up. But you're wrong. My leaving wasn't courageous. I had to leave, I knew I had to, I couldn't breath."

Karin looked up. "How d'you mean?"

"Well," Anni cleared her throat, "I felt suffocated by the whole system. I'd been thinking about leaving for a long time." She took a sip from her glass as she tried to find the words.

Karin waited.

"There were so many reasons…" Anni paused. "I must have applied to every university and got nowhere; my life was going nowhere. Perhaps you remember that."

Karin nodded.

"Well, after the first rejections I opted for every subject but chemistry. 'You have not been successful in your application', was all they said. Except, in one case they gave some reasons, starting with my 'unsuitable background'. Then there was my school report." Anni grinned irreverently. "They did me a favour, I was positively out of favour."

"I remember, you were at a disadvantage, but I suppose that helped later. What was in the report anyway? I've forgotten."

" 'Non-co-operation with the Youth movement, class discussions negative, generally unenthusiastic,' and so on."

"Oh yes, that's right! So, you had it in black and white."

"Mmm," Anni grinned, "and they said if I became 'a worthy member of society' I could reapply in a couple of years."

"Yes, I was accepted and you weren't, that's why I felt guilty," said Karin. "I couldn't talk to you properly afterwards, I felt like a traitor, and I made it worse by not answering your letters. I've never stopped feeling bad about that. I meant to tell you, but not on our first evening together. Trust me to pre-empt myself, but I'm glad it's out." She managed a smile. Her facial muscles relaxed and she sat more easily in her chair, her body becoming less rigid.

Noticing that Anni had reached for her empty glass, Karin downed hers in one gulp, but trying to talk too soon caused her to choke. "I'll get some more," she said when she had recovered.

Left alone in the room, Anni pondered over Karin's dilemma.

I told her it was all right, but I wonder what I would have done. I think I might have been stubborn and written anyway, and bugger the consequences. But who's to say...? I'm glad she didn't hide the truth though, it would have created a barrier between us. After all those years they didn't manage to destroy her integrity!

Anni's thoughts turned to her own last years in the East and it made her appreciative of what Karin had endured.

There had been no getting away from the incessant propaganda. It had pounded at Anni with painful and nauseating regularity. She remembered the loudspeakers; every classroom had had one, so wherever you were you could not avoid hearing the official morning news—followed later by several updated versions.

There were loudspeakers in all the public places too. From strategically placed amplifiers in the market square the latest speeches of the Party bosses would blare out, and they were repeated at intervals. When there were no speeches, revolutionary music was played.

You looked up at the buildings and what did you see? Red banners, slogans plastered over walls, pictures of Lenin, Karl Marx, Walter Ulbricht and other socialist heroes.

If you went to see a film you had to pass through the cinema foyer, suitably draped with politically correct messages. More indoctrination by way of the newsreels before the film started—which in any case had been thoroughly vetted so that it did not offend the purity of the doctrine or, heaven forbid, pander to what the censor called bourgeois moral corruptness and decadence.

In the restaurants, cafés and dance halls you saw huge photographs of Party dignitaries benignly smiling down.

Anni groaned wearily. "Enough," she muttered and started to get up, then let herself sink back into her chair.

"What's the matter?" said Karin, coming back into the room with an opened bottle and several packets of crisps.

"Oh! I've just been thinking about red flags, banners and slogans," Anni sighed. "It makes me angry. No wonder I used to fear I'd do something rash."

"Like what?" Karin said, pouring their drinks.

"Oh, I don't know. Tear down some damned placards for starters."

"Calm down!" Karin said.

"I suppose I'd better, but I'll tell you something." Anni shook her head. "Never mind, doesn't matter."

"You can't stop there," Karin urged.

"Right, yes, well," Anni said self-consciously, "the thing is, I was afraid I might go mad." She felt embarrassed at the revelation but continued. "It started at school," she nodded towards Karin, "near the end of our time. I acquired a hysterical sort of laugh. Nothing like a normal laugh, but ugly, unhealthy." She stared into her glass. "There didn't seem to be a reason for it; it just happened." Karin made as if to interrupt. "No, let me finish; it didn't happen very often. But that wasn't all. I had a sense of unreality, like you're not really connected to the ground. Feelings of coming apart."

Anni's hands were clasped tightly together as she spoke and struggled to express herself. She unclasped her hands, quickly got up from her chair and went over to the window. She stood there, looking out. Then, very quietly she said, "I thought I was actually going mad."

"My God!" said Karin, I had no idea."

"I never told anyone," said Anni, still staring out of the window. "I didn't think anyone would understand. Now you know why I had to leave."

Anni returned to her chair and stood behind it. She rested her hands on the back of it. "Of course, it was all academic really, because of what happened with Rudolf."

Karin looked at her friend. "I was going to ask about him, you caused quite a stir."

Chapter Fifteen

With Rudolf's office and workshop being nearby, he had often come to the café, mostly in the early evenings.

Anni had noticed his good looks. He was extremely tall—well over six feet—slim, intelligent looking with grey eyes and longish, very dark hair. He was usually accompanied by two or three others, friends, she assumed. They would have a couple of drinks and talk together animatedly. From as far away as the shop she could hear bursts of laughter coming from their table. It would make her look up from whatever she was doing, simply because there was little of their kind of carefree laughter about.

One evening, when she was helping out behind the bar, Rudolf introduced himself. His gaze was probing; he would not just glance at her but looked her straight in the eyes.

Later, whenever she saw him in the street, they exchanged greetings and the odd few words.

She remembered that she had always blushed when their eyes met, no matter how hard she tried not to! She knew he noticed it, and the instant it happened a mischievous smile would cross his face.

"It was in the summer of 'fifty-nine when I first saw Rudolf," Anni explained, "not long before you left for East Berlin—the place he came from."

Being a newcomer to Aschersleben, people wondered why he had set himself up in such a quiet town. The explanation turned out to be quite simple; he had inherited some large premises from his aunt. This allowed him to indulge his passion for restoring antique clocks, while at the same time, but as a sideline, practising as an accountant. His main function there was to advise clients in tax matters as well as preparing balance sheets.

It was shortly before Christmas that Anni's father sent her to Rudolf's workshop to take her grandfather's antique watch for repair.

"I can't tell you how nervous I was," she said. "It felt a bit like a visit to the dentist and winning a raffle prize all in one. I had a couple of hours' grace so I worked out what to say, memorised it all." Grimacing, she looked at Karin, "After all, I didn't want him to think I was a country bumpkin. He was very polished, in manner and dress. But, of course, when I actually got there all my well-laid plans came to nothing. I mumbled something about grandfather's watch."

Karin laughed. "So, the game was up."

"Well, he pretended he hadn't noticed anything. 'Why don't I make some coffee?' he said. I followed him into the workshop, sat in one of his visitors' chairs and he went into some annex room. By the time he came back, I'd pulled myself together. While he laid out the coffee things I managed some small talk."

Sitting at Karin's table Anni moved her chair far enough back to be able to cross her legs. "He really went to town on the coffee," she said, "expensive-looking china, cakes and all the trimmings."

"I should think so," Karin smiled. "He was probably trying to impress you."

"He wanted to know all about my hobbies and favourite subjects at school. Anyway, talking about my interests loosened my tongue, and with one or other of his clocks chiming every few minutes and us having to wait for them to finish…well, it broke the ice. He seemed like an ordinary mortal, despite his big-city origins. He made me laugh, he was very entertaining and I stopped worrying about making an impression. We even discovered we had some common interests."

Karin looked up quizzically, and Anni went on to tell her about Rudolf's and her own love of reading science fiction. "We talked about several titles we'd read. This led us to discuss books in general and English books in particular. I mentioned my private English lessons and of course…"

"He offered to lend you his books," Karin said.

"Yes, at the time it was all very plausible, and he made it sound quite innocent. I found books in English difficult to get hold of and I was pleased he offered…an ulterior motive didn't occur to me. Anyway, not until later. I can hear him now: 'I've got the complete works of Shakespeare at home. You're welcome to drop in, any time.' Before I left he gave me his address."

On the way home Anni felt elated; she had spent a most enjoyable hour with Rudolf and he had flattered her with his attention.

During the following weeks she agonised over whether or not to go to his flat to borrow a book.

"Actually," she admitted to Karin, "I did go round but I passed his house by."

"Yes, I can just see you getting flustered," Karin said.

"Because I was shy, you mean?"

"Yes," said Karin. "But obviously, that wasn't the whole reason, was it?"

"No," said Anni, "there was more to it than that."

She had been thinking of Rudolf; she pictured him sitting opposite her in his workshop as he had done over coffee during her visit. His slim fingers had turned the pocket watch over several times before putting it almost lovingly down on the small table next to him. She wondered what it would be like being touched by him. She wanted to see him again but she sensed that it could be dangerous.

Thinking about him had diverted her mind from the boring office work at the farm co-operative. She had taken the clerical job after her last hope of getting a place at university had been dashed. For the first time since she had started work there, she forgot how miserable she had been feeling. She was also worrying less about her strange fits of laughter.

For a while, she wondered if he had forgotten about her. She could not think of any reason why she should be of interest to him. She did not consider herself attractive. It seemed to her that she lacked colour, and looking into the mirror, she saw a very pale face with a nose she thought too long and a mouth too wide. Her green eyes, which she thought to be her best feature, were hidden behind spectacles.

"I hated my hair. I still do, it's too fine," Anni said. "Anyway, all the boys courted you, remember?"

"Nonsense." Karin waved her hand in belittlement of her successes. "I was just more outgoing. You were the serious one, that's probably why Rudolf fancied you. But you did go, to his flat, I mean?"

"Yes," Anni said.

Not long after her aborted attempt to visit Rudolf, they

had met by accident near the town hall and he pretended to be cross because she had not come to see him. He made her promise that she would do so soon.

As soon as she arrived she realised she need not have worried. He was friendly and matter of fact. She picked a book of short stories in simplified English. But, carrying it home, she felt that the visit had been disappointing.

Her mother was alarmed when she discovered where Anni had been. She warned that Rudolf had the reputation of being a ladies' man, and that it would be better not to go again as he lived alone.

"He was older than you, wasn't he?" Karin said.

"Yes, forty-four."

"Crikey! He was old."

"Do I hear disapproval?"

"It depends," said Karin. "I can't really say, I never met him. I'm not surprised your mother was worried though."

"I told her there was no need to—he wasn't interested in me anyway. But I didn't promise not to go again."

"Did you?"

"Yes, a couple of times. Then everything changed."

Karin got to her feet. "Wait a minute," she said, let's be more comfortable. Bring your glass." She walked over to the easy chairs, sat down and put her glass on the floor.

"That's better," she said when Anni had settled opposite her. "Right, I'm all ears."

Anni took a sip from her glass, then put it down on the floor next to her. "After our usual coffee, we sat on the sofa, looking at his photos. Well…he put his arm around my shoulder; I didn't think anything of it at first. But I could feel his warmth through his silk shirt. Then he started to stroke my hair." She paused and ran her fingers across her forehead. "He wouldn't stop!"

"Well, what did you expect?"

"I don't know," Anni said. "I wanted him to touch me but…I didn't know what to do." She picked up her glass and took a big gulp. "Can you imagine! I'd no experience with men. So when he started to kiss my neck I went rigid."

Karin giggled. "Yes, I can imagine!"

"You can laugh, but you weren't there… . Anyway, he took my glasses off, very carefully, and kissed me on the mouth. Then everything seemed to happen at once…"

"Go on," said Karin, "don't stop now."

Anni looked a little embarrassed. "All right, all right, don't rush me… . Well, the next thing; I was lying on the sofa and his hand was inside my blouse. One of the buttons pinged off."

Karin moved forward in her seat. "Oooh!"

"Oooh, nothing!" said Anni. "I was absolutely terrified, and I panicked. I tried to move away but he wouldn't let me."

"Oh no!" said Karin.

"Oh yes!" said Anni, picking up her glass. "I screamed at him to stop," she took a quick gulp, "really screamed! And he did; stop, I mean. He looked as if he'd been scalded."

"I bet he did," said Karin. She refilled Anni's glass. "So?"

"We just sat there; at opposite ends of the sofa; there was an awful silence and…"

"And what? What?"

"I got up and straightened my clothes," Anni said, as she recalled the scene.

"He looked angry. I didn't say anything; I was too shocked. I turned to go and he said, 'Don't come back until you've grown up.'"

"Oh dear!" said Karin.

"Yes, all the way home I kept hearing his last words. I was too naïve. It was my fault, partly."

"Well," Karin said, and she fell silent.

"I had no idea…"

"You went back, didn't you?"

"Yes… . I knew I would; as soon as I left the house I knew." Anni thought for a moment, then she continued. "When I did go, he was pleased to see me; he apologised." She smiled. "He looked like a little boy, promising to be good."

Karin laughed.

"That's just what we did, laugh, and everything was all right. I kissed him, and we made love."

From then on they met frequently. Eventually, Anni took to going out almost every evening and came back home late. That caused trouble with her parents and she had to come up with all sorts of excuses, including working late. Her parents suspected where she was going but she would not admit it.

It was around Easter before her affair became obvious. Her parents insisted she stop seeing Rudolf, her mother stressing that he was still married, even though his wife was living in the West. "He's old enough to be your father, and he's not going to divorce his wife to marry you."

Anni replied that the thought had never entered her mind, but her mother did not believe her.

"There's no future in it," she said, "and what about the scandal? He's only interested in one thing; why else would a man of his age want anything to do with a young girl?"

Anni did not stop seeing him. If anything, she grew more determined to continue the affair, despite the distress she was causing.

Anni cleared her throat and looked at Karin. "I wasn't as callous as I sound. I knew my parents were worried, but Rudolf was like a drug."

"Hmm, I suppose he was," Karin said.

<hr />

One day, towards the end of May, something happened …

Anni had finished work and was hurrying down the steps of the office building. She was on her way to meet Rudolf.

Across the road two men got out of a black car—she had noticed it parked there earlier in the afternoon. She wondered why it was still standing there at this late hour— the farm co-operative was in an otherwise derelict area and the offices stood alone, so it seemed strange as they had had no visitors during the course of the day.

The two men walked quickly over and placed themselves one on either side of her. Ignoring her protestations and shouts for help, she was dragged to the car and pushed onto the back seat. They clambered in after her, sandwiching her between them. One of them leaned forward and tapped the driver on the shoulder and the car moved off sharply.

The thought of abduction momentarily crossed her mind, but she dismissed the possibility almost immediately as the idea seemed too fanciful.

Squeezed tightly between the two men, her demands to know who they were and where she was being taken to were met with total silence.

After a short journey the car stopped outside the entrance to the local Party headquarters. She was hauled out roughly and manhandled up a flight of steps and into a room on the first floor of the building. They unceremoniously shoved her inside, making her stumble. Then they left and locked the door behind them.

Once Anni had regained her footing, she looked around. Facing her were three men and a woman, all middle-aged. They were sitting at a large ornate table—she vividly remembered it for its beautifully sculpted legs and inlaid mother-of-pearl top; it was totally out of place in the almost bare, white-washed room. Opposite them, on the other side of the table, stood a single blue metal chair. Without saying a word the woman motioned to it, indicating that Anni should sit down. She complied and sat looking into their expressionless faces. Clinically, as though she were a specimen, they studied her. For long minutes, none of them spoke.

After being seized Anni had expected to be taken to the police station. The events of the past few days ran through her mind. She thought of the people she had been in contact with and wondered if she had made any careless remarks; she could think of none. But during the journey she began to suspect that there was something odd about the situation. If they were policemen, why had they not come into the office to snatch her? They had been waiting outside; the police did not usually hesitate to bring someone in.

Now that she was at the Party offices she was sure that this was not a police matter. But what could it be about? Whatever it was, and whoever these people were, she resolved she was not going to be intimidated. Pointedly, she kept looking at her watch and yawning, her eyes wandering disinterestedly around the room.

Eventually, one of the three men present asked her about her association with Rudolf: how long had she known him, when had she last seen him, did she intend to see him again and finally, did she think it right that a young girl should be having an illicit association with a married man? The last question brought incoherent muttering from the others.

162

As the interrogator spoke he looked with piercing eyes at Anni over the top of his spectacles. His huge, domed head kept bobbing up and down as he talked, only briefly coming to rest with each pause for breath. He proceeded to preach to her about morals; trying to convince her that he was concerned about her social well-being.

As though pre-arranged, the second man took over. He was exceptionally small. Anni noticed it even though he was sitting down. He twittered, in a high-pitched voice, saying that a number of well-meaning citizens had asked them to talk to her. His smile was sickly sweet. "We from the committee," he chirped, smiling all the time and encompassing his comrades in a sweeping gesture, "feel duty-bound to help you see the error of your ways." He opened a small handbook and quoted various sections from the guidelines for young people's behaviour. He concluded his jargon-cluttered speech with: "It's our responsibility to make you a better citizen." He smiled even more sweetly: "You'll thank us in the end."

Throughout Anni's corrective schooling, the grim-faced woman had only grunted. Now, she became animated, nodding her head vigorously.

The third man had said nothing at all; he seemed to be there solely to take notes.

The questioning went on for a couple of hours. If they had expected to make Anni humble herself, they were mistaken; she had made up her mind to keep her silence.

The twittering little man seemed about to speak again but he was prevented from doing so by the sudden entry into the room of the two men who had delivered her. Without a word to the committee, they pulled her from the chair by her arms and she was hustled back to the car. Its arrival outside her home did not go unnoticed by the neighbours—it was much too luxurious to have belonged to a common citizen.

The following afternoon she was again removed to the Party headquarters and the quizzing was repeated. Anni continued to say nothing.

Even though her parents lodged an official complaint about their daughter's treatment, the interrogations carried on; each day the same questions were asked and the speeches were repeated.

At the end of the first week the grim-faced woman spoke: "We can always send you to one of our rehabilitation centres if you don't co-operate. You remember Schulz, don't you?"

Anni still did not speak.

As she sat on the hard metal chair, harassed by the self-appointed protectors of her morals, but becoming well versed in closing her ears to them, she reflected on her situation. She was grateful that it was not the police who were interrogating her; even so, they, the committee, had been interfering in her private life and had kept her from Rudolf. She was powerless against them and it angered her. They had no idea that the more they persisted with their teachings the more frustrated and stubborn she was going to become, and consequently the less likely she was to give them satisfaction by repenting. She wondered what they had to gain by lecturing her and depriving her of her freedom of association. All the same, not giving in to them did not make her position any better. She knew she was going to have to solve the problem; they were not going to leave her alone. She needed to do something…

On the thirteenth day—by now even the sickly smile of the chirpy man was a thing of the past—Anni made the following announcement: "I'm going to take my annual holiday and visit my grandparents," she stared at them defiantly, "and, I'm going in three days!"

The interrogators glanced at each other, and then, as of one mind, they left the room.

Twenty minutes later the man with the domed head returned, alone. "We of the committee," he said gravely, his head bobbing, "have decided that you seem to have shown some common sense, and you may go on holiday. In view of this we are suspending your attendance to our meetings until your return. After which, if you continue your association with Herr Darrenbach, we will start our little discussions from the beginning. Next time," he said, taking off his glasses and glowering at her, "we may not be so accommodating."

It was a victory of sorts for Anni.

Later that day, she managed to get a note to Rudolf explaining that she was going to visit her grandparents. One of Rudolf's trusted colleagues passed the note on, and when she returned the next day to his office she was able to pick up the reply.

Rudolf proposed that they meet at Palace Sanssouci near Potsdam. It was not far from her grandparents' home.

Chapter Sixteen

W e met in the grounds of Sanssouci. It was a lovely afternoon. It means 'without worries', Sanssouci, you know," Anni said.

In a secluded area Anni and Rudolf had found a grassy spot and they lay on their backs looking up at the white puffs of cloud in the sky. But this was going to be good-bye.

He did not know she had decided to leave East Germany for good.

"I couldn't stay after all that interrogation business," Anni said, "so I made up my mind to leave."

"What, just like that?" Karin said.

"No! I'd thought of it for days. I had no choice. There was no hope of anything better."

❦

Anni had worked out the practicalities beforehand. She would try to make her way from Potsdam to West Berlin. Once there she would ask the first policeman she saw for directions to the refugee camp. She knew she would have to spend two or three weeks there, that she would be screened and, when cleared, flown out to one of the resettlement centres—around this time, up to five thousand people a week defected.

She had everything with her that she was going to take across the border: the Abitur certificate, the outspoken rejection letter from the university and her handbag—she carried the rolled-up documents hidden inside her collapsible umbrella. As for the suitcase containing the rest of her belongings, she had left it at her grandparents' house. At breakfast that morning she had told them that she was going on a day-trip.

With Sanssouci and Potsdam being close to Berlin she would not have far to travel. She would go to the eastern part of Berlin and then, using the city's internal rail system, she would get off at the nearest station in the Western sector—the divided city would become her springboard to freedom.

With no heavy luggage, and an identity pass which she hoped was in order—there was always the possibility that she was listed as a potential escapee—she thought she might succeed. The point of greatest danger was at the last station on the eastern side. The police usually at least spot-checked passengers before allowing the train to go on.

❧

Once Rudolf had become accustomed to the idea that she was leaving he reluctantly agreed that this was the best thing for her.

"There we were," Anni said, "hugging and kissing and discussing the future."

Later, it was difficult to say which of them had first thought of that utterly mad but exciting plan of how, before the final goodbyes, they could snatch a little more time together, back in Aschersleben, under the noses of the authorities. Once they had thought of it, the plan took shape and seemed to stand there squarely in front of them, refusing to be moved aside.

❦

"You mean you returned to his flat in Schiller Street; stayed a while, then left for real," Karin said slowly. She paused. "I'm surprised it worked; and you didn't tell your grandparents?"

"No," said Anni, "too dangerous for them."

"They must've worried when you didn't come back. Didn't they contact your parents? You might've been murdered!"

"I thought of all that."

Anni had set out for Sanssouci in the late morning. Before leaving the house she left a note in her grandparents' letterbox telling them that by the time they read it she should be in the West and that they need not be concerned about her. She told them she would write to confirm her safe crossing as soon as possible and she would also let her parents know. She knew her grandfather always collected his paper between six and seven in the evening so he would find her note.

"I see," said Karin, "you crossed into the Western sector, and came out again!"

"Yes, that's right," said Anni.

Rudolf and Anni said their goodbyes in the evening and she crossed into West Berlin alone. He went back home, to make everything appear normal.

"I stayed in a hotel and wrote my letters; to my grandparents and parents. I said, 'I've made it.' I didn't say much more, just that I didn't have any future in East Germany, and not to worry. I said it was my own decision; anyway, something like that."

"Hmm, so nobody could be implicated," said Karin.

"Exactly." Anni leaned back in her chair and looked thoughtfully at Karin. "That's it really. Next morning I went back into the East and set off to meet Rudolf."

"And nobody saw you?" said Karin.

"No," said Anni, "we met after dark as arranged."

❧

Anni got off the train two stops before Aschersleben. It had been a long and anxious trip. She had been on the move since breakfast, and for much of the journey she had deliberately used slow, local trains. She was anxious because she was on territory she had renounced.

But all that was forgotten as she walked quickly towards the village pond where, as they had planned, Rudolf was waiting for her.

They had about an hour's walk ahead of them, and the last stretch of it, through her home town, was the most dangerous. Rudolf had allowed for that and as a disguise for Anni he had brought along an apprentice's blue working overalls. She changed into them and hid her handbag inside the tool-pouch. Rudolf, who normally dressed very carefully, was also less than elegant in his oldest work clothes.

They were both very tense and stepped out quickly, keeping their heads low. Hardly a word was exchanged between them as they hurried along the darkened country lanes. The nearer they came to the town the more anxious Anni grew.

A light drizzle had started and they used the opportunity it afforded to pull their collars up closer around their necks.

Hunched into overalls and work clothes, as they were, made it easier to negotiate the lamp-lit streets without arousing suspicion.

Anni's heart was pounding as they approached Rudolf's flat. She looked casually around to check that nobody was paying attention to them. Once she had satisfied herself that it was safe, she waited in an unlit doorway across the road whilst Rudolf went into the flat. From his ground-floor bedroom window he had a clear view up and down the street. He gave her a sign to indicate that everything was all right and she walked briskly across the road. As soon as she closed the heavy outer door, he opened the door of his flat and she quickly slipped inside.

They stood very still for a while, just looking at each other, almost in disbelief. Then pure joy took over and they fell into each other's arms.

※

The sound of a cork popping interrupted Anni's thoughts.

She looked over Karin's shoulder at the clock on the wall behind her. "Goodness!" she said. "It's past two and I think I've had enough for one day. What about you?"

"I suppose you're right," Karin said. She re-corked the bottle. "This will keep. Right," she said, seeing that Anni was already standing near the door, "bedtime!"

※

Despite her tiredness, Anni could not sleep. Her thoughts kept returning to Rudolf...

She remembered the yearning for him, and her horror when he had first tried to make love to her. She had found it disappointing when eventually they did. She remarked, quite bluntly, that the experience had been far from pleasurable and that she could not understand why so much fuss was made about sex. Smiling, he assured her that it would get better, much better. And indeed he was proved right.

He had liked to undress her slowly, removing the individual garments one by one, kissing each area of newly exposed skin and taking his time over it. When there was nothing left to be taken off he would run his fingers lightly along the length of her body. She could feel his warm breath; from the nape of her neck and down along her spine, making her shiver in anticipation.

At other times he had driven her into a frenzy by kissing her breasts and belly, sucking her nipples and connecting with her, then ceasing all movement. Playfully, he would forbid her to move, but she could never hold herself still for very long. She remembered bringing herself to a climax while Rudolf remained immobile. He was pleased when she praised his self-control.

His friends flattered him when they jealously, or so he told her, commented on his ability to attract a lover who was so much younger than himself.

During their time together he dreamed up new ways of touching and pleasuring her; she sensed that for him making love was a perfectly natural thing, and that it was creative.

As she lay there with sleep eluding her, it occurred to her that he had played her like a musical instrument, finely tuning it and encouraging sweeter and more beautiful melodies from it.

No wonder he had had nothing but scorn for what he called the two-minute-man and the fumblings of spotty-faced youths from whom, he declared, he had saved her.

When her inexperience made her feel insecure she had let Rudolf convince her that he adored her boyishly slim figure and small breasts. But, even though she pestered him to do so, he would never talk about the women he had known, except in the vaguest of terms.

Chapter Seventeen

Despite their late night, Anni and Karin got up just after eight the following morning. While they were eating breakfast, Karin said, between mouthfuls, "Eduard's having a small get-together tonight. It's in his studio flat. D'you want to go?"

"Mmm, I've been wanting to meet him. He's more than a friend, isn't he? Any special reason for the party?"

"Yes, he is." Karin took another bread roll and hurriedly sawed through it. "I'm hungry," she said, her mouth partly full of sausage. "Sorry," she mumbled. "And the party's to the success of his one-man exhibition in Bavaria."

"Ah, Bavaria. Does he exhibit locally too?"

"Hardly at all now." Karin swallowed the remains of the sausage. "He does better in Munich; he's making quite a name for himself now."

"He must be pleased."

"Mmm, but I'm not happy about the implications."

"I see," Anni said, leisurely stirring her coffee—she had finished eating a while ago. "He's thinking of moving there, isn't he? That's what you meant yesterday?" She was watching

Karin in fascination, amazed at her friend's insatiable appetite for buttered rolls and cold sausage.

"He wants me to go with him," Karin said. "He needs to be near the gallery. He'll get a regular income and his work's on permanent display. He'd be stupid to turn it down."

"And you don't want to go."

"No. I'm happy here in my flat. And," she said, taking a stab at the last piece of sausage, (rather viciously, Anni thought) "I enjoy my work! I've been here for two years and for the first time in my life I'm appreciated. I've got good colleagues, good friends, good prospects and," she said, twirling her fork around in the air and making another attempt at the sausage, "I'm ambitious!" The sausage remained elusive. Impatiently, Karin picked it up with her fingers and bit hard into it. "Never liked forks anyway," she muttered.

"It's important, isn't it, your work?" Anni asked.

"Yes, but so's Eduard."

"There must be a need for eye surgeons in Munich, so…"

"I know, but that's not the point, is it?" Karin pushed her plate aside. "Okay, so it's career or Eduard; right?" She leaned into the hard back of her chair. "Look, I had a rotten marriage and I don't want to make the same mistake. We've got our own flats and we return there every night, each to his own. Well, almost every night. It's hours to Munich!" She threw her hands into the air, got up and started to pile the dishes. "Maybe we're too independent. Eduard was married before too; and there's another thing," she said, wagging her finger at Anni. "His politics make me angry. His attitude to the East for one thing. But I don't want to influence you before you've met him. No, don't get up, I'll do this, you sit there," she said, pointing at the table.

She's bossier than I remember, Anni thought; *or am I getting touchy? Maybe I'm more English than I realised. She certainly seems more relaxed than she was last night.*

❦

Karin had told Anni about her ex-husband, Detlef. Their marriage had started out harmoniously enough but Karin had not foreseen the awful quarrels that became everyday occurrences. She had not forgotten the bitterness and the hurt. They had agreed not to have children, but it was only later that Karin discovered Detlef had not been serious. He had hoped he would be able to change her mind, and after only four years they had divorced; that had been five years ago.

"There aren't any guarantees about anything," Anni called out as Karin disappeared into the kitchen.

Guarantees, Anni repeated to herself. *Who am I to talk? I haven't even worked out what I want with Victor.*

Only a few weeks ago he had jokingly suggested they live together. "To save travelling expenses—what else?" he had teased. But she knew he had been serious. Some of their colleagues had remarked on Victor's obvious fondness for her and joked about wedding bells. "You've got it wrong, we're only friends," she had told them. She had not let the relationship go further. She and Victor had kept their lives separate, and he had not pressed her for more.

A few days before Anni left England to meet Karin, Victor had flown out to Austria on a college-organised skiing holiday.

I wonder how he's getting on with the students, she thought, picturing him on the ski runs...

She knew there were some rowdy elements amongst the students. *But he can deal with them all right. What's more, everyone in the class likes him. The staff do as well!* The image of pretty Marlene, their new colleague, racing downhill at Victor's side gave Anni a sudden pang. *Come off it, you're not jealous, are you? Marlene's friendly with everyone, and the fact that she baked him an apple pie is neither here nor there. Don't forget, she did you a favour by agreeing to substitute for you.*

But was Marlene really being generous? "Don't be naïve!" her mother had warned. "He's an eligible bachelor."

Chapter Eighteen

It was a cold, crisp but sunny day, and after Karin had cleared the breakfast dishes she suggested that they walk the two miles to the nearby shopping centre. Eduard had telephoned earlier to say he was short of olives and cheese and could she pick some up from her local supermarket.

As they made their way along the suburban streets, towards the park, Karin again brought up the subject of Rudolf.

Anni told her that three days after her secret return to Rudolf's flat, the letter she had posted to her parents from West Berlin arrived.

The police delivered it. It had been opened. They suggested her parents write immediately and persuade Anni to come home; no proceedings would be taken against her if she did so. (One of the officers said allowances would be made for her age, but he added ominously that she was too young to have come to the decision to leave and someone must have influenced her.)

"Even if my parents had believed them," Anni assured Karin, "they wouldn't have wanted me to come back."

Her parents thought that under the circumstances, she

had done the right thing in leaving and they were relieved to read that she had crossed the border safely. They pointed out to the police that she was over eighteen and of an age to make up her own mind, and that they would not interfere with her decision.

As might have been expected, her parents' refusal to co-operate resulted in recriminations. They were blamed for not having guided Anni in the right way and were also accused of being obstructive. When the police came no closer to success, after several weeks of daily visits, the harassment suddenly stopped but soon after, an order was given that the flat be divided: it was deemed too large for two people. A young family was moved into the greater part of it. At the same time, the pressure to hand the café over to the State increased. "Over my dead body!" her father said. "Work here as an employee! I'd rather sweep the roads or clean the public lavatories."

There were other consequences of Anni's defection. Rudolf was put under surveillance. Even before he was tipped off about it he had noticed that he was being shadowed. It was not hard to imagine why; he was suspected of planning to leave.

❦

During the time Anni was in Rudolf's flat, he kept purposefully to his normal routine so as not to draw undue attention. He left for work at the usual hour in the morning, returned home for lunch every other day—on alternate days he lunched with a colleague—and finished at the usual time.

When she was alone in the flat she kept away from the windows, did not listen to the radio, fill the bath or flush the toilet.

On the afternoon of her fourth day, she was crossing the hall, having just come from the kitchen and intending to go into the living room, when she heard the sound of a key being turned in the front door. She was not expecting Rudolf yet. She hesitated. The way the key was inserted into the lock made her suspicious. It was as though it was being used by someone unfamiliar with the mechanism. Shoeless, she dashed back into the kitchen, knocking the toes of her right foot against a heavy wooden box which was partly obstructing the entrance. She was barely able to suppress a shriek of pain. Bending down and massaging her toes, she peered carefully from behind the kitchen door and watched as the door to the flat opened. The figure of a tall young man came briefly into view, but it was long enough for her to see she had never met him before. Without lingering, he headed straight for the living room. Anni noted that one foot thumped on the floorboards as he shifted his weight from one leg to the other, as though he were lame. But as he did so, there was a metallic clicking sound.

She could hear him moving about in the living room, switching on the radio and rummaging in the drinks cabinet. He seemed to know his way around.

She controlled her panic sufficiently for her to come to grips with the situation. She knew that she must not be found in the flat. Quickly weighing up her options, she looked around. There was nowhere in the kitchen to hide. Who the hell was this young man? What on earth would she do if he came into the kitchen?

To make her way to the bedroom was out of the question. It was situated directly across the hall, and to get there she needed to pass the living-room door which the stranger had left wide open. The chances of him seeing her were extremely high. Furthermore, the bedroom door was shut and always needed a hefty pull to get it open. Even with the radio switched on the young man was bound to hear the noise of the door.

While she was still trying to think of a solution to the problem, and as she surveyed her immediate surroundings for a possible hiding-place, her eyes came to rest upon the grandfather clock. It was only steps away in the hall. Rudolf had recently bought it and it was in need of repair. She remembered he had taken out the movement, which meant that the heavy wooden casing was empty. He had also oiled the hinges. Anni tiptoed the short distance and hid inside the case.

It turned out to have been a timely move because soon after she had settled onto the floor of the clock case, she heard the stranger, click, thump, click, thump on his way into the kitchen where she heard him open the refrigerator.

It was not long before she began to feel very uncomfortable. Her legs, her back, even her arms ached. She was afraid of making a noise, and hardly dared to move. She carefully alternated between sitting on her haunches and kneeling. To make matters worse, in the stale, dry and dusty air, she had to fight the urge to sneeze.

After about half an hour, by which time she was getting painfully stiff, Rudolf returned. From the few words she could hear, she realised that the young man was Rudolf's son Fabian. He had been passing through town and, on the spur of the moment, he had decided to pay his father a visit. Having his set of spare keys on him he had let himself into the flat. Fabian had not seen his father for some time and he had rather a lot to talk about—which was unfortunate for Anni in her cramped hiding-place.

Eventually Fabian departed and an anxious Rudolf tried to locate her. By now, she had managed quietly to get herself into a sitting position with her knees drawn tight to her chin. Feeling more comfortable, the situation had begun to strike her as rather comical. So when he called her, she did not answer; instead, as he came near, she made him jump by doing a poor imitation of a ticking clock.

The incident had highlighted the precariousness of her presence in the flat and they decided they needed to plan more carefully to safeguard themselves. Rudolf emptied the airing cupboard in the hall. He took out its shelves and put in some soft padding. It was not long before she had reason to use this more luxurious hide-out.

The very next day, around eight in the evening, the doorbell rang. Before Rudolf went to open the front door she made a dash for the airing cupboard and hid inside. The visitors were two well-known Party members. One of them wanted a French mantel clock, a particular one. Rudolf had had dealings with them in the past but this was the first time they had turned up at his flat and he suspected the real reason they had come was to snoop.

❦

Originally, Anni had planned to stay for up to ten days. That self-imposed limit was getting close, and she was still there.

Another weekend came and, as usual, Rudolf went to the corner bakery. When he asked for six crusty rolls, the baker's wife remarked; "You're eating well lately; are they all for you?" and she gave him a knowing look. He was quite certain that her comment was innocent enough as it was made in a flirtatious way, referring to his reputation as a ladies' man. But what did worry him was that there were other customers in the shop, any one of whom could report the lady's comment. Even if the remark was repeated innocently, it was always possible for someone to read more into it and get ideas.

"We both knew the risks," Anni told Karin, as they entered the supermarket. "If I had been discovered, it would've meant prison for both of us. I knew I couldn't stay much longer."

She related to Karin the bittersweet atmosphere of that last weekend and told her how they had planned her impending journey; how they had tried to make the most of being together, not thinking of the parting to come.

❦

Anni was to leave on the following Wednesday. They thought the border checks might be easier to get through in mid-week. Because of her train connections, Rudolf would leave the flat earlier than usual and walk to his workshop. If he could draw his "shadow" away with him she would slip out soon afterwards, but if the man could not be lured away her attempt would have to be abandoned for that day and they would have to rethink their plan.

On the pre-appointed morning, as she watched from behind drawn curtains, she saw Rudolf disappear around the corner; his "shadow" was close behind him. She waited for ten minutes, as they had agreed, and when everything in the street seemed quite ordinary she stole out of the house. Dressed in the apprentice's overalls she had worn before, she hurried away in the opposite direction. She kept up her pace until she reached the outskirts of the town; only then did she dare slow down and look behind her.

Everything appeared to be quite normal; the people on the street were going about their daily business and she had not attracted any unwanted attention. Fortunately she saw no police.

So far so good, but she knew this was only the beginning. She thought of Rudolf and of how anxious he would be. It was worse for him, just waiting, not knowing what was happening. But she had to go alone; they had both agreed it would be safer.

In theory, she had already left and nobody should be looking for her. Rudolf's name, on the other hand, was probably on the wanted list of the border police. It occurred to her that she was now, as far as her status as a citizen was concerned, a nonentity.

Her next hurdle was the village station near to where Rudolf had been waiting for her not all that long ago. That now seemed an age away.

After she had walked for some considerable time she looked at her watch; she was ahead of schedule. To make her arrival at the station coincide with the rush of local commuters she needed to slow her pace; she had planned to blend in with them and lose herself in the crowd. She was in possession of a ticket which would allow her to pass through the small station building without having to stop at the booking kiosk first.

Shortly before the train was due she made her way to the platform, sat down on one of the benches and opened a popular weekly magazine. After the train arrived she boarded it; it was a slow train, stopping every ten minutes or so. At each stop more passengers were picked up but none alighted and after a while she relaxed a little. There was a bit of a scramble in Magdeburg where everybody had to change trains, and she gladly merged into the crowd of people heading for the exit. The journey had taken her closer to the West, but now she had more than two hours to wait.

Her stomach was grumbling so she decided the best thing

to do would be to go to the railway restaurant and have some breakfast—it was too early for the eating places in town to be open and she had been too wound up earlier that morning to eat before she left the flat.

But first, she had to change into the floral summer skirt and white blouse she had worn in Sanssouci—to be seen sitting in the restaurant in overalls when the working man's day had already begun would draw people's attention to her. Any nosy policeman on a routine check, in and around the station, might have wondered and decided to ask some awkward questions. Luckily, the ladies' cloakroom was unattended, so she was not seen as she stuffed the overalls into the waste-paper bin.

Even after lingering over breakfast and taking her time buying the ticket for the next step of her journey she still had almost an hour to wait until she could board the train, so she decided to take a look at the town.

Even though she had hardly slept the night before she was not tired…

From the moment she left Rudolf's flat she had felt uncommonly wide awake to everything and everyone around her. It was as though the sense of danger had given her extra eyes and ears.

The colours of the sky, of people's faces and of their clothes struck her as being intensely vivid. And in the morning sunshine it seemed as if the streets of Magdeburg were flooded with brilliant light. The singularly vibrating sounds of people's voices, of cars passing by, of a dog barking added an almost painful intensity.

It was an odd idea, but she remembered comparing herself to a powerhouse which could convert the multitude of impressions into energy.

All through the day she experienced a range of emotions. There was her acute unhappiness at having to leave Rudolf, the ache of cutting herself irrevocably loose from her parents, her home, Aschersleben; there was guilt too. She was fearful of getting caught, apprehensive about the refugee camp and her future. On the other hand, there was the excitement and exhilaration of the adventure which, although she did not like to admit it, she enjoyed. Added to all of this was the anticipation of getting out of the clutches of the suppressive regime. It was only tempered by the realisation that she would be shutting the door behind her permanently—or so she thought at the time.

When it was almost time to board the train in the direction of Brandenburg, Anni walked back to the station. Several policemen were standing around in the ticket hall but none of them demanded to see her papers. Punctually, the train departed and this stage of her journey went well.

Brandenburg was the last major stop before going on to Potsdam. And of course from there she knew her way, having crossed the border successfully before—she had been superstitious about choosing an alternative route.

She arrived in Brandenburg in the early afternoon and because there was another lengthy wait for her connection she strolled into town and found somewhere to eat. Afterwards she walked to a local park, following directions from a signboard.

The sunny, warm morning had given way to a hot and sticky afternoon. There was hardly a breath of air but the clouds began to thicken and the sun kept disappearing behind them. She sat for quite a while on an empty park bench and watched some children playing in a nearby sandpit. Every so often they would squabble over a red toy bucket, intermittently lose interest in it and continue to play absorbedly without it. Watching the children seemed to have a calming effect on her for it temporarily took her mind off her situation, and when one of the mothers accompanying her children joined Anni on the bench they chatted of ordinary things.

She felt much more relaxed as she walked back to the station to catch the train going towards Potsdam; it was already waiting.

She was making her way along the platform to the middle of the train when she noticed another one pulling in; it stopped on the other side of the platform. Almost at once the passengers spilled out along the length of the carriages. Among the people getting off, she noticed a number of noisy young conscripts. But instead of walking to the exit with the rest of the arrivals, they stayed on the platform, grouped in a semicircle and looking around. They seemed to be waiting for something.

※

Impatiently, the checkout girl ushered Karin towards the till. "Come on, other customers are waiting," she said sourly. "It's not the place to have a conversation, is it?"

Karin looked at Anni and raised her eyebrows. "Tell me when we get out of here," she said, as she paid for the groceries.

Having put her few items into a carrier bag, she suggested that once again they walk through the park.

"You were talking about the conscripts," Karin said, as soon as they had left the supermarket.

"The conscripts? Oh yes," said Anni. (*So I haven't been bending her ear*, she thought.) "Well, I noticed them but didn't pay them any attention. But just as I walked past, one of them called out my name."

"No!" said Karin, slowing her pace.

"I couldn't believe it either," said Anni, shaking her head. "I started to turn; all I could think was, who the hell's that! I'm not supposed to be here! I didn't dare look so I swiped at a wasp; there wasn't one, but I wanted to get a quick peek at him and I couldn't think of anything else. That's why I swiped at the wasp, you see."

"Who was it?"

"Gerhard; you know, Gerhard Fichte."

"From school?"

"Yes, I thought he was going to ruin everything, so I kept walking and pretended I hadn't heard, but that idiot came up and tapped me on the shoulder. I knew it was him. He asked me what I was doing there—he'd heard I'd left, you see. Imagine that!" Anni shook her head again. "I asked him who he was talking about. He said 'Anni', and I said, 'I'm not Anni.' And I called him an idiot, and told him to stop pestering me."

"Mmm! Quick thinking," said Karin.

"I had to; it could've been disastrous. Afterwards, I felt a bit sorry, he wasn't a bad sort, he just didn't think. He kept saying, 'You must be Anni.' "

"What about his friends?"

"They just jeered and whistled, so I rushed for the train; I couldn't hang about and get involved, could I? I suppose they thought it was a chat-up."

❧

As Anni ran along the platform she could hear the continuing jeers and whistles of Gerhard's companions and his querulous voice doggedly insisting that he had been in the same class as her at school. She reached the furthest carriage and got in.

She took the nearest available seat; her hands were shaking and her heart was pounding. She wondered whether Gerhard would keep quiet about her defection. She listened for the sounds of soldiers' feet hurrying along the platform and she visualised being hauled from the train. But nothing happened.

After a few minutes the train moved out of the station on its scheduled journey. All at once she felt relieved, but with the relief came anger; anger at Gerhard for putting her into a potentially dangerous situation. Did he realise what a mess he had nearly made of her life, and if so, would he think about it and see how stupidly he had acted?

An elderly woman who had watched her break away from Gerhard leaned towards her and said, "They'll stop at nothing nowadays, even in broad daylight."

Anni closed her eyes and pretended to sleep. *If only you knew*, she thought.

❦

"All this walking's making me thirsty," said Karin, as they reached the park." I thought we might sit by the lake and have an ice cream, but it's nearly lunch time and I'm more hungry than thirsty."

Anni laughed. "Again!"

Karin made no reply.

Oops! Anni thought and looked at her, but Karin's mind seemed to be on other things.

"Mmm, I wonder if Gerhard did say anything," Karin mused. She quickened her pace, "I bumped into him once; he didn't mention you."

"I've wondered about him for years," said Anni, trying to keep up.

❧

At Potsdam, Anni stood on the platform waiting for her next connection. The Gerhard incident had dented her confidence and she was apprehensive about the final stages of her journey. But all being well, by nightfall she should be safe.

It was almost six o'clock in the evening when the Berlin City train approached the border. It stopped on the Eastern side and the police got on for their customary check.

Anni was sitting in the third carriage behind the engine and, looking out of the window, she saw two policemen enter a carriage much further down the line. She knew the train would not move off until it had been cleared.

It was quiet in the compartment. Most of the seats were taken but some passengers preferred to stand. A few of the people sitting were reading. Some were holding whispered conversations and others, like her, were doing nothing in particular. Every so often, she craned her neck to look out of the window and along the length of the train. The curve in the line enabled her to see the last carriage at one end and the engine at the other. She watched as the policemen stepped out onto the platform and walked along to each carriage in turn.

She noticed that the platform on her side of the train was uncared for and in need of repair. Grass and various weeds were growing out of the cracks. Her eyes were drawn to a clump of pale blue wild flowers with bright yellow centres. They were growing from one of the cracks not far from where she was sitting. It pleased her to look at the flowers and, for some reason or other, she took them to be a good omen.

189

I shall count up to ten, she said to herself, *and if at least three of them nod their heads towards me with the next puff of wind, then I'll get through.*

The two policemen—she thought one of them might be a sergeant—had checked as far as the middle of the train. Now that they were closer to her carriage, she saw that each of them carried hardback notebooks. On her last border crossing she had not noticed the police carrying them; she wondered what the significance was.

She sat and waited. There was nothing she could do. She felt quite calm now—the nearer the policemen came the calmer she grew. It seemed as though it were happening to somebody else—*a kind of detachment*, she thought.

Only after they had entered her carriage did she notice that the younger of the two officers looked little older than a boy. She could not tell his rank and presumed him to be an ordinary constable.

The middle-aged sergeant proceeded to inspect the passengers on one side of the carriage, while he ordered his young colleague, Frank, to check the other. The sergeant went through the passengers' documents thoroughly.

Anni's side of the carriage was being checked by Frank, and it was not long before it became clear that he worked much faster, but less carefully, than his superior. He seemed to be anxious to finish the job quickly as he kept looking at his watch. She was glad it was Frank who was almost certain to check her pass and not the miserable looking, pedantic sergeant who kept opening one of the notebooks and leafing through its pages every time a document was handed to him;

Anni was heartened that Frank missed checking the occasional passenger. Also, she had only seen him open his notebook a few times and suspected that he went more through the motion of checking names against the register than seriously comparing identities. He did not appear to be concentrating on his work, and when he held a pass upside down the people nearby exchanged meaningful glances.

Just as he was about to check the passengers sitting opposite her, there was a disturbance four rows further down the carriage. Anni tilted her head slightly to one side, enough to see what was going on whilst at the same time trying not to show too much interest.

It seemed a young man had been trying to leave the carriage. But before he could make it to the door, Anni saw the sergeant grab him by the arm and force him violently back onto his seat. The policeman rammed his knee against the young man's chest; he wheezed as he struggled to breathe. "Don't move!" the sergeant shouted, and he called to his colleague, "Come 'ere, Frank! Quickly, man!"

The passengers looked on passively as Frank dropped his notebooks and rushed to give support.

"Watch 'im!" the sergeant growled. He took out his revolver before removing his knee.

At the sight of the weapon, the people in the carriage went very quiet and avoided looking at each other.

The sergeant thrust his hand inside the young man's jacket and drew out a small bundle of papers. "These yours?" he said.

The young man nodded.

The sergeant studied the papers minutely. For long seconds he looked from the young man to one of the documents. "That you?" he said, pointing to what must have been a photograph.

The young man nodded again.

"If that's you, I'm your twin brother! Come on, whose pass is it?" he sneered. He nudged Frank and grinned, holding the photograph in front of his face, "What d'you think, Frank?"

Frank looked embarrassed and shrugged his shoulders.

The sergeant turned to the passenger again and pointed the revolver at him. "Out!" he ordered, waving it towards the carriage door.

Once on the platform he pushed the young man, face downwards, to the ground, the revolver aimed at the back of his head. Without taking his eyes off the prone figure, the sergeant commanded: "Frank! Flag the train on!"

The train started to move, and when Anni looked out of the window she saw Frank pulling the young man's arms up behind his back as the sergeant kicked him in the face.

"I didn't see much after that," she said, "except that the sergeant grabbed the poor man by the hair and made him watch the train move out of the station."

"So, you were safe," Karin said after a while, quietly.

Anni did not answer straight away…

❦

Nobody in the carriage so much as whispered and the silence persisted long after the train had crossed into West Berlin.

Out of the corner of her eye Anni suddenly spotted the notebooks Frank had dropped. She stared at them for a moment, then glanced at the old man at whose feet they had fallen; he was scowling at them. She looked around the carriage; other passengers were eyeing them too, but nobody made a move towards them; it was as though they were contaminated.

Aren't they curious,? More likely, they're afraid; Big Brother's still watching. They're going back, and they know that anyone could report them.

Slowly, Anni reached out and picked up the books. She put them on her knee and placed her hand on top of them. Her fingers played with the edges of the pages, partly separating the leaves of the top book. She hesitated, then decided she did not want to know its contents so, letting the cover flick shut, she pressed her hand firmly back on the neat pile.

Through the window she watched as the scenery seemed to speed by. She was looking along the length of the train as it approached a bend over an embankment. The train slowed to negotiate the curve and she noted the dereliction of the surrounding area. As the train pulled out of its trajectory she stood up and holding the notebooks in her right hand she thrust them through the open window, still clutching them, waiting a few seconds. Then, with a flick of her wrist, she tossed them out into the slipstream. She followed the books with her eyes as the air snatched them; their leaves fluttered madly as they tumbled down the embankment. She tracked them until she could see them no longer; only then did she sit down.

The old man caught her eye. He was smiling. But he said nothing.

Chapter Nineteen

Having enjoyed the refreshments after their bracing walk to the supermarket, Karin piled the lunch dishes into the drip-tray, then turned and leaned back against the kitchen sink. Meticulously, she wiped her hands on the hand towel and placed it with the same care over the handle of the oven door. "I'm glad you told me about Rudolf," she said. "Did you see him again? You did love him, didn't you?"

Anni shifted her position on her stool and placed her hands together, gripping them firmly between her knees. "I thought I did, at the time, but when we..." She looked at her friend.

"Not sure?"

"I changed; so did he." Anni shook her head. "It wasn't the same."

Karin folded her hands in front of her apron. "Too much time between?"

"Maybe.... It was only about a year."

❦

Anni was living in the students' hostel near the school she attended. She was on a course, studying to validate her East German Abitur, when, unexpectedly, Rudolf turned up.

She had been sorting through her clothes, trying to find something suitable to wear for a performance of the local symphony orchestra later that evening. A neighbour knocked on the door and told her that downstairs, in the reception room, there was somebody to see her.

She recognised him instantly, even though he was the last person she expected to see. He was standing by the French doors, looking into the garden, but turned to face her when she came in.

They stood, looking at each other. Then Rudolf stretched out his arms and, hesitantly, she walked towards him. "Aren't you happy to see me?" he asked.

"Yes, of course I am," she said. "It's j—just that I'm—surprised."

As she told him that she was delighted to see him, she knew she was covering up for her lack of reaction, and it disturbed her.

For the first few months after she had left home she imagined what it would be like to see him again, though she thought this was unlikely. They had not even exchanged letters; for fear that it would leave him open to accusations of complicity in her escape.

As the months passed, she found herself thinking of him less often; lately, she had hardly thought of him at all. On the occasions she did, she felt the pangs of guilt for not missing him but she told herself it was only natural; it being a subconscious defence to make it easier to accept that she was not going to see him again. She made excuses for herself: she was busy studying; she needed to come to terms with her new way of life.

As Rudolf persisted in reminding her of their charmed times together, she became aware that she was beginning to be irritated by him. It was clear to her that she did not feel the joy and happiness she had imagined anyone in her position would experience. She knew her feelings were not appropriate, but pushing the uncomfortable thoughts aside, she asked him how long he had been in the West and how he had managed to find her.

Over a drink in a nearby beer cellar, he told her that he had left the East quite recently. Despite the fact he had always said he would never leave, and that all the while there was the possibility of escape he did not feel an overpowering need to do so, he had come to believe the rumours that the building of the Wall was imminent and had begun to fear he would be stuck behind it for good.

"My parents had heard the rumours too," Anni said, "but they took longer to make up their minds."

With great seriousness, Rudolf told Anni how he had traced her. He had had contacts in the area's education department. Knowing she had hoped to settle in Westphalia he thought she might be attending one of the schools or colleges, so he had made enquiries about her.

After their drinks in the wine cellar she returned to her hostel, but not before he had made her promise to visit him at the weekend—he had told her he had rented a small flat in a nearby town and that they would be able to celebrate their reunion in private.

As the weekend drew near, she became uneasy about seeing him. Apart from the feelings of doubt, there was something about him that was worrying her. Then, on the Saturday morning as she awoke, it suddenly became clear what it was that had eluded her. His attractive free and easy manner, recklessness almost, was gone. During their meeting at the hostel, and then again in the beer cellar, there had been no laughter, no joking. Instead, she had sensed an unfamiliar tenseness in him.

❦

He was standing on the platform when Anni's train arrived. As he greeted her with a happy grin and a bunch of deep red roses, he seemed more like his old self. He lifted her off the ground and hugged her. He twirled her around until she begged him to put her down. There was great tenderness in his face and he looked altogether elated. She could not help being touched by his greeting, but at the same time she was overcome by sadness and tears filled her eyes.

Rudolf's flat was not far from the station, so they walked. He had only recently moved into the small apartment and had not had time to stamp his individuality upon it. But there were flowers in the living room and with the pretty table-cloth and soft curtains the room looked inviting.

After several more hugs he installed her into his armchair; she put her feet up and relaxed while he took himself off to the kitchen to put the finishing touches to their meal. He told her that preparing it had given him great pleasure. She had not forgotten what a good cook he was. During her stay with him he had insisted on doing all the cooking, after a couple of mishaps on her part when she had offered to help.

From the kitchen came the sounds of drawers being pulled open and of crockery and cutlery being taken out. Rudolf's intermittent humming reached her ears and the appetising smell of a roast wafted through the partly open door. Only a year ago she had dreamed of such a situation.

I should feel gloriously happy, but instead…

❦

197

They had finished their meal but were still sitting around the table. The empty plates and dishes had been stacked and pushed to one side and Rudolf had uncorked a second bottle of wine.

Anni's head was no longer clear and her dormant senses were beginning to awaken. She moved closer, leaned against him and took one of his hands into both of hers. She lifted it to her lips and lingeringly kissed it. He put his free arm around her shoulders and squeezed her hard, but he did not kiss her.

He smiled and said, "I want to tell you something, something I wanted to say when I first saw you again, only you seemed distant. It's all right," he added, noticing the furrow on her brow, "I understand. You must've thought I was a ghost." He tilted her head towards his and looking at her searchingly he repeated, "I want to tell you…I made up my mind… ." He paused again.

Once more she was struck by the unfamiliar earnestness in his voice. In the past there had been times when she had seen fit to scold him for not being serious enough. Now he was too intense and it made her feel jittery. She would have preferred him in his more jocular mood, to counteract her mounting sense of foreboding. She suspected that he was preparing the ground to ask for her commitment to him; she did not want that. As she dwelled on the change in him, she felt a sinking feeling in her stomach.

Finally, he said, "I went to see my wife," and he proceeded to tell how he had found his wife living with another man and that the man appeared to be overly jealous, refusing to allow him to speak to her privately.

Rudolf went into the minutest details of the meeting, to the extent of describing the layout of the flat. He was fidgeting and blustering as he spoke. Anni had never seen him so nervous and uncontrolled.

He suddenly stopped speaking, got up from his chair, sat down and, again, looked intently at her.

Is that what he wanted to tell me so urgently, Anni thought, refilling her glass?

He waited until the glass was full before repeating what he had already told her.

Her last doubts evaporated. She was sure he was afraid to come to the point.

As she drank yet another glass of wine she realised she had had too much. Feeling an oppressive lethargy taking hold, she struggled to keep her eyes open. She was dimly aware that she was missing whole chunks of what Rudolf was saying. Through her semi-stupor she heard him say that his wife had asked him for a divorce. He droned on about how much her request had pleased him, in fact he had expected it and had agreed they needed to make their separation legal. He elaborated on his wife's open hostility towards him but insisted that he still thought of her as a friend.

While he was describing the court proceedings to come, she could stay awake no longer. Her head sank down onto the table, narrowly missing a soup bowl. At that, Rudolf jumped up from his seat. Full of apology, he picked her up and carried her to the bedroom. She vaguely remembered hearing him scold himself for not realising how tired she was.

❦

Even before she opened her eyes she could sense Rudolf's presence, but because she needed more time to compose herself she pretended to be still asleep.

As she lay there, her thoughts went back to their time together in his flat, and how once, just once when she felt particularly emotional, she had told him, "I love you." She had wanted to say those words to him before, but something had always prevented her from doing so. "No, you don't," he had said, putting a finger against her lips. "You only think you do; you'll soon forget me. And that's just as it should be," he had added. Then he had taken her in his arms, kissed her forehead and asked her to try to enjoy their last few days together. He had refused to use the word "love" when she pressed him to tell her how he felt about her.

She lay there thinking about what he had said, and for the first time she dared to admit to herself that he had been right. The veil of self-deception was lifting and beneath it she could see the truth: she had needed to purify her passion for Rudolf and only love could cleanse the tainted image of sex her upbringing had conditioned her to have.

❧

"I wonder if I would've thought differently if I'd never met him again," Anni said to Karin, "or would I have tied him up in pink ribbons and cried over him. Anyway, when I did open my eyes, he was looking at me. He said he'd been there for quite a while, watching and thinking about our future."

"Your future? Oh, so he did want to marry you?"

"Yes," said Anni. "He was very sincere."

"Poor man," said Karin.

"I felt sorry too," Anni said. "How else could I feel?"

She had been overcome with compassion as Rudolf stretched out his hands to her. She was struck by the same sadness she had felt on the station platform. As she stroked his head she felt as though she were mourning a loss.

She knew she was going to hurt him whether she broke with him or not; the result would be the same. But how, she wondered, was she going to tell him?

Anni did not mention to Karin that Rudolf had kissed her and that she had responded. She did not say that she had been tempted to continue with their relationship.

Chapter Twenty

Rudolf spent almost the whole of the first week after Anni's defection in a state of anxiety, worrying whether she had managed to get across the border. He was only reassured when he received her coded card.

🎋

Some time before, a West Berlin firm had sent Rudolf an invitation to attend an exhibition of old clock mechanisms. The invitation card was typewritten and addressed to his workshop near the town hall. He had not attended the exhibition but he had kept the card. He gave Anni the card and asked her to post it to him once she was safely in the West. He had smudged the date to make it illegible, and he had also removed the stamp. Anni agreed she would put a new stamp exactly where the old one had been and add the initials OK under the text on the card to indicate that everything had gone well.

🎋

Rudolf had expected to miss Anni but was unprepared for

the strength of feelings her leaving had generated. He did not seem to be able to settle into anything. In the evenings, alone in the flat, he would pick up a book but after reading a few pages his mind would wander. Listening to music made him sad and only increased his longing for her. He forced himself to go out to pubs and to visit his friends, but coming back to an empty flat made his loneliness worse, so he took to staying at home. In any case, several of his friends had told him that he was "boring company nowadays". He found his work, which he had always enjoyed, could not in itself compensate for Anni's absence. Still, throwing himself into work was better than sitting and brooding over his loss, so he stayed late at his office or workshop. He did not like his state of mind and told himself that it was ridiculous to feel the way he did. He resolved, after weeks of misery, that the best way to get over what he, privately, called his laughable teenage love sickness was to re-establish a relationship with Frau Knopf.

She was an attractive widow in her early forties. He had known her for about a year before his wife left him but had stopped seeing his long-time mistress when Anni came onto the scene. (Actually, his affair with Frau Knopf had been more then his wife could take; it had been one affair too many. She had told him that she would not put up with his philandering any longer.)

One evening in late November, after a couple of stiff drinks Rudolf felt audacious enough to turn up at Frau Knopf's country cottage. "Hi, Erika," he said brazenly, as soon as she opened her front door. As she stood, stunned, inside her lobby, he flashed what he intended to be a most disarming smile. And as if they were still on the best of terms, he suggested, "Why don't I pick you up at eight tomorrow? We can talk over dinner? Okay? Can I—?"

"You've got a nerve!" she snorted, cutting him short. She was glaring at him now as she took hold of the door handle.

"Just let me come in for a moment," he begged. He was about to step over the threshold when, bending his head forward, he felt the painful knock on his forehead as she shut the door in his face. *Oh well*, he thought, *must have overestimated my charm. Never mind.*

"Come on, don't be silly," he said, loud enough for her to hear from behind the door. And even though he realised it was futile, he repeated his plea several times. Then he noticed a neighbour's upstairs curtain twitch and a pinched face looking down at him, so he decided it was time to go.

He whistled a tune as he stepped nonchalantly out towards home. He was not too unhappy with Erika's response. She had not threatened him with the police, neither had she told him not to come back. He was confident she would see him eventually, if he persisted.

He told himself, *she's far too nosy not to want to find out what I have to say. Anyway, it'll be good to get together again. I've been missing the gossip, and her taking the mickey out of the townsfolk had been a scream. I need a good laugh, there's been too much gloom already. I know she enjoyed my company. "You're just what the doctor ordered", was a saying of hers.*

An image of Erika's auburn locks against white skin flashed through his mind and he stopped suddenly in the middle of the road. "Christ!" *I am in a bad way. How could I have forgotten about her allure…?*

He returned to the cottage the next evening at eight o'clock. As he had expected, Erika did not answer the door, so he pushed a note through the letterbox:

AT LEAST LISTEN TO WHAT I HAVE TO SAY!

I'LL BE BACK TOMORROW.

YOU KNOW WHO.

When Rudolf came back the next day as promised, Erika did allow him into the house. "Shut the door behind you and come to the living room," she said, smiling sweetly.

She was wearing the black cocktail dress he favoured, black stockings and stiletto-heeled shoes. Walking behind her, he noted the wiggle of her voluptuous bottom, which she knew he had always found seductive.

"Sit yourself down," she said, pointing to a group of easy chairs. "Coffee's made." Once he had sat down, she lowered herself into the chair opposite his. Leaning forward, she fixed her blue eyes on him, but she did not speak.

There's steel in that gaze, he thought. *She's ready to forgive me but wants me to cringe a little first; wants her pound of flesh, she does. Well, what did I expect?* He sipped from his cup. *A bit of generosity would've been nice though…*

He had worked out a lengthy and detailed apology, but being faced with Erika's self-assured demeanour he suddenly felt like denting her superior air so he came straight to the point. "You know," he said, looking at her, "when I made the excuses that I was too busy to see you, I was courting Anni. I should've told you, instead of blaming it all on the clocks. I'm sorry you had to hear about it from others." He paused, waiting for Erika to respond. She still did not speak and was regarding him with a hurt expression. "We'd been together for a long time and you deserved better," he said. "I mean it. To my credit," he smiled as he touched his chest, "when I was ready to tell you about it, you refused to listen. Remember?"

"So, you thought to keep me in reserve," she said coolly. "I thought as much at the time."

"Well," he started, "I didn't know if Anni—"

"Never mind all that now," she interrupted. She leaned back in her chair, crossing her legs and showing an ample length of thigh. "What did you expect from that slip of a girl? The whole thing was just a laugh for her. How could you be so stupid?! She was bound to dump you. She—"

All at once he felt angry. His face turned red. "Shut up!" he interrupted her. "You don't know anything, so don't jump to conclusions."

"I would've thought you'd be glad to be shot of her," she continued, sneering. "Why come to me if you're not?!"

"That's it," he said, jumping to his feet. "I don't have to listen to you slagging off Anni. I'm through with you."

"Fuck you too!" she shouted, as he stormed out of the room. One of her shoes thudded into the doorframe behind him.

※

Christmas turned out to be one of the bleakest Rudolf could remember. He spent the festive days at home, alone, from choice. He brooded over failed relationships, including Erika, and could not face being in the company of friends. Neither could he be bothered to prepare a proper Christmas dinner for himself. So, on Christmas Eve he had cooked a large pot of vegetable stew; what remained he warmed up for the next three days.

Luckily for Rudolf, with the dawning of the New Year his spirits had lifted enough for him to realise he had, for his own good, to snap out of his black moods.

I really must make a new start, he decided, *and find a companion…*

❧

Mindful of his New Year's resolution, Rudolf gave up his recent reclusive life-style and became a partygoer once more. The annoying thing to him was that while he had never failed to appeal to women in the past, now that, for the first time since his marriage, he was free to look for a partner, he seemed to have lost his touch. When he later thought about why this should have been so, he came to the conclusion that his eagerness, combined with an ill-disguised calculating attitude, must have been putting the women off. Maybe they had sensed his heart was not in his courting.

However, he eventually started to take out Doris to whom he had been introduced by a friend.

Rudolf hoped Doris might be the one who could make him forget his longing for Anni, but he soon had to admit this was not happening. Perhaps it was because Doris and Anni were markedly different that he continually found himself making comparisons.

He missed Anni's questioning attitude of mind. She would not accept any theory merely on his say-so but required evidence. Doris' way out of disagreement was to capitulate smilingly: "I suppose you're right." And it was Anni, who, despite being half Doris' age, had not made demands on him—at that time he was not ready to give of himself.

He knew Doris sensed that he did not feel emotionally involved with her and her resulting insecurity made her increasingly possessive, a character trait he did not like. She also thought that by going out of her way and doing his household chores, she would make herself indispensable to him. Her constant attentiveness, (fussing, as Rudolf called it) only made him irritable. What was more, he did not like Doris' suggestion that she move in with him. He reminded her that he was still married and that he worried about her reputation. All were excuses, as they both knew very well. Privately he acknowledged he was not being fair to her.

What more do I want? After all, Doris is good-looking, good-natured, caring, even loving.

The trouble was, of course, he did want more, more than Doris had to give.

By the time Anni had been gone for six months, Rudolf thought of her and of their brief stay together more often, rather than less. In retrospect, their relationship, which he had taken to analysing and re-evaluating, took on a deeper meaning. He remembered that when he first noticed her interest in him he had been flattered—any woman's interest made him feel good, but the fact that Anni was so young boosted his vanity more than usual. As he recalled, he had felt attracted to her from the beginning, and when he started talking to her he found that he actually liked her. The comments made by some of his friends, that surely he was past the age where he had it in him to seduce such a young woman, only made him more determined to succeed.

When Anni rejected him that first time in his flat, he had been very angry and imagined she was playing what he thought of as a silly girl's game. Then he thought about it again and realised it must have been due to her inexperience and he blamed himself for not having been more considerate.

Later, when she had delivered herself to him, in her spirited way, he felt very protective towards her. Her candidly voiced disappointment of the sex act became a challenge to him. What he did not foresee was that he was going to be too good a teacher and she too eager a student. Her physical abandonment fuelled his desire and intoxicated him.

However hard he tried, he could not expel the ever-present image of her. The vivid picture he had of her became part of his mind's landscape and the most natural thing of all was to imagine how it had felt to touch her. He could still sense, almost physically, her smooth skin and longed to hold her small but firm and erect breasts with their tiny nipples pointing ever so slightly outwards. Her naked body had been quite a surprise to him. With her slender build, he had not expected such strong, though softly rounded shoulders. Her thighs were full and beautifully shaped, culminating in the mass of red-blonde pubic hair, slightly curly and feeling springy when he let the palm of his hand rest on it. She used her powerful thighs to grip and hold him, preventing him from disentangling himself from her as in a tug of war. She had the sort of thighs to which he was partial, and he had told her of his distaste for what he called broomstick thighs between which a large coin could easily be passed, horizontally.

His respect for Anni's independence of mind grew when she showed she was not going to be frightened into submission by the pressures applied to her by officialdom. He had been prepared for a visit from the local Party representatives, but when they did not come he was furious at their cowardice; he felt she was being singled out deliberately. He was humiliated at having to stand by while the remnants of personal liberty were taken from her; it made him feel impotent. He had resolved then that as long as she wanted to keep seeing him he would not let them break up their relationship.

The days spent with her had been special, unique, and

the knowledge that their time together would be so brief made those days particularly precious. Living in constant danger of being discovered in the flat had brought them closer; but above all, to the bonds of the flesh were added the important seeds of friendship.

The more Rudolf thought of their past the sweeter the memories became. Gradually, almost imperceptibly, he turned her into the kind of idealised figure that Doris did not, could not, measure up to.

As time went by, he began to accuse himself of having been heartless in response to Anni's declaration of love. He had made light of their age difference and he tried not to dwell on what he had said to her: "You'll forget me soon enough." He started dreaming of seeing her again, to tell her, explain, rectify his image in her eyes and he began flirting with the idea of following her to the West.

Then suddenly the rumours of the building of the Berlin Wall reached his ears. Fearing he would be a captive and that their separation would be final, the decision to leave before it became too late was surprisingly easily reached. Once he had made up his mind to go, he felt strangely elated and he was quite amazed that he did not mind as much as he had thought he would at having to leave his treasured belongings behind.

❧

As a potential escapee, he expected to be still on the lists of the police and thought it wise to plan his departure carefully. Even though he believed he was no longer under direct surveillance he did not allow himself to assume that the authorities trusted him; the Party was renowned for having a long memory and he was sure his wife's and Anni's illegal border crossings had not been forgotten. (Soon after his association with Doris he had noticed he was no longer being openly watched. At first he thought that his regular "shadow" had been replaced by someone else, but after making many and sudden changes to his normal walks and haunts to try to catch out any new surveillant, he was convinced there really was no one following him. He remembered that, at the time, he had viewed the withdrawal of his "shadow" with something approaching disappointment. He would no longer have the chance to vent his repugnance of the authorities—surreptitiously, of course—on one of its representatives.)

Preparing for his escape, he sold his most highly valued possessions, foremost amongst them his clocks, though he had to be careful not to arouse suspicion; for that reason, he knew he would not be able to dispose of the two grandfather clocks even if they were removed from his flat at night. An additional complication concerning the disposals was that Doris visited frequently, not always allowing enough time to cover up for the missing pieces.

"What happened there?" she inquired, as soon as she had stepped into Rudolf's hallway. She was eyeing a rectangular patch of pristine wallpaper.

"Oh, yes, the empty space…" he said casually, playing for time. Only the evening before he had carted the antique clock which had been hanging on the facing wall to a neighbouring village and sold it to a farmer. *Blast*, he thought, *I should've hung the substitute in its place the minute I came home. Wonder why the previous tenant didn't take it with him.* "Well…" he hesitated, then suddenly thought how he might explain it. "The fact is I needed the money."

"But why? You're not short, are you?" she puzzled.

"Actually," he said, still working on the details of his idea, "it's to pay for a holiday for us. It was meant to be a surprise." His mind was ticking over fast. The fictitious holiday had to fit in with the date of his planned escape.

"Oh," she beamed, "that's lovely. Going away together. I'm so pleased." She stretched her arms and managed to fling them around his neck. Holding him tight, she smothered his mouth and chin with kisses. "What did you have in mind?" she said after she had let go and got her breath back.

"I rather fancy the Baltic coast, I haven't been there, it's supposed to be glorious."

"It is," she said. "Only, the trouble is," her features darkened, "it's too late to book a room in any of the resorts now that the holiday season's started."

"Come here," he said, drawing her close and gazing over her shoulder into the distance. *What a shit I am*, he thought. Aloud he said, "Don't worry. Leave it to me. I know how to butter up those seaside landladies."

After Doris had gone home, Rudolf got some papers, a pen and a calendar and settled at his desk. He wrote down some possible holiday dates, taking into account Doris' allotted time slot from the hospital where she worked as a nursing sister.

He decided he would defect two days before the start of Doris' vacation. "As soon as you stop work," he planned to say to her, "we'll be off to the Baltic coast." He had no intention of booking a room but would tell Doris in a week or so that he had managed to find "just the place" and that the destination was a "surprise".

He felt sorry for deceiving her in this way but he knew he could not confide in her, fearing she might give him away out of jealousy—he remembered on several occasions that she had accused him of caring more for Anni than he did for her.

He poured himself a cognac and as he sat down with it on the sofa he thought about the coming days. Having brought the date of his escape forward, he would be hard pushed to sell the rest of his moveable belongings. Also, he had to finish all work in progress, ask his regular customers to collect their pieces and make sure he did not accept anything new.

To keep Doris from noticing his home become bare, he would tell her, "Don't visit me while I'm decorating. I'll come to you." And of course, once he had deliberately damaged his two grandfather clocks so that no Party boss would enjoy them, it was imperative that nobody be allowed into his flat.

❦

A year or so before Rudolf had moved away from East Berlin, he found cause to distance himself from Willi, one of his colleagues. Willi had chosen to become an active Party member. This was reason enough, but Rudolf was further dismayed when he discovered that Willi had also joined various socialist committees; a move which had greatly speeded up his promotion.

Willi was a rather plain man but similar in height, hair colour and age to Rudolf whose company he had always liked to be seen in and whose polished manners, appearance and ease of conversation he appreciated but also envied. Rudolf was aware that by this association Willi hoped to increase his chances of meeting the kind of women he desired, but which he, so far, had never managed to attract. So when Rudolf contacted him, instead of feeling annoyed, Willi readily agreed that they meet in East Berlin. That was two days before the scheduled holiday with Doris.

Rudolf was a little late as he entered the public house

he had chosen for the meeting. (It was a quiet place, out of the way, not usually frequented by either his or Willi's friends, so the chances of encountering anyone either of them knew would be greatly reduced.)

Willi, with flushed face beaming, walked very unsteadily towards his former colleague; his clumsy greeting was followed by some hearty back-slapping. Normally Rudolf would have objected to this sort of reception but tonight he suffered it gracefully while noting, with satisfaction, that Willi had already had quite a lot to drink.

Clutching Rudolf's arm, Willi steered him back to the table he had been occupying. He slumped into his chair and almost immediately wanted to know all about Rudolf's new life. "Why for heaven's sshake did you move to the provinsshes?" he slurred. "I've misshed you, you've been hiding away," he babbled into his drink. "Mussht've been woman trouble." He winked salaciously, "Sschome female after you?" He roared with laughter, nudging Rudolf in the ribs.

Rudolf noticed that people's heads were beginning to turn. One or two of the clientele were making disapproving noises and he raised his eyebrows in apology to them.

"Wouldn't you like to know!" he replied quietly to Willi, disguising his contempt by adopting a mysterious tone. "Truthfully," he continued, "it was nothing like that, I only moved for the business premises."

Playing along with Willi's wisecracks, he said, "You're right though, life's really boring; nothing happens in the provinces. Never mind, I'll get the drinks." He grinned, and leaning closer he whispered, "I fancy the waitress."

Slowly Rudolf turned the conversation away from himself to Willi's good fortune, encouraging him to talk and also to drink more.

"Between you and me," Willi said, slurring even more, "bessht thing I ever did, joining the Party, I'd sshtill be sshlaving in that rotten offish-block. Money'ssh better now." He gave his empty glass a quick glance before thumping it down on the table.

"I'll get the drinks," said Rudolf.

A few rounds later, Willi was struggling to put his sentences together. "You alwayssh sshaid you weren't inter—inter," he could not get his tongue to pronounce the word, "bothered about politicssh…nor am I, becausshe…" and he breathed what followed conspiratorially into Rudolf's ear: "Go on, g—give it a go." Slapping the table, he bragged, "I'll put in a word…not wisshout influenssh, y'know."

"Yes," said Rudolf, "you do that." Under his breath he added, "Integrity's not in demand, nor's honesty." Speaking more loudly, he said, "I'm turning over a new leaf, you'll see."

"Prossht," smirked Willi.

"Prost," replied Rudolf, attempting to clink glasses with him.

What a despicable little creep he's become, Rudolf thought, but he raised his glass again. "To you and all your help."

Willi nodded vigorously, grinning stupidly, then a puzzled expression crossed his face. "My help," he slurred, "have I…?" He seemed to have forgotten what he wanted to say.

After a few more glasses of schnapps Willi was getting really drunk, his face was perspiring profusely. Every so often he pulled out his handkerchief and shakily tried to wipe his brow.

"I'll take you home to your wife," Rudolf said, getting up from his chair. "Home to your wife," he repeated, bending over Willi.

"Wife?"

"Right," said Rudolf, "I'll take you home anyway." *Not before time*, he thought. He was beginning to feel light-headed himself.

❦

Rudolf settled the bill and asked the waitress to call for a taxi. When it arrived, with the help of the driver, he installed Willi on the back seat and climbed in next to him. "Where's your door key?" Rudolf said. Willi fumbled in his pockets and eventually found it. "He's really pissed," said the driver as he started the engine. Rudolf just nodded.

Willi fell asleep almost immediately and soon began to snore.

By the time the taxi got to Willi's flat Rudolf found it impossible to wake him. Once again the driver helped and Willi was manhandled up the flight of stairs and into his flat. Before he was deposited on the living-room sofa he briefly lifted his head and grunted, but as soon as he was stretched out he began to snore again.

After the taxi had left, Rudolf made himself some sandwiches and a pot of strong black coffee to clear his head for the task in front of him. *Fortunately*, he thought, *he still lives alone*, recalling Willi's incomprehension at the earlier suggestion that he might have a wife. (Actually, Rudolf had expected his former colleague to still be single and the question had merely been calculated to make sure there would be no third party in the flat to stand in his way.) He picked up Willi's jacket which the taxi driver had carelessly thrown over the back of a chair. In the inside pocket he found Willi's identity pass; he opened it and studied the photograph. He took the pass to the kitchen table, put it down, removed from his own pocket a bundle of passport photographs of himself and spread them out on the table. He examined the way Willi's photo was fixed to the pass and, after careful consideration, he decided not to try peeling off the photograph but to shave off, with a razor blade, as much of it as was possible, down to the glue, and cover what was left with a picture of himself—he knew it would be a laborious task. Keeping the extra thickness of the glue was a risk he felt he had to take.

From the assortment of photographs he selected one which was an almost perfect fit. He applied a very thin layer of adhesive over the remains of the original picture, placed the chosen photograph of himself over it and pressing with the utmost precision, he stuck it down.

Once the glue had dried, he took the round rubber stamp he had expected to find on Willi's desk and, holding it at an angle, he marked the bottom left-hand corner of his photograph very lightly with his thumbnail. By using the outer edge only of the seal he managed to complete the missing segment of the official seal's outer circle.

Then, tilting the page from side to side, holding it up to the light and feeling the edges of the photograph, he checked his workmanship. It would have to do. Since his picture fitted in with the personal description in the pass, he thought his chances of getting through a border check should be good.

He found Party membership papers as well as a number of letters from the various committees in Willi's desk and decided to take these documents with him.

Before leaving the flat he collected the mound of shavings from the kitchen table, plus the surplus photographs, and put them in a paper bag to be disposed of at the first opportune moment. (He considered it unwise to flush them down Willi's toilet for fear of rousing him.) He hid his own identity pass in the lining of one of the shoulder pads of his jacket. Putting Willi's identity pass, the one he had tampered with, and the documents into the inside pocket, he took a final mental inventory and, hearing the reassuring sounds of rhythmic snoring, he let himself out of the flat, shutting the door quietly behind him.

❦

At the border, when Rudolf's turn came to be checked, he unhurriedly took the official papers, including the pass, from his jacket pocket, making sure they were all in one batch. As he sorted through them he allowed Willi's Party membership document to slip from his fingers onto his lap where it would be noticeable. He made a show of locating the pass, deliberately lodged between the letters bearing prominent seals, and he offered it to the policeman while apologising for having taken so long. The officer waved his hand indicating that he was satisfied, and briskly moved on and turned his attention to some other traveller.

A week later, before Rudolf was flown out from the refugee centre to the Federal Republic, he posted Willi's pass and the rest of the papers together with a short note to his former colleague. In the note Rudolf thanked him for the loan of the documents, mentioning how invaluable they had been in enabling him to "turn over a new leaf".

❦

Though Rudolf had made light of it when he found Anni at the students' hostel in Wuppertal, it had not been easy to locate her. The difficulties had not deterred him but had spurred him on, and as soon as he knew where she lived he set out to see her. He remembered waiting in the reception room and feeling as excited as he had been as a little boy, eager to open his Christmas presents.

With a pang of disappointment he had noticed Anni's reserve but, being ready to rationalise her lack of reaction, he soon convinced himself that the shock of his unexpected appearance had made her undemonstrative.

He felt relieved that he had managed to make her promise to visit him. Consequently he spent the waiting time in happy anticipation and did not allow his excitement to be dampened. He was filled with great warmth, his heart full of tenderness and love. There was so much he planned to say to her. Their first meeting, he told himself, had not been in the right place or at the right time. He could not have declared himself then.

❦

Rudolf could not say how long he had been sitting by Anni's side as she lay on his bed after succumbing to sleep at the dinner table. He sat watching over her, thinking, remembering, analysing. He wished he could penetrate the space behind her closed eyes, thereby entering into her mind and discovering how she felt about him.

He was troubled because he was no longer sure she would welcome his proposal that they should share their lives. He pictured their meting at the hostel, and as he did so the doubts which had crept into his mind—the doubts which he believed he had laid to rest—surfaced again.

He thought he had detected a sadness in her when he greeted her on the station platform. He, for his part, was unreservedly happy to be with her. And during their meal, it seemed to him, she had kept herself at a distance. It was not that she had said anything in particular which led him to form this conclusion, for she had not. He reasoned that

219

it was solely because he cared that he was sensitive to the atmosphere with which she had surrounded herself. Even the fact that after the meal she had moved closer to him had not helped to placate his worries. He could not help comparing the way she was now to the way she had been only a year ago and he could not deny that she had changed. She was so sincere then, so easy to understand, but now he sensed an undercurrent. He realised that because he had not been confident of her acceptance of his proposal, he had subconsciously delayed making it. This was why, he told himself, he had waffled on in the way he had at the table. Because he did not feel in control, he could not simply take her in his arms, make love to her, and ask her to stay with him.

❧

After Anni left late the following afternoon, Rudolf persuaded himself that the weekend had gone well. For one thing he had kept his promise to himself by talking to her about his hopes for a future life together—he refrained from using the word "marriage". Admittedly her response had been vague, but while she did not agree to live with him, she had not said she would not. She had made her reply sound very reasonable. She really could not move out of the hostel so close to the end of her course. After that, it depended on which university would accept her. She might have to live a long way from his flat. This, of course, would make living together impractical. It had sounded plausible and Rudolf had had to agree. Also, she had promised she would come to see him the following weekend.

That Friday he received a postcard from her cancelling the visit. She said it was because of heavy schedules and deadlines she had to meet. She apologised for having to

220

postpone the visit and assured him she would be in touch soon to arrange another date.

The weekend passed and it was Friday again, but he was still waiting to hear from her. However hard he tried, he could not calm his growing misgivings about her sincerity. In an effort to lift his low spirits he tried to be angry, first with Anni and then with himself. He accused her of being self-centred and thoughtless, and himself of having been so stupid as to think that she could really care for him. But working himself up into an angry mood only temporarily relieved his heartache and his painful longing returned.

After Anni had not contacted him for three more days, he wrote to her. (He had been offered work in a bookkeeper's office and he thought telling her this piece of news gave him a good reason to write. He would, he explained, be working as an assistant. Admittedly, quite a comedown after he had run his own office practice—even though it had been part-time—but it was going to be only temporary while he was waiting to be considered for a government training programme.) He announced he would come to see her in a couple of days' time, and because he wanted to share his good news with her he was going to take her out for a meal to celebrate. Purposely, he did not allow her enough time to reply and perhaps cancel his visit.

❦

As he walked towards Anni's hostel, he felt increasingly apprehensive. He wondered how she would receive him. He had always disliked being pursued by women, but he persuaded himself that what he was doing now was not quite the same. She should, he thought, not object to celebrating with him.

When, to his relief, she congratulated him and appeared genuinely pleased that he was starting work soon, he made up his mind he would not fault her for not contacting him.

During their candlelit dinner he manipulated the conversation, keeping away from the subject of their relationship, even though that was what he was most anxious to talk about. He inquired about her studies. She was only too keen to discuss the various aspects of the course which she had just completed, telling him how different the teaching approach to the subjects had been. In turn, she encouraged him to speak about the training programme she knew he hoped to take part in, and wondered where he would be sent to if he were accepted. Half in jest, Rudolf debated the chance that, come the autumn, he and she could find themselves in the same place, together.

Encouraged by Anni's noticeably relaxed tone and manner, he suggested that the two of them ought to go on a short holiday now that her studies were completed. But his idea drew a long silence from her.

To break the suddenly charged atmosphere he asked, "Don't you think you could do with a few days' away? There's nothing wrong with that, is there?"

She still did not answer but merely played with her food, looking uncomfortable.

"What's wrong with wanting a few days together?" he doggedly persisted. "Give me one good reason why you can't take a short holiday…I thought you'd be pleased."

He knew his tone had sounded harsh and accusing. As soon as he had had his say, it was obvious it had been a mistake, but he felt quite unable to control himself and blurted out, "You've found somebody else, haven't you?"

"No, I haven't," she said sharply. And before he could say anything else she accused him of being possessive and pressuring her at a time when she could do with some peace of mind after the last hectic weeks. "I was going to tell you about my holiday job," she added. "I'm starting at a newsagent's and my work'll clash with your holiday plan. You haven't given me a chance to tell you. I can't go on holiday!"

"I don't believe you," he sneered, raising his voice. "You've no intention of seeing me again, have you?"

They had never quarrelled before, but now they were making a spectacle of themselves. People at neighbouring tables stopped talking and looked up from their plates.

They want to be entertained, Rudolf thought, seeing their expectant eyes on him and Anni.

Why am I doing this, he asked himself? *I didn't come here to fight...*

Hoping to relieve the tension between them he apologised, over and over.

After a while Anni suggested they put their differences behind them.

Later they talked, at first coolly and then more amicably, as he walked her back to the hostel. Neither of them referred to the unpleasantness of the evening; everything seemed to be as it should.

❦

Three days later Rudolf received a letter from Anni:

Dear Rudolf,

There is no way I can say this without hurting you and, I think, without making you angry. I must tell you I cannot continue with our relationship. I hope you will forgive me.

223

I know I should tell you to your face, but in my cowardly way I am preventing you from hitting out at me in reproach, and me from retaliating. I do not want to end our relationship in a hail of mutual accusations.

I cannot explain why it is that for me being with you has lost its magic. There is nothing you have done (quite the reverse) that deserves the change in my feelings for you and there is nobody new in my life, yet my tie to you has become unravelled. In my quiet moments I can recall what my feelings for you were but I do not have these feelings any longer.

Please don't attempt to change my mind, that will be pointless. Don't write to me and please do not come to see me. Maybe sometime when the wounds have healed we can meet again.

I shall never forget you. Please believe me when I say I do not regret a single moment spent with you. What we had together was, for me, of great beauty.

I know you feel much, much more for me now than you did in the beginning. The stupid and ironic thing is that in the old days I wanted you to feel more for me, and now that you do your feelings are weighing me down. I can't explain about my emotions, I'm still trying to work them out. I only know that I'm not willing to be a captive. No, that's wrong, I think I shall never be willing to be that. One day I shall be ready for commitment, but only when I don't perceive myself as a prisoner, but that isn't now; I have a great need to feel free.

Anni

He sat down slowly, holding the letter. His face showed no emotion. Without realising what he was doing he lifted the letter to his eyes again and looked at it, unseeing. Then the hand which had been holding it dropped slowly to his side and he loosened his grip. The letter fell to the floor.

He stood, facing the open window.

So that's it.

His lips twitched and he repeated the words aloud, over and over again…

Chapter Twenty-one

They had taken the lift to the underground car park of Karin's apartment block. Whilst Anni followed her friend to the car, she dropped her handbag. The clasp loosened and a number of photographs spilled out.

"'Who's this?" said Karin as she picked them up.

"Victor," said Anni, gathering up the rest of her belongings.

She had told Karin that he had accompanied her on her return visit to Aschersleben the previous summer but had not said anything about their relationship.

Karin handed her the photographs, "Looks nice," she said.

"Mmm," said Anni, "I meant to show you yesterday, but your neighbour came in."

"Looks intelligent…" Karin winked.

"We're good friends."

"Just good friends?"

"Yes," said Anni. She brushed the hair from her face in embarrassment.

Karin grinned. "What about the heart?"

"Just good friends," Anni repeated firmly.

"Oh! Shame!" Karin said, unlocking the car door and holding it open. "He does look nice though."

"Mmm." Anni got into the passenger seat and fastened her safety belt.

Karin was a snappy driver and as she weaved the car in and out of the busy traffic lanes, Anni realised with a jolt just how much she was missing Victor.

At first, she was grateful that Karin did not ask any more probing questions about him. Apart from briefly referring to him as "your good friend, Victor"—which convinced Anni that Karin had seen through her—the two women exchanged only occasional remarks. Karin concentrated on her driving.

But as the minutes ticked by, Anni found herself wishing for another chance to talk about how things stood between her and Victor. She regretted not having said anything earlier.

Well, it's the old story, isn't it? An unexpected question throwing me off-guard because I haven't had time to prepare for it. Haven't changed have I?—still lacking in spontaneity, still denying Victor's importance in my life, much in the same way as I did with Maria when I denigrated him to the status of colleague.

A wry smile on her lips, she glanced at the passing traffic, and beyond it at some flashy shop fronts, not really seeing either. She kept thinking about her damned reserve.

Then remembering the telephone call to her mother, shortly before setting out on the trip to see Karin, Anni wondered whether she was being too hard on herself. Maybe there was hope for her yet! Without any prompting she had started talking about the new ski outfit Victor had bought specially for the Austrian college-holiday. And then, after mentioning Marlene—which had prompted her mother's warning—Anni somehow, without having intended it, went on to say, "You shan't have to wait much longer before you meet Victor." The curious thing about that was, she had not yet confirmed it with him—though she was sure he would readily agree.

Gazing out at the city lights as they made their way towards Eduard's flat, Anni let her head drop back against the headrest. She thought of the coming meeting with Victor. He had promised to pick her up from the airport on her return from Germany. Almost certainly he would give her an enthusiastic hug.

Homecoming…that's it, she said to herself. *That's what it'll be, yes…coming home.*

The glare from a car's headlights dazzled her. She squinted and immediately the intruding light from street lamps and other cars created flashing plumes of colour. She did not altogether like the sensation, so she resisted being drawn into the mesmerised state that often happens with flickering lights. She opened her eyes again unlike she had done on a previous occasion, when she had allowed herself to become drawn into the spell—on another Saturday, as it happened.

Victor had been driving then, humming a familiar tune. The rain had turned to a steady drizzle. Beams of light were catching her eyes from every direction. It was late; they had been to see a film and she remembered feeling cocooned by the warmth of the car. *He must have made me feel particularly secure…*

❦

"I'll show you how a capitalist lives," said Karin as they approached a large country house. Seeing Anni's surprised expression and not being able to keep a straight face, she chuckled, "No, it's not Eduard's, he only rents the top flat of the east wing. The owner occupies the rest."

Karin drove slowly towards the great iron gates which gave on to the estate. As the car came close, an unseen mechanism clicked and the gates swung open.

Only a short time ago they had been in busy Düsseldorf but the noise and the fumes of the city seemed very far away now in these elegant country surroundings.

In the diffused light of several old-fashioned street lamps, Anni saw that the estate included a number of large outbuildings, as well as a range of kennels and a stable block. The driveway was flanked on one side by a stone wall which, as Karin explained, ran almost completely around the perimeter. Iron lattice openings with oval insets appeared at regular intervals along the upper half of the wall; figures of animals were set into them.

Karin parked near the front of the building, which had been largely renovated. The years had been unkind to the old house and the present owner had spent as much as he could afford on its restoration, but funds had run low and he had rented out the upper floor of the east wing to Eduard.

The two women passed by the tall stone columns of the main entrance and headed towards a small door on the extreme right-hand side of the building. They entered the doorway and climbed a narrow stone staircase which led to Eduard's flat.

Even though Anni had seen a photograph of him, it took her a few moments to recognise him. He looked quite different in his washed-out jeans and loose cotton shirt— the photograph had shown him in a dark suit, white shirt and bow tie. She thought the clothes he was wearing at present gave him a much more relaxed appearance, more approachable. He also looked younger than she had expected. His finely chiselled face was framed by a mass of unruly red hair and he sported a full seaman-style beard—the few grey streaks did not detract from his youthful appearance. His eyes were kind, but Anni suspected that little would escape their searching gaze. When he shook her hand she was struck by the powerful grasp of his delicately tapered fingers.

The only other guests to have arrived for the party, so far, were Ina and Theo. Ina was a colleague of Karin's, and Theo, Ina's husband, was a graphic designer. While Karin and Ina were exchanging departmental gossip, Theo talked to Anni. On Eduard's return from the kitchen, Theo suggested that their host show them his latest paintings. "It'll keep his mind off other things," he said.

Eduard gave him a sidelong glance.

On entering the studio, Anni was surprised by its vastness, which was accentuated by a sparsity of furniture. Apart from two easels, the only other items were a sturdy table covered with dried patches of streaky paint, a stylish old leather sofa and a chest of drawers; the drawers were exceptionally wide and shallow. Anni had seen this type of chest before and she knew it was designed to hold large, unframed, watercolours or pastels. The centre of the floor was protected by large squares of linoleum, leaving a border of highly polished floorboards. Two large skylights dominated the studio while all the side windows were angled from floor to ceiling, allowing maximum daylight into every part of the room. But on this winter's evening they had to make do with the illumination offered by fluorescent lights. They gave the room a slightly bluish tint, reminiscent of natural north light. "They're not the usual kind of fluorescent tubes," Eduard said.

Leaning against the walls were at least a dozen oil paintings; also some drawings and several framed pastels.

The easels held canvasses at different stages of completion. One was of, what seemed to be at first glance, an autumn landscape with a small lake at the edge of a forest clearing. Sunlight filtered through the trees onto a leaf-covered floor. The painting struck an immediate chord with Anni. The scene seemed so alive that she expected the leaves on the ground to begin swirling at any moment. It reminded her of the Gondelteich, the lake she had played beside as a young girl. (When she was older she had spent many peaceful hours sitting near its edge, reading and dreaming.) Yet, as she looked closer at the painting, she could see that it was not the place she had known as a child. It was not even, as it were, a real lake and, in the same sense, they were not real trees; the image of the lake and of the trees around it was an illusion, an illusion that was created by the patterns of colour that sprang from the canvas, giving merely an impression of a lakeside scene; a subtly surreal scene.

Eduard spoke about his struggle to paint the view. It had taken him four months of intermittent work already and was nearing completion. He had worked on it for periods of up to ten hours at a time, only to leave it for weeks without touching it. On other paintings, he would work from start to finish, taking no more than five or six days.

"I studied the techniques of the old masters," Eduard said. "They've influenced me a lot."

"So have women," Theo cut in.

Anni wondered what was meant by the remark. She looked at Eduard, but he did not comment. Casually, she said, "I suppose you hate the current fashion."

Theo laughed. "To my friend here, Minimal Art's like a red rag to a bull. Just talk arty-farty. You know, paint thrown at canvasses and all that crap."

"If you mean abstracts, you're wrong," Eduard said. "I like paintings with harmony of colour, shape and line; even splashes! But I don't call empty canvasses art!"

"I couldn't agree more," Anni said.

She had recently looked at some catalogues and come across an illustration of a study called *Homage to the Square*. There had also been pictures of canvasses covered entirely with nails, as well as natural substances. It seemed to her that art critics only had to praise such constructions and sections of the public went along with it, convincing themselves that the experts knew best.

"Fashion's the bane of artists," Eduard said. "It always has been." He sighed as he adjusted the height of the second easel.

"Anyway," he said to Anni, walking over to the chest of drawers, "have a look at my pastels, I really like that medium." He slid open the top drawer. Taking out a painting and holding it by its extreme edges, he lifted it high. "I think it's as good as oils, but it's difficult to paint out mistakes; too many and you have to start again. They're a bit delicate so you've got to handle them carefully."

❧

"Can we come in?" asked Karin, gently pushing the studio door open with her foot. She was carrying a tray of glasses; Ina followed with several bottles clasped tightly under her arm.

"We knew you'd get stuck in here," Ina said. "It's always the same, so we thought we'd bring you something to drink, we've already started."

"Speak for yourself," Karin said. "I had orange juice, remember."

"Oh!" Theo looked at his wife: "I'm condemned to drink mineral water, am I?" He attempted a peeved expression but failed.

"Your turn to drive," came Ina's quick reply. "Don't quibble, come here and uncork the wine."

Anni's eyes followed Theo as he moved towards his tiny wife. With his massive frame, his dark-brown pullover, heavy corduroy trousers and soft shoes he appeared to be a cuddly gentle giant. But she wondered.

"I'll help," said Karin. Turning back to Eduard, she suggested, "Let's go to the living room, it's more comfortable."

❧

New guests had been arriving in ones and twos during the course of the evening, and, as Anni learned, most of them were Eduard's artist friends and their spouses.

Bertrand was the most recent arrival and had come along on his own. Anni had already heard of him through a London gallery and knew that some of his paintings were in the Vatican. Karin had met him through Eduard and she had told her more about him and had said that he would be coming to the party.

He was Malayan by birth and came from a family of long-established landowners. He was educated at Oxford, but after his studies he moved to Hong Kong where he had been living for most of the time.

"Anni, this is Bertrand," said Karin. "I told you a bit about him, so I'll leave him in your care."

He was of indiscernible age, but might have been anything between forty and sixty years old. The well-spoken little man seemed quite excitable—while holding his glass in one hand, the other would constantly move in expression of what he was saying.

Anni was aware that he was renowned in Europe for his paintings of emaciated figures with hollowed faces, mythical oriental beasts and felines. "I've seen one of your paintings in London," she said, "of a Siamese cat, and—"

"He paints lots and lots of cats," interrupted Frieda from close behind him. "I've seen some, they're lovely. I don't paint them, I make them; in glass. You've given me some brilliant ideas, haven't you?" she said, resting her chin on the top of his shoulder and purring into his ear. (She might have been considered plain if it were not for her misty grey-blue eyes.)

"Leave him alone," said Siegfried, draping an arm over her shoulder.

Frieda purred again. "My little hubby doesn't want me to play pussy cat," she mewed petulantly.

"I want my pussy cat to come with me for a moment," Siegfried laughed. "Leave these two to talk about nasty little governments, or other things."

Left alone again with Anni, Bertrand said, "He knows me well. I do want to enquire something of you though. Karin has talked about you, and so has Eduard. But allow me first to fill up your glass. Please don't go away."

❦

"I'm so sorry I was so long, but it took me a while to locate the red wine," said Bertrand, handing Anni her glass. "Where were we? Oh yes, I remember, Eduard told me you once resided in the East."

"A long time ago; I was young then," she grinned.

Bertrand laughed. "So was I, young I mean." Then, abruptly, he said, "How do you feel about the Stasi? Do you think they should be punished?"

Anni was taken by surprise at the little man's directness and did not reply immediately, so Bertrand added, "I was in Hong Kong during and after the Tiananmen demonstrations. I spoke to some students who had escaped. They felt most bitter about having to leave. Do you feel that way?"

Anni raised her eyebrows a little. "I'm not sure now, but when I left... .Time makes a difference, doesn't it? I haven't forgotten; I don't think you ever do, but for many years I hated them; I mean, really hated! Then it wore off a bit." She took a sip of wine and thought for a moment.

Bertrand's eyes were intent, but he said nothing. He waited.

"The fall of the Wall brought it back; full force; in here," she said, and she tapped her temple with her index finger. "But emotions, they're hard to speak about; it's not easy finding the words."

"No," said Bertrand quietly, but that was all be said. His face was serious and his hand had become still.

"I've thought about it a lot and I don't think they should get away with it, the Stasis," Anni said, "but I wouldn't like a witch-hunt."

She had come to that conclusion after visiting Aschersleben the previous summer.

She told Bertrand how she had heard the opinions of some of the locals; they had said it would be better to forget about the past, easier to start afresh. Rather than settling old scores and creating a lot of antagonism, they believed it would be better to channel their energies into making the country prosper. She had not been convinced that leniency towards those who committed the worst crimes was justified, although she had thought the argument, to let the past be, was persuasive. There were so many collaborators and exposing them all could undermine society, and it would make it harder for people to live together.

As Anni continued to deliberate, she could see that Bertrand was getting quite agitated. He shook his head vigorously and his small frame quivered, so much so that the wine sloshed over his glass. "I can see it would be harder for people to commune, but even so…I could not justify it…ever. I recall Tiananmen all too well; the 'big bananas' were not called to account. Do your people really think they can live with these Stasi policemen?"

Again, Anni did not reply immediately. She had asked herself the very same question but had been unable to come up with an answer. "I don't know," she said.

Bertrand was about to say something more when Susie, who had been standing nearby, took her chance to join in the conversation. "Hello," she said, "I'm Susie, can I play?"

"We're talking about Stasis and the Wall," Bertrand said.

"I know, I heard. I saw it on television. It was brilliant, all those people hacking away."

"Yes, yes, it was!" said Bertrand, nodding and waving his arms to such an extent that he almost dropped his glass. He looked at it. "Oh dear!" he exclaimed. "I think I need refreshing." He held the glass up, looking around the room.

Eduard caught his eye. "You empty? Hang on."

"Ina! Bring the drinks," he beckoned, as he sauntered over. "You lot look a bit serious, let's liven things up!"

He held his hand up for attention. "Listen everyone," he shouted above the buzz of the party, "Ina's going to do the Charleston!" He scanned the faces in the room. "We want to see it, don't we?"

Shouts of approval came from around the room.

He gestured to Ina to park the drinks trolley, and before she could object to having been volunteered, he took her arm and pulled her away. "You can choose the music."

Bertrand tapped Anni on the elbow. "Maybe we can talk later."

"If I'm still capable," she grinned.

Loud dance music was soon reverberating around the room. Anni and Bertrand looked at each other in resignation and moved towards where Ina was demonstrating her sidekicks.

※

"I think I'll sit this one out, Siegfried," Anni said, still puffing from the exertions of their last dance.

But in the event, she did not settle in the living room, she was drawn inexplicably back to Eduard's studio.

Slipping quietly away from the party, she entered the room. It was bathed in moonlight. Being alone in the half-light appealed to her and she did not switch on the fluorescent tubes. The leather sofa glinted in welcome and when she sat down on it, she felt its cool tautness. Putting her plate and glass down on the floor she looked around. A beam of moonlight shone across one of the easels, lighting up the autumn landscape she had so admired earlier. In the shimmering glow the painting assumed an other-worldly appearance.

She looked at it for a long time, and gradually her viewpoint shifted. Seemingly, as she peered into the landscape, she became part of the scene. There was no surprise when she appeared to be standing on the lake's edge, staring into the still water.

The noises of the party had fused to an indistinct thrum, and as she continued to stare there came the anticipation of something important. It was as if under the water's surface lay some vital piece of knowledge. It was elusive, there, at the fringes of consciousness, one second within her grasp, the next, gone. She remembered a similar sensation she had experienced after waking from a dream.

Then, all at once, it was solid.

Really, she had known it all along; it was just that she had not voiced it to herself before—not all of it at one time anyway. Now she could understand why she had held back with Victor. The fear of repeating the mistakes she had made with Rudolf, and compounded in later relationships, had stopped her from seeing clearly.

In the past she had looked for excitement and adventure; the unconventional, with a hint of danger, had attracted her. Through Rudolf she had found the additional element of rebellion against her parents. Because of her association with him, she had felt the oppressive political atmosphere more keenly. She had been in love with the idea of love and had leaped into the relationship without thinking of the consequences, neither for herself nor for Rudolf. As her passion for him cooled, the emotional demands he made on her became burdensome. To be accommodating had not been the answer. Ultimately it had made her feel a prisoner and the only solution had been to break free.

She had not started out in the same way with Victor and had avoided making her previous mistakes. The value they had placed on their friendship had led them to consider each other's needs.

She thought of her letter to Rudolf in which she had written that she was not willing to be a captive, that she would never be willing to be that, and she realised that with Victor she could remain free, at the same time committing herself to him, knowing that her trust would not be abused.

Anni looked again at the painting and walked slowly back to the party; it had become clear what she was going to do on her return home.

❦

From across the living room, Anni saw that Karin had finally been cornered by Hans and Hilda, Eduard's neighbours.

They were hypochondriacs and Karin had been trying to avoid them all evening. She had told Anni that they had bored her to tears on previous occasions.

During Anni's absence, the tempo of the music had changed and she was drawn to watch the dancing couples as they glided leisurely about the floor.

She noticed Theo standing close by. He was no longer wearing his pullover and one of his shirt-tails had worked itself loose. She could see that he was unsteady on his feet. "Come and sit down, Theo," she suggested, "you look a little wobbly." She moved over on the sofa to make room for him.

"I'm all right," he said gruffly, but he turned and walked over to the sofa. He had a half-bottle of whisky in one hand and a full glass in the other.

"What a relief! I can hear myself talk again," Anni said, as he settled next to her. Looking at him more closely she saw that his cheeks were flushed and, when he yawned, the smell of alcohol was overpowering.

"Should you be drinking?" she said, remembering that he was meant to be driving home later.

Theo did not answer; he was staring at his wife. Ina was standing close to Eduard; he said something to her and they began dancing. When she rested her head against his shoulder he bent down and brushed her hair with his lips.

Stony-faced, and grinding his teeth, Theo continued to stare at his wife. As she put her arms around Eduard's neck, Theo gave an angry snort and the grip on his whisky glass tightened. The sinews on the back of his hand bulged against the skin and his fingers worked on the side of the glass.

Anni watched as his knuckles turned white. "Theo..."

"Don't interfere," he growled.

Anni flinched under his hostile glare. He struggled to his feet and swore as the glass slipped from his hand.

※

Karin took the shattered pieces of glass from Anni and placed them into a dustpan. "You look upset," she said, taking Anni aside. "I saw you talking to Theo. Was it something he said?"

"No. But I don't think he likes Ina dancing with…"

"Oh, with Eduard, you mean. It's all right, you can say it. I'm not jealous. Ina's always been a bit of a flirt, but Eduard's fond of her. It doesn't go any further but it bothers Theo. He denies it when I joke about it; and I do. But he's been drinking and that makes him moody, so I thought…"

Still holding the dustpan, Karin looked straight at Anni. "He doesn't like me; I'm not sure if he really likes Eduard."

"Why doesn't he like you?" Anni said.

"Difficult to say; nothing positive, apart from the odd sarcastic remark." She emptied the dustpan and put it next to the waste bin, then wiped her hands on the sides of her skirt. "I just feel it," she said. "Ina thinks I'm imagining it; Eduard does too, but something tells me…I don't know."

"Talk of the devil," Anni said, inclining her head towards the passageway. Theo and Ina were fighting for possession of the telephone receiver. The tussle lasted until Ina jabbed Theo's toes with her stiletto heel. He squealed and let go of the receiver and Ina slammed in onto the cradle. "You're drunk!" she shrieked and pulled him towards the kitchen.

A little while later they emerged. Theo was holding a mug of steaming liquid.

"Coffee, I suppose," said Karin.

※

The dancing had finished some time earlier and the party had quietened down; some of the guests had already left. Those remaining were sitting in small groups and talking— apart from the few who had wandered back to the kitchen to help themselves to more food.

Anni was talking with Eduard and Karin, and Susie's partner, Axel, when Ina breezed in. With a sigh she allowed herself to collapse onto the carpet and crawled to where Eduard was sitting. She settled her back against his knees.

"Right!" Theo snarled from the other side of the room. He scrambled to his feet, towering above everyone. "We're going!" His voice was icy. "I'm getting a taxi."

Ina sat up. "I'll go when I'm good and ready."

Everyone stopped talking.

"It's early yet, Theo, come and sit down," said Axel, pointing to a chair.

"Yes, cool it, man." Eduard spoke lightly, getting up from his seat. With his hand outstretched he took a step towards Theo.

Theo stomped up to his wife, brushing Eduard's hand aside. "We're going! Now!"

Before Ina had time to say anything, Eduard placed himself in front of her. "Come on, Theo, there's no need for that," he said quietly.

"Don't tell me how to speak to my wife!" Theo exploded. "I don't tell you how to treat your fucking Stasi-bitch!"

Eduard looked stunned and shook his head in disbelief; his fingers formed into a fist. He looked at it abstractedly, as though it did not belong to him. Then suddenly he threw himself forward.

Theo staggered as he took the full force of a shoulder charge on his chest. He stumbled backwards and his whole frame shuddered as it struck the wall behind him. One of

Eduard's glazed pastels crunched under the force of the impact. Splintered pieces of glass fell out of the frame as his crumpling body slid down the wall, dragging the picture with him.

Eduard rushed forward and grabbed hold of Theo's shirt. Holding it tightly in his left hand, his right fist drawn back, he stood over him, an expression of incredulity still on his face.

"Stop it, both of you!" Karin shouted. "Stop behaving like bloody imbeciles!"

Eduard stepped aside, his body shaking and his fingers opening and closing. He looked again at Theo and turned away. Still shaking, he walked to a chair and sat down.

Axel and Bertrand were starting to lift Theo as Ina hurried to him. "Wait, don't move him, he might have glass in his back."

She leaned him forward, carefully removing what glass she could see, then gently peeled her husband's shirt off. When she had assured herself that he was basically all right, apart from a few small cuts, the three of them helped him into a chair.

Karin was too angry to be concerned about Theo's well-being. "That's it!" she said, facing him, "I'm sick of your innuendoes. Now you accuse me of being a Stasi. We might as well settle this right here, and sod your bleeding back!"

Theo avoided looking at her. He rubbed his chest and moaned.

"For your information," she continued, shoving her face close to his, "I've never had anything to do with the Stasi. What do you know about me anyway? You know nothing! You weren't even there. You were safe in the West. We were living with those damned creeps." She turned away from him, her hands clenched. Then she faced him again. "You know nothing about the Stasi! But you accuse me of being one. Why the hell d'you think I never made it to consultant! I had nothing to show when I left; no villa, nothing!" She kicked the leg of his chair. "Why d'you think I joined in the mad rush and got out through Hungary? You didn't know that, did you?"

Theo cringed under Karin's onslaught and he looked very small, but she went on. "You sit in judgement over me! Why don't you pick on Honecker?"

She moved away from him, a sneer spread across her face. Looking at Eduard and then at Ina, she said over her shoulder, "By the way, Theo,"—she made the word 'Theo' sound like a dirty word—"Eduard and Ina aren't having an affair. That's another thing you've been getting up my nose over." She spun around and said very quietly, "It stops right now."

Nobody uttered a word.

❦

Tempers cooled but the party atmosphere had evaporated.

Ina rolled up her husband's torn shirt and put it in her handbag. "Your pullover will have to do till we get home," she said.

While the couple waited for their taxi, Ina took Karin and Eduard aside to apologise for having provoked Theo's behaviour. "I didn't realise he'd be that jealous; and hateful," she said.

"Don't worry, I won't let it spoil our friendship," Karin reassured her.

The taxi arrived and Ina said a hasty goodbye, but Theo ignored his hosts.

After a while the other guests started to leave and soon only Bertrand was left. When he prepared to go, Anni and he exchanged addresses and telephone numbers as he had invited her to the preview of his forthcoming exhibition in London. She, Karin and Eduard accompanied him for the short walk to his hotel car, but even though they wore their winter coats they were shivering from the cold when they returned to the flat.

Reminders of the party were everywhere: chairs scattered around, rugs upturned, plates with remnants of food left on them, half-empty glasses, wine stains on the floor.

"Apart from the broken picture, nothing more than the usual," Karin said, unperturbed by the disorder. She and Anni helped Eduard to tidy up some of the clutter. Afterwards, he made some coffee and the three of them mulled over the events of the evening.

Eduard sighed and leaned against the pantry door. "You can see, Anni, I have my differences with Theo, but he's not normally spiteful." He rubbed his shoulder and winced. "I don't understand it, he sees everything in black and white. He wants all collaborators locked up; he's said as much to me. He's got it into his head that Karin was one of them." He sighed again. "God knows how he came by that idea."

"I told you he was like that!" Karin burst out, jumping up from her chair. "You didn't believe me, you pooh-poohed it. So did Ina!" She was indignant and glared at Eduard. She sat down again and folded her arms across her chest, her face wooden.

"Simmer down," Eduard said, "I'm on your side, remember?"

Karin exhaled noisily. "All right," she said, more calmly, uncrossing her arms, "assuming that I'm not a collaborator," her eyes searched Eduard's face, "what would you do with them, treat them all the same?"

"No! It depends," he said, pausing for thought.

"On what?" Karin said, scornfully.

"How much they were involved...and why."

"How d'you decide that?" Karin enquired, her voice less cutting now. She shuffled her chair to the table and poured herself another cup of coffee.

"I don't know," said Eduard, "get the BIG BOYS first, that shouldn't be too hard, then work your way down."

"Oh!" Karin said. "So you agree with me."

Eduard laughed. "Don't look so surprised."

"Well, I suppose..." She stared at her hand. "I..." struggling for the right words, her fingers started playing with the teaspoon. Returning it to the saucer, she aligned it with its geometric pattern. (A foible, Anni thought, which the neat arranging of surgical instruments might have fostered. Still looking down at her hand, Karin said, "I assumed that you thought along Theo's lines, I don't know why; we don't talk about it much." She lifted her cup from the saucer, then set it down again without having drunk from it. Resting her elbows on the kitchen table and looking into Eduard's face, she said, "You've always been scathing about the old East, so I thought... . Think what you said about the hospitals. I put everything into my work, everything. I..."

"Scathing?" he repeated. "Critical, maybe. I think you misunderstood... . Yes, we should've talked about it."

"Yes, we should," Karin said, "but we didn't, not properly. I'm not saying it's your fault, I'm not very approachable."

The silence that followed was accompanied only by the hum of the refrigerator and the occasional clink of cups on saucers when one of them took a sip of coffee.

Anni kicked off her shoes and, with legs stretched out, she made herself more comfortable. She was relieved that the discussion between Karin and Eduard had not ended in discord. Being the outsider among them, she had sat on the sidelines and just listened, feeling embarrassed at times. Even though she had told herself it was none of her business, she had thought that Karin had been touchy, and maybe a little unfair towards Eduard. But thinking about it more, while she was finishing her coffee, she wondered if she had been objective. After all, Karin had experienced the regime for much longer and had had time to accumulate resentments. It was she who had been exposed to the snide remarks from Westerners; Anni had avoided all that by living abroad.

After a while she said, "Theo's done you a favour."

Eduard frowned, then he laughed. "I suppose that's true. Theo, the catalyst." He grinned at Karin.

For a moment her face remained impassive, then she forced a smile. Speaking to nobody in particular, she said, "The last couple of days have made me think. Meeting Anni after all those years, the party, even 'good old Theo'," she grimaced, "and I actually admitted for the first time I was too cowardly to answer Anni's letters after she'd left."

Anni dismissed the confession with a wave of her hand. "We're all the same, we're all cowards at some time."

Karin would not be appeased, "But I'm still responsible for my own actions; and omissions." She went on to point out that only a small number of people had openly opposed the regime; most, including herself, whilst not in favour, conformed or at least adjusted. She talked about the silent majority and their failure to protest against injustice. "I was part of that; I'm to blame too. I could've got out; Anni did."

"I was running away," said Anni, "so I'm guilty too."

"Maybe," said Karin, "but I was too damned scared to do even that. All I could think about was my bloody medical career. I didn't even distribute leaflets. I did nothing; Nothing! With a capital 'N'!" She looked thoroughly dejected.

For a while neither Eduard nor Anni spoke. Then Eduard stretched out his hands towards Karin. "Who knows what I would've done? We're not all heroes. Stop blaming yourself! I dare say we in the West wouldn't have been any different."

Chapter Twenty-two

I've been thinking about last night," said Karin as she drove Anni to the airport. "I'm glad I said what I did, to Eduard I mean." She switched off the radio. "I thought his criticisms were attacks on me as an Easterner, so I got defensive and couldn't see my own contradictions." (Karin had resented what seemed to be Eduard's lack of appreciation of her hard work in the East. But she now realised that while she was devoted to her patients, that same devotion had helped to keep the system going, a system to which she was completely opposed.)

"If you two can't agree, there's no hope for anyone," said Anni.

"You're right," said Karin, "I must stop seeing people as 'Wessis' and 'Ossis'."

Anni suddenly remembered Peter Hopfenstange's shrill voice as he had cursed the 'Wessis'. "It took me a while before I understood that that's what Westerners and Easterners are called."

"I suppose I saw Eduard as a 'Wessi', an outsider," said Karin. "And if somebody like that makes criticisms, even when you know they're right, you don't admit it."

❦

Anni boarded the plane and settled into her window seat.

Soon the aircraft rumbled, like an old bus, down the approach to the runway. It hesitated, as if it were a big cat waiting to spring. The engines picked up speed and started to scream and she tucked her thumbs into her seat belt. The brakes were released and the machine moved forward; slowly at first, then it was tearing down the runway. Its nose tilted sharply up at the sky and all at once the rumble was gone, and they were floating. She felt herself being pressed against the back of her seat, but, as the plane gained height and banked towards the open sea, she relaxed.

Anni watched the unfolding patterns of grey as the clouds hurried by, at one moment enveloping the aircraft and the next, keeping their distance. The newspaper she had intended to read lay unopened on the empty seat next to her. The ever-changing cloud formations conjured up faces from her past. At one point she imagined she saw Rudolf, beckoning to her. Then the shapes which had made up the features of his face disintegrated and made way for the form of Herr Wagner, sitting in his characteristic way.

Rudolf's face appeared again and she wondered if he might be living somewhere below the flight path.

Is he still alive? If I'd spoken to Fabian when I had the chance, I'd know.

After Fabian's expected return, she had gone back to Bahnhofstrasse 13, intending to ask him about his father. But the nearer the house she came, the less sure she was about the venture. *Maybe nobody's at home*, she thought, half-hoping for a get-out.

But as she approached, her steps faltering, she could see

Fabian through a gap in the fence. He was bending down doing some weeding. He looked awkward with his artificial leg sticking out at an angle from his hoe. All she needed to do was to go up to him, but as the distance between her and the fence narrowed, she turned away from the house and crossed over to the other side of the road.

Suppose Rudolf's alive and well, what do I do, get in touch? Surely that was the whole point. But what do I say? Tell him I hope his life's turned out to be happy, that it took me all this time to come to terms with myself. Do I tell him about Victor? No, that would be cruel. It's not worth risking upset just to satisfy my curiosity.

She knew Rudolf had once contacted her parents and spoken to her mother on the telephone. He had wanted to leave his number and had asked for Anni's address—at the time she had been living in England for a number of years—but her mother would not take his number and had refused to tell him where she lived. He had referred to Anni as Fräulein Niklas. "There's no longer a Fräulein Niklas," was her mother's abrupt reply. "My daughter's married now," she lied, "I suggest you leave her alone!"

Anni did a quick calculation in her head. *Goodness,* she thought, *it was twenty-seven years ago, during one of my regular visits to West Germany, that mother told me about Rudolf's phone call. I remember we were standing on the balcony; it was the first time since I left Aschersleben that his name had come up. "You did the right thing, Mother," I said, looking into her blazing blue-grey eyes. Then I hastily changed the subject. After that time, she never mentioned him to me again, and I didn't speak about him...*

As always, when Anni thought of her avoidance of Rudolf's name, she felt uncomfortable. Part of the reason for feeling that was that she had never apologised to her mother—well, nor to her father—for the hurt she had caused.

Many times, when she returned home late after having been with Rudolf she had seen her mother's tear-stained face.

She leaned back in her chair and shut her eyes. *I could've stopped their suffering; I knew what I had to do. Yes, I know,* she mocked, *but I couldn't give him up, could I? Couldn't I?* She thought for a moment. *More a case of wouldn't!*

Being that frank about it to herself made her sit up. *Well! I didn't admit that before! I suppose it's a case of the truth wanting out…*

She had made excuses for herself, justifying her affair with Rudolf. While it was going on, she had convinced herself, or thought she had, that she was doing the right thing. After all, she loved him and nothing and nobody would stand in her way. So, she defied her parents' wishes, but, when she ran up against the Party machinery, she realised she could not win. In later years, she had put her behaviour down to an obsession. "Rudolf was like a drug," she confessed to Karin—implying she could not have done otherwise. But addicts can, and do, kick the habit!

Turning her head, she looked down at the clouds again. Given her overpowering feelings, she had argued for many years, she only did what anybody else in her situation would have done. But deep down, she never completely believed it, hence her guilt and her shame. Hence also, her avoidance of all talk with her parents about Rudolf—their silence on the matter was very convenient.

The time's come to explain myself to Mother. And there's another thing, my secrecy over my escape; but not the return to his flat, I'll keep that to myself…

❦

Sipping from the glass of wine the stewardess had brought her, Anni tried to turn her thoughts away from the last couple of days in an effort to concentrate on her home-coming. But she could not stop thinking about her time spent with Karin.

Her thoughts kept returning to the problematic situation between the two Germanys. The discussion at Eduard's party came back to her. Some of the arguments had illustrated the difficulties lying ahead. Putting her mind to the problems only served to magnify them. Her heart sank as she wondered whether or not it was true that a new Wall was being erected, a new invisible divide which threatened to keep the old East and West apart.

Anni's visit to her old school friend had been exhausting, both physically and mentally, but she fought to ward off the sleep closing in on her.

The continuous twisting and turning of her mind finally took its toll and she started to doze, and then to dream.

In the dreams she relived the conversation she had had with Karin on the way to the airport, except that the setting had changed. She was walking with Karin along one of the walkways of the Promenadenring which had been formed from Aschersleben's medieval moat, only the walkway was not as she remembered it or, as she had ever seen it. They seemed to be walking along the original dried-out moat before it had been filled in and paved over.

Suddenly the dream sequence changed and they were standing in front of the school they had attended as girls. They entered the building and walked up the stairs to where their classroom had been. They sat down in their old seats; two phantom figures alone in the room. Then, as Anni looked towards the teacher's desk, a form materialised. She could not recognise the hollow-faced apparition as it tilted forward and glared at them. It was leaning on the desk, its chin resting on crossed forearms. Almost imperceptibly, as she puzzled over the apparition's identity, its features became sharper and an excessively red mouth, beneath icy-blue eyes, started to sing. It was a kind of singing anyway. The voice wailed, robot-like, screeching its message; the same three syllables, over and over again: VO-ZI-DA, VO-ZI-DA, VO-ZI-DA... After a while, with a smile of stupidity, the two friends joined in the hypnotic chant.

❦

Anni was startled into wakefulness by the sound of her own voice, "VO-ZI-DA..." She wondered about the significance of the syllables and quickly glanced around to see whether she had been overhead. A lady sitting on her right, by the gangway, smiled at her. Blushing self-consciously, Anni smiled back.

Chapter Twenty-three

When Anni arrived at Heathrow Airport Victor was not there to meet her as they had arranged. Suppressing her disappointment, she told herself that he must have been held up in the traffic.

She decided she would wait for twenty minutes or so, and if he did not make an appearance by seven o'clock she would make her own way home.

Fifteen minutes later she saw him limping towards her.

"Oh, it's nothing," he said, when she voiced her concern. "I twisted my ankle, it's not as bad as it looks. I did it towards the end of the skiing week."

Apologising for his lateness, he told her he had been in a rush to get back to the airport to meet her. "It's my second time here today," he said, "I only arrived this morning."

"How come?" Anni looked surprised. "I thought..."

"Well," he said, "it was all fun and games yesterday afternoon. Fragrant Wayne," Victor tapped his nose, "gave us a good old run-around. It was time to leave for the airport and he'd disappeared. Anyway, I stayed behind to sort things out. When he showed up at the hotel the plane had already taken off."

"I see, so you came back with him today. What did he say for himself?"

"Nothing, to begin with, until we were in the air. Then he told me about this girl, Beate—he pronounced the name all wrong—showed me her photo." Victor grinned knowingly, "His watch had stopped! Well," he grinned again, "we were all young once."

❦

"We'd better stop off at my place," Victor said, as he unlocked the car, "you left your work schedules behind. I meant to bring them with me but I forgot; sorry." He gave her a doleful look and hung his head.

"I don't mind," she said, "especially if you've acquired some new bronzes."

He winked. "I have indeed." Then, giving her sleeve a light prod, he said, "Won't you be hot in that heavy coat?"

Putting her handbag on the bonnet of the car, Anni took off the coat and handed it to him, but before he could get hold of it properly it slipped from his hand. They both bent down to retrieve it at the same time and, in the process of doing so, they banged their heads together.

"It's nice to be home," she laughed, rubbing her forehead. "One lump or two?"

"It's that magnetism of yours," he sighed, and he slung the coat over his shoulder. "I'll just have to kiss it better." He hesitated a moment before smothering her forehead with kisses; she did not object.

"I'm so happy you're back," he said quietly as he helped her into the car.

❦

Anni had always liked Victor's flat. There were often new pieces of art to be discovered, a painting she had not seen before or a new carving. Every bit of wall space, windowsill, mantelpiece and shelf bore witness to his passion for collecting. Even if he had bought nothing new from one visit to the next, there were still surprises in store. Because of the limited space he was continually rotating the paintings, drawings and sculptures. It seemed he had an inexhaustible supply of treasures in the loft.

Anni was well aware of his latest penchant for Nepalese bronze figures and ritual objects, so it did not surprise her that the first thing he did after closing the front door was to go straight to his study to show her his newest acquisition, a bronze figurine. It was still in its box. His face beaming, he took it out and handed it to her; he had discovered it in an obscure Austrian gallery.

"Whatever else you do," he implored, "don't abscond with that one."

Anni looked at him in surprise.

Victor seemed embarrassed. "Sorry," he said, "I'd better explain. I never told you about Helen and my Japanese lacquer boxes. I treasured them, they took me years to collect."

He coughed several times in quick succession and looked down at the carpet. Then, straightening up, determination in his eyes, he said, "I think I told you that I fell in love with her. Well, after I went back to Nepal she came out to visit me. When she went back she stayed here in the flat. We were going to get married in a few months. She said she loved me." He coughed again. "By the time I got back, she'd gone. So had my lacquer boxes—she knew they were valuable. Oh, and she'd emptied my back account too." He went on to relate how for weeks he had gone about in a daze. "Luckily, I was still on holiday, I couldn't have done any work." He spoke in unemotional tones saying, as he had once before, that he had got over his hurt. "But until you came along I found it difficult to trust women."

Standing by his desk she felt for him. No wonder, it had been hard for him to talk about being jilted; his self-esteem had been badly knocked and his pride would not allow him to broach the subject. His confidence in his judgement had been further dented when some of his friends had implied that he had been partly to blame for the heartache and financial loss he had suffered, and he had feared she might think so too. "If you will be impetuous and overgenerous, you must take the consequences," was how one friend had put it and his words, accompanied by a self-satisfied expression, had added insult to the injury. Anni realised she had gained Victor's trust enough for him to risk appearing naïve and rather silly in her eyes.

"I'm glad you told me," she said. "I wondered what happened between you and Helen. I appreciate your honesty, it must have been hard to talk about."

As she spoke, she was still holding the figurine. She looked at it properly now. "It's beautiful," she said as she stood it on the desk and studied it for a moment longer. Then she turned to Victor and brushed his hand, "I think we need some coffee."

❧

Until very recently—before her visit to Karin and before she had become clear in her own mind about her feelings for Victor—it would have alarmed her to hear him talk about his emotions. She knew she would have wondered how to react, and she also knew she would have been very tense. But now, settled next to him on the sofa and feeling very snug, being told more about his relationship with Helen somehow seemed right. When, in quiet empathy she felt for his hand, he pressed hers and did not let go of it. After a while he turned and looked at her warmly; he cleared his throat as if he wanted to say something important, but instead he stood up. "I'll make the coffee this time," he said and went into the kitchen.

Feeling at ease, Anni leaned back into the soft furnishing. She had taken off her shoes and tucked her legs up onto the seat. On the wall opposite, to one side of the window, she noticed the Russell Flint had been replaced by another painting. Captivated by its unusually vivid colours she got up from the dark-red velvet sofa and went closer to it.

"*Beginnings* by Eric Mahler," Victor said coming back into the room. "Good, isn't it? Can you see the skull?"

"Skull?" She moved nearer in an effort to see... . "No," she said.

"You're too close," he said. "Here." He took her by the shoulders and stood her further back. "It was hanging in a gallery near Boston; Swineshead of all places," he said, with his hands still on her shoulders. "I must find out more about the artist. Abstract Surrealism I'd call it. What d'you think?"

"Hmm, yes..." she muttered. "Whatever the style...it's very striking." She started to turn around and Victor let go of her shoulders. But having lost the support, she momentarily stumbled, and she realised how heavily she had been leaning against him. "Yes, striking," she repeated.

They sat down and drank their coffee slowly. "Photos of last week's skiing," he said, picking up a bulky envelope from the coffee table.

Looking at the photographs with Victor, she was reminded of the incident she had so recently described to Karin. She had been sitting on a different sofa then. Rudolf had been showing her photos too. She smiled to herself as she remembered how frightened she had been.

The memory of the events in Rudolf's living room gave way, and she saw herself in Eduard's studio, bathed in moonlight as it had been. Standing in front of the autumn landscape, she again stepped into the scene and recalled her resolve to talk to Victor about her feelings for him.

Why not tell him now? As soon as the thought entered her head, she started to make excuses for doing it some other time. For one thing, she had not had a chance to work out how to put it, had she?

But then, she came straight out with it. When she thought of it later, she was amazed at the ease with which she had spoken the words. "I love you," she said.

Victor turned towards her, his smile held a hint of surprise. She held his gaze. "I love you too," he said, "but you know that, don't you?"

"I'd never have guessed," she grinned.

They sat immobile, each immersed in the simplicity of the moment.

After a while they kissed; their lips touching then letting go. As she buried her face into the side of his neck, she breathed in the aroma of sandalwood, and she thought she could also detect the faintest smell of jasmine, mingled with hot wholesome skin.

❦

"Funny thing, lovemaking," Victor said, as they lay side by side. He gave a quiet chuckle and lifted himself up onto his elbow. Still smiling, he bent down and brushed the hair away from her face.

He started to kiss her again, ever so gently.

Epilogue

In the spring of 1995, almost four years after their first visit to Aschersleben, Anni and Victor were back. On Herr Klein's invitation they had come to spend a few days with him. Tomorrow they would be travelling to Berlin to attend the court case against Schulz and four of his co-defendants.

"I'm too old to go myself," Herr Klein said, leaning against the kitchen doorway. "But such is life." He sounded sad and sighed heavily. "Anyway..." he paused, then forcing a smile and focussing on each of his visitors in turn, he said, "the two of you, and Maria as well, will be my eyes and ears."

Using his walking stick he slowly crossed the tiled black and white diamond-patterned floor. And, pulling a file from under his arm, he put it down onto the small round breakfast table. The label on the file, hand-written in bold red capitals, read *KASPAR K SCHULZ*. "This is in case you need to reacquaint yourselves with some of the details of the case."

Victor looked at Anni. "You did remember to bring your folder?"

"Of course." Turning to Herr Klein, she said, "I kept all your letters, the newspaper cuttings, and all the other bits you sent that had to do with Schulz. But if there's more in your…?" She pointed to the file on the table.

Herr Klein shook his head. "You have all there is."

There had been a number of letters from Herr Klein. The first one especially, Anni remembered well. She had good cause to do so. It arrived at her Wimbledon flat about a year after her and Victor's previous visit to Aschersleben— Herr Klein's later letters always included Victor; they came to Anni's and Victor's new home, a small cottage at the edge of Epping Forest. The two of them had purchased the run-down place, renovated it and restored the garden to its original Italian style.

In that first letter to Anni Herr Klein reported some recent developments which he thought would interest her. Apparently, Schulz's reply to Herr Klein in "Letter to the Editor" had resulted in rather unfortunate repercussions for the one-time Stasi operative.

Schulz's turn of phrase, and his admission to having worked for the Ministry of State Security, had brought him to the attention of a certain Frau Lichtblick; that was despite the fact that he had not used his own name in his dealings with her. Once her private enquiries had confirmed her suspicion that he was indeed the person who had swindled her out of property and money back in 1972, she initiated an official investigation which eventually resulted in his forthcoming prosecution in the Berlin Court.

Herr Klein had been right in thinking that Anni would be interested in reading about Frau Lichtblick's successful tracking down of Schulz. But there was more to that particular cutting. Anni had turned it over. Something about a small black and white photograph at the top of the page attracted her attention. She looked more closely. The picture showed a mature couple on the occasion of their first wedding anniversary. The printed text below the picture named the smiling pair as Rudolf and Doris Darrenbach.

In amazement Anni had stared at the newspaper copy, lifting it closer to her eyes, then holding it further away, tilting it sideways. *So, he is alive,* she thought, *that's marvellous; and he's living in Aschersleben. They really look happy, just as well I didn't intrude.* It occurred to her that she could easily have bumped into Rudolf by chance during her last visit. She was sure she would have recognised him. *That would have thrown me,* she thought.

❧

Herr Klein picked up his file from the table. "Right," he said, nodding to Anni and Victor, "you won't need this. Back it goes into my desk for safe-keeping."

He hesitated at the doorway. "There's something though you may not know, it's been coming out in dribs and drabs." He hobbled back to the table, pulled out a chair and sat down. He waited until his visitors had joined him before speaking.

"During the 'sixties, 'seventies and 'eighties, West Germany paid vast sums of money to the East Germans, ransom for political prisoners. But that's not all, billions disappeared before and on unification, through corruption and fraud; most went into the pockets of the Stasi. A figure of twenty-six billion marks has been quoted. Can you believe it?" He shook his head. "Not much has been recovered; the Stasi have hidden it well." He gave a pained laugh. "As far as Schulz is concerned, he was, as he said himself, 'small-fry'. But you know all about his rackets."

"He only pretended to buy the freedom of political prisoners," said Victor. "He was in no position to buy anybody, but he had no scruples."

Herr Klein put his file down. "I suppose it's not surprising that he came up with that idea, he's that sort of person." Drumming his fingers on the red lettering of the file's label, he continued, as if rehearsing a text from memory. Apparently it had been easy for him and his fraudsters to deceive would-be victims into believing that husbands, wives, sons, et cetera would be selected for freedom. He promised them that, providing he was paid, he would see to it that their names were put onto an official list. However, after the bribes were paid over nothing more was heard from him and the prisoners served out their sentences." With a grave expression he looked at Anni and Victor. "Only during the investigation of Schulz did Frau Lichtblick realise that she was just one of many victims. She, like them, lost everything." Herr Klein's fingers drummed harder on the red lettering.

"How long will Schulz be put away for?" Victor said.

"Not long enough," said Herr Klein.

❧

Now, on the eve of the court case, Anni and Victor stood once more in front of the café. Looking at it, Anni could see that there had been major changes since they had last visited. The flat above where she had spent her youth was gone. All around lay the materials for the reconstruction of the upper floors. It was rumoured that the new owners were to let the top two storeys for use as insurance offices.

At the moment the Café Vienna stood unused, gutted, its old name plate fixed to a now empty shell. Anni stared at the obscured windows…

She raised her eyes and, through and beyond the scaffolding, she could see the highest of the ancient towers. For centuries they had endured, standing like sentinels over the town, separate and aloof.

THE END

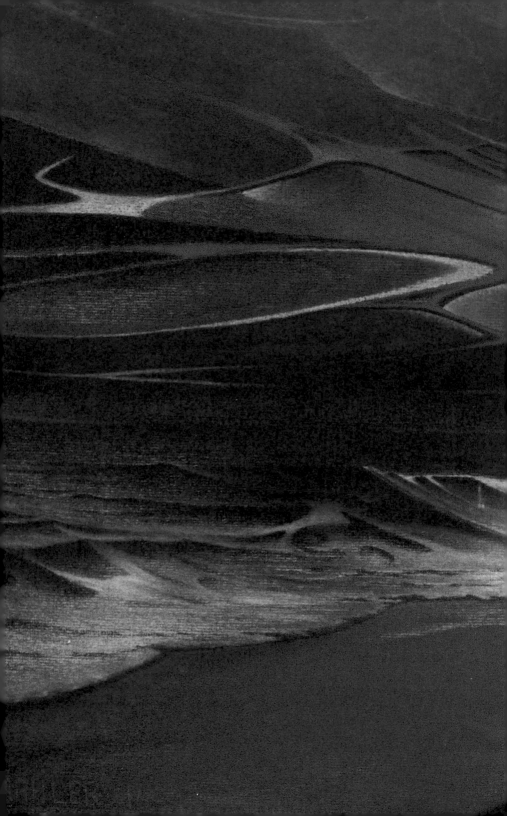